Opening Acts

'It's Ben's birthday tomorrow,' said Mr Briars. 'He'll be nineteen. I'm going to give him a magnificent birthday present, though God knows I want it myself.' He ran his hand up Holly's thigh and she suddenly realised what he was talking about.

'Me?' She couldn't believe it.

'I want to teach him how to make love to a woman. He's a virgin, you see.'

'How dare you?' said Holly. She felt like slapping him.

'Oh, come on. I've seen the way you look at him. You'd love it as much as he would.'

She had to admit, he was right.

Opening Acts

SUKI CUNNINGHAM

Black Lace novels contain sexual fantasies.
In real life, make sure you practise safe sex.

First published in 2001 by
Black Lace
Thames Wharf Studios,
Rainville Road, London W6 9HA

Copyright © Suki Cuningham 2001
The right of Suki Cunningham to be identified as the
Author of this Work has been asserted by her in
accordance with the Copyright, Designs and Patents Act
1988.

Typeset by SetSystems Ltd, Saffron Walden, Essex
Printed and bound by Mackays of Chatham PLC

ISBN 0 352 33630 7

Chapter One

*S*he was sitting back on a crowded train. She never knew so many commuters lived all the way out in the West Country, in their stiff jackets and doing their *Times* crosswords. She closed her eyes and allowed the rocking locomotive rhythm to take her over. Her legs were more open than they should be. Was the guy opposite sneaking a look? Was she dreaming or were her legs opening wider? Was there a whisper of breath against her thigh? She swayed with the jerking movement of the train, and woke up.

Holly stood just off the step of the doorway, her green eyes squinting slightly in the August evening sun. Behind her the sound of the sea brushing the pebble beach reminded her of childhood holidays. A lock of her auburn hair blew into her mouth and she could taste the salty freshness of sea air on her tongue. She sucked the end, enjoying the flavour of the sea. A change from London taste – all artificial and choked.

She knocked on the door for the second time, her long artistic fingers curled into a fist. As she waited, she smoothed down the lilac cotton of her dress, still crumpled from her long train journey. There was no answer. Did she have the right house? It would be

1

typical of her to turn up on some deranged stranger's doorstep, she thought. She knocked again, louder this time, and began to rummage in the messy chaos of her hastily packed bags for the digs list that the theatre had sent her. She had thrown anything to hand into her bag last night and now it all tumbled around in there – clothes, papers, her mobile, an unopened letter from her ex that had lain ominously on the doormat a few weeks ago – it was all chucked in there along with her script, which she had not had time to read. But still she couldn't find this stupid digs list. She was sure they had said it was number 15, although in all the panic of her last-minute arrangements she could easily have made a mistake. She was used to the actor's life of living out of a suitcase and sudden surprises, but this time it had been bizarrely rushed. She had got a call on Saturday night that she was to start rehearsals for a play in Cornwall on Monday morning. A remote village, her agent had said, quite prestigious in theatre circles. Her agent had a way of dressing things up. Holly had spent most of Sunday in a panic, tearing around her London flat washing clothes, making calls and finding a neighbour to water the plants. She hadn't had time to take in that she was to play the leading role (her agent had told her) in a play she knew nothing about with a director she had only met once, hastily, in a small office in Knightsbridge. He had been humorous but imposing, older, European.

Her thoughts were interrupted by the door finally opening.

'Miss Parker, is it?' The voice seemed to come out of the breeze, rough and rich with the curl of a West Country accent. She peered up to see a man in his early forties eyeing her with obvious curiosity, his blue eyes twinkling. He stood in the doorway, clothed only in a white vest and dark tracksuit bottoms, which were spattered with white paint, as was the mop of black curls that framed his weathered face. He had the stocky

2

muscularity and leathery skin of someone who leads an outdoor life, living off the land or the sea.

'That's right.' Holly smiled and extended her long hand. He took it formally in his, not without a sense of irony. His hand was warm and brown, enveloping hers almost completely in its rough grip. 'Mr Briars, is it? I thought I'd got the wrong house . . .'

'Sorry about that, love. Me and the wife, well, we had things to do if you know what I mean.' He cracked a smile that left her in little doubt. 'And it's Briar. No "S". Come on in.'

Holly followed her host through into a dark hallway, lugging her heavy bags inelegantly behind her. The house was warm with the musty air she had come to expect from theatrical digs. The wallpaper was pale pink and slightly tatty at the edges, with a raised pattern of large roses. She glanced around her and saw the kitchen door open, glimpsing a big oak table and an open fire, which had not been lit.

'Use the kitchen whenever you like.' Mr Briar had followed her gaze, and fixed his eyes firmly on her. 'Although it doesn't look like you eat much. My wife'll soon build you up.' He smirked and led her straight up a narrow stairway and onto the landing. Holly didn't much like that smirk.

'Bathroom, toilet, Ben's room, our bedroom, your bedroom.' He pointed as he went, walking straight into her room. Holly looked around, smiling. After the musty drabness of the hallway this room was large and airy, painted brilliant white, still faintly smelling of fresh paint. The double bed looked soft and inviting enough, covered in a puffy white duvet embroidered with tiny red roses. Opposite the bed stood an old mahogany dresser and chair with a matching full-length mirror in the corner. From the window she could spot the pale blue and gold wash of the sea at sunset, and next to it was the obligatory washbasin, soap, hand towel and kettle. 'All mod cons.' Mr Briar was obviously rather proud of the room. Holly flung her heavy load on the bed and looked around.

'It's great,' she said rather belatedly.

'It'll do.' Mr Briar stood for a moment, his eyes again fixed on her slender frame. 'It'll do.' Holly felt her skin shiver slightly under his gaze, so steady and penetrating. His eyes rested on the full orbs of her breasts, which strained slightly against her summer dress. She was used to this, having developed large breasts at an early age. But this guy was taking the piss, his eyes fixed on her. Her natural indignation at his rudeness gave way to a curious tingling at the unabashed appreciation in his eyes. She was horrified to feel her nipples harden against the slight material of the lilac dress. His face registered with pleasure the tight points of her nipples, and Holly felt the tingling sensation travel downwards, awakening the hidden nerve endings between her legs.

'Well, Miss Parker, I have to finish off my business, so you just make yourself at home. Keys are on the dresser. You look cold – put the fire on if you like.' With a loaded smile he turned and pulled the door shut behind him.

Left alone, Holly gazed for a moment at her broad sea view, still flushed from Mr Briar's overfamiliarity. She brought her hands up to her engorged nipples, and reddened. She had always felt that her large, heavy breasts seemed incongruous on her slim frame and they constantly attracted unwelcome attention, but that they should respond so obviously . . . ! She felt let down by her body. She threw herself on the bed, her head buried in the soft pillows that smelled of lavender and fern. If she was to stay here for the duration of the play, she would have to start avoiding that man. She should be concentrating on her work.

She had been single for a few months after discovering that her boyfriend Jeff, also an actor, had been seeing his leading lady of the moment, and she missed a man's attention. She closed her eyes, her body still disturbed by the arousal of Mr Briar's gaze. She turned full onto

4

her stomach, bunching up the covers slightly between her legs. The gentle pressure on her sex was comforting and warming, just as the rhythmic rocking of the train had been on the way down here, and she began to dreamily remember her trip. On the train her imagination had conjured up all sorts of fantasies, and she had let her legs fall open slightly as she leaned back in half sleep. She had let the sheer lilac cotton of her dress gape open and ride up, affording the row of middle-aged commuters in front of her the pleasure of a rare glimpse of her white cotton panties. She had been well aware of this, had felt the heat of their eyes on her, had even (she was sure) noticed a stiffening in the trousers of the man opposite. She was quite an exhibitionist when she wanted to be. She had imagined that man suddenly kneeling before her on the crowded train, parting her smooth knees and taking in an unashamed view of her. In her mind he had kissed gently up the inside of her leg, asking her to let him taste her – she had said no, until he begged some more. So with everyone staring, she had allowed her fantasy man to kiss her through her flimsy panties – she had felt the wet, warm kisses soak the fabric, the tongue eager to get inside her, straining against it, the deep vibration of his groans dancing over her clit. Her pussy had almost felt these sensations as she imagined them, filling with moisture like a hungry mouth anticipating a feast. In reality her legs had opened wider at this point, under the pretence of sleep and the shaking of the train. But then, as now, she had succumbed to her weariness, and fell into a doze.

After a while, Holly became aware of a noise. At first she thought it was part of her dream or the wind groaning over the sea. Her eyes fluttered open and saw that twilight had fallen, sending a blue shadow through the room. The sound came again, a low, slow moan, a woman's voice, echoing through the wall. It became louder, more urgent and Holly's consciousness came back to her with a jolt. Whoever this woman was, the pleasure was palpable in her voice. As she lay listening, the moans became shorter and more frequent, and Holly's body started to respond in empathy. There was a whimpering now, the woman was saying something, and Holly felt suddenly curious. She listened intently, but the sounds were confusing. She tried to go back to sleep, turning on one side and puffing up the pillow with a fist. Her eyes shut but her head filled with suggestive images. Presumably it was that rude man Mr Briar who was pleasuring this woman. She didn't think he'd be so good at it. Sleep wasn't coming, so she gave in to curiosity.

Quietly, she slipped off the bed and made her way to the bedroom door. She silently turned her door handle and eased it open. She instantly saw a reddish spill of light oozing from the crack in the door of the Briars' bedroom, which had been left widely ajar, and she crept towards it like a moth to the flame, her cheeks burning with anticipation. She leaned silently against the door-frame gaining full view of the couple's bed.

In the orange lamplight Holly saw Mrs Briar's voluptuous body crouching over her husband as he lay defenceless and naked on the bed. At least, Holly assumed it was Mrs Briar. She looked a little younger than him with curly blonde hair and a generous body that moved wantonly over his. She was straddling his stomach and binding his hands to the top of the bedposts with a thick black scarf, her pendulous breasts swinging teasingly over his face. He sometimes caught a large pink nipple in his mouth and sucked hungrily, grunting with pleasure, his eyes flitting between her full curves and her determined face. He obviously enjoyed his bondage, his thick, sturdy erection was jumping and straining as he was being bound. Holly could see his wife's brown eyes glinting with power as she undulated her pelvis over his taut belly, circling lower and lower, leaving a shining trail of her desire on his skin, until her sex was directly over his. Holly focused her eyes in the strange light. She didn't know why she was being so nosey – maybe it was the fact she had gone a few months without sex. And maybe it was to do with this man's obvious interest in her own body. She let her hand absently stroke herself through her dress as she saw Mrs Briar rotate her hips slowly over her husband's naked groin making him grimace and jolt with need, although he was constrained and could barely move. Holly's knickers became wet as she found herself imagining that rigid shaft pushing against her own body. She gasped softly as she saw Mrs Briar lift her hips, reach down between his legs and deftly lower herself onto the fat cock, moaning open-mouthed at the size of him. He bucked and struggled as she moved her hips slowly up and down with studied control, her plump hand pressing onto his belly to hold him still. Her full buttocks tightened and released with each deliberate movement. He soon acquiesced to her gentle rhythm, letting out a deep groan which sent a gush of gooey pleasure into Holly's knickers. He groaned again, louder.

'Be quiet. You make noise when I tell you!' Mrs Briar's voice was hard even in a whisper. She lifted her hips petulantly, releasing her husband's livid cock from its moist home and causing it to twitch in frustration.

'Come on, woman,' he hissed, bucking his pelvis up to meet her dripping sex again, but she flinched, pressing her hand insistently down onto his chest. She moved up his body, trailing her juices over his brown stomach and chest and finally pausing with her sex poised over his mouth. She hovered there, smiling down at his helplessness.

'Let me taste you. Let me lick you,' he begged, his tongue darting out to meet her fleshly lips, not quite able to reach. 'Please, Delilah!' Again his tongue reached out to taste her. Holly didn't know how she could even hesitate. The woman's bushy dark-blonde pubes tickled his chin, and Holly saw his hard penis glistening from her juices, straining for attention. 'Please!' Without looking round, Mrs Briar reached behind her with her left hand and grasped her husband's cock, at the same time lowering herself onto his eager mouth. Holly's fingers pressed harder as she saw Mr Briar's lips and tongue gobbling ravenously at his wife's mound, whilst Mrs Briar whipped his stiff cock into its own frenzy. His mouth and her sex squelched noisily in their heated union. She was moaning and panting, losing some of the control she had shown earlier as her husband worked furiously on her cleft with his mouth, licking and sucking rabidly. Her hips began to tremble uncontrollably as her excitement grew, and she took her hand away from his shaft for a moment to concentrate on her own orgasm. Her large bottom began to wobble. She grasped the bedpost and gyrated wildly on her husband's face, pressing herself onto his mouth, whimpering and crying out in delight, her head thrown back, her blonde curls swaying in the orange light, her mouth open wide. She finally came in violent spasms, her full breasts and dimpled bottom shaking with the tremors of her orgasm. Holly's fingers worked up a frenzied pace as she imagined it was her aching sex that Mr Briar was stimulating so enthusiastically, and she too came stealthily, her knees buckling and her throat just catching the yelp of pleasure that threatened to betray her.

As she caught her breath, Holly saw Mrs Briar return to her position straddling her husband's now enormous cock. She lowered herself onto it and began to fuck him with gusto, bouncing full-bloodedly up and down and staring into his face to clock the unbridled joy of his reaction. The pressure of his huge member inside her ignited her passion again and she began to groan with lust – a different noise this time, primitive, guttural, urgent – as her heavy bottom moved up and down to meet his desperate thrusts. His face was contorted in extreme pleasure, Holly noticed breathily, and soon it was all too much for him. He suddenly let fly an enormous howl of release as his climax wracked his body, his bound hands tightening the black scarf as they yanked against their constraint. They both panted in sweaty relief and, still sitting on him, Mrs Briar began to laugh a throaty, lusty laugh, her swollen bosoms wobbling as she did so. The laugh became infectious, and soon Mr Briar was laughing too, his blue eyes glinting with spent desire. Holly slipped back into her room, closed the door shakily behind her and collapsed onto the bed. Her clit was still tender and her white cotton knickers sodden from her what she had witnessed. She climbed into bed and listened to the continuing laughter from the next room. She had an unnerving suspicion that the laugh was on her.

Chapter Two

'Christ!' Holly squinted in disbelief at her alarm clock, which had characteristically failed to go off. Perhaps in the heady arousal of last night, she had set it wrong. The sun flooded her room, and half blinded her as she stumbled out of bed. She hurriedly filled up the basin with warm soapy water and pulled her nightdress over her head. She liked a leisurely morning, but perhaps it was a blessing that she only had twenty minutes to get to rehearsals. She would just worry otherwise, and also she wasn't keen on a meeting with her lecherous landlord at this time of the morning. She had seen rather too much of him the night before. She splashed cold water on her cheeks, and then rubbed the soap over the full swell of her breasts. Feeling herself getting turned on at the memory, she rubbed herself dry vigorously with the guest towel.

Mr Briar grinned at her as she came running down the stairs. 'Oversleep, did we?' His eyes, again, gravitated stubbornly towards her breasts, which bounced obviously with every step. 'Bad girl.'

'Can't stop.' Holly smiled tightly back at him, and went for the front door. 'Oh, I . . .'

'Don't know where you're going?' He came up

behind her and leaned over her to push the door open, his solid arm brushing her cheek. The fresh air and sharp light of morning hit them full in the face. Mr Briar walked onto the porch and took a deep breath. 'Bet you don't get air like this in London.'

'Look, I'm in a bit of a hurry. Could you point me in the right direction?' Holly couldn't quite meet his eye, and instead threw her cool green gaze down the slope of the street and beyond, where the horizon was just a blue band of sea.

'OK, miss. Go down the hill till you get to an alley on the right – bit overgrown and that, wouldn't try it on a moonless night. Watch out for brambles, you'll snag that dress of yours – very pretty, isn't it?' His eyes strayed to the curve of her hips. 'Bit see-through in this light, mind. Still, the green brings out the colour of your eyes.' He smiled at his own smoothness. 'Anyway, get to the end of that and you'll be at the beach – turn right along the shore and the old theatre is there. Can't miss it.'

'Thanks.' She nodded and smiled wryly, and hurried off down the lane, conscious of the way the sun sliced through the sheer fabric of her dress. She turned back for a moment and saw him still standing there, staring.

'Thank you for joining us. Do come in.' Holly peered around the curtains in the wings as the man she remembered from the auditions as Max Biemeyer, the director, beckoned to her with an impatient gesture. 'You're late.'

'Sorry – I . . .'

'Everyone, this is Holly Parker, our leading lady. Well, come on, come on!' Holly stepped onto the stage, where the other actors had all assembled, seated in a circle. 'Looking lovely, my dear.' His voice still had the traces of some middle European accent, which along with his thick bush of greying hair gave him the air of a mad psychiatrist. But his grey eyes were steely, and Holly felt their displeasure at her lateness. She had heard he didn't like to be crossed and was a strict

11

taskmaster. 'Holly, sit down for God's sake, don't stand there like a spare part.' She glanced hurriedly around the circle, and a kindly looking actor in his early fifties patted the chair next to him.

'Got a free one here, my dear. Come and make an old man very happy and join me.' She smiled and gratefully sank into the chair. 'Nathaniel, by the way.' He extended a big hand, which she shook, relieved at his warmth.

'Yes, yes, we are coming to our introductions, Miss Parker – don't just stroll in here and take over. I heard you were a bit difficult, please don't prove the gossip-mongers right.' Holly was astonished at the man's rudeness. She bit her tongue and looked at the ground, feeling with shame that her cheeks were burning. 'Right, everyone say your name and what you are playing. Miss Parker can go first as she is so keen. Yes?'

'Well, I'm Holly – as you all must have gathered by now . . .' She laughed nervously and shot a glance around the group. It was only then that the bolt of recognition thundered through her body. Her gaze met a pair of all too familiar eyes. She drew a sharp breath and stared for some time, shocked into silence and disbelief. But her senses came to her slowly, and she checked the contours of the face, the tight mouth, the handsome jaw, the carefully coiffed chestnut hair, the mean smile. 'Jeff?'

'Hello, sweetie. Fancy meeting you here!' Holly baulked at his voice. The last time she had heard it had been in the heat of an awful row – when she had learned of his betrayal, his affair. What had his words been then? 'This isn't the end,' he had said, and he had smiled as he did now. But she had thrown him out, and spent a good six months recovering from his callousness. She had seen him for what he was, a handsome monster. 'Go on, my love. What are you playing?' He was studiedly cool.

'I – I'm not sure.' She glanced back at Max who was watching her anxiety with a measured gaze. 'I haven't had a chance to read it – I only got cast a few days ago. Sorry.'

'Holly is playing Dolores. The whore.' Max looked about the room. 'For those of you who did take the trouble to read the play, you will know Dolores has sexual contact with each and every one of you. I need you to be open to this. There is no room for inhibitions in my production. When it says you touch a breast, touch it. When you kiss each other, I want to see your tongues in each other's mouths. When you grab her cunt, or caress it, or kiss it even, I want the real thing. No pretending. This isn't a school play. It's about sex, about a woman who loves to fuck, and the people she destroys with her lust. It will be ground-breaking – no real theatre has put on something like this before. Do it right and we'll get the publicity we need to go into the West End, maybe Broadway, who knows? Do it wrong, and you can kiss your careers goodbye. Are you all up to this? Sweet Miss Parker? Can you get wet every night? Can you leave the men on and off stage hard?'

'Oh, she can do it all right.' Jeff chuckled. 'She's only twenty per cent frigid.'

'Fuck you!' Holly spat.

'Already have, my love.' Jeff smiled back. The rest of the cast was shuffling uncomfortably in their seats.

'Nathaniel!' The older actor once again rescued Holly from her humiliation. 'Playing Dolores' uncle – Lord Hunter. Lord Humper more like, the man's obsessed. He teaches her a few things.'

'Thank you, Nathaniel. Next.' Max sat back and pointed to a handsome, tall black actor who had caught Holly's eye when she had first arrived.

'My name's Oberon. Please don't laugh.' They all did. He smiled defeatedly, used to this reaction. 'My parents both read *A Midsummer Night's Dream* while they lived in Nigeria – it stuck, what can I say. I play Derry – the foreign knight who falls in love with Dolores. It won't be too hard!' He grinned playfully at Holly and every-one smiled, except for Jeff who spoke up hurriedly.

13

'I'm Jeff. Old friend of Max, Holly's ex if you hadn't guessed, so no new territory for me here. I'm playing Dolores' husband – poor cuckolded man. Bit of role reversal, eh, Hol?' Holly scowled at him and prepared to launch into a tirade, but checked herself.

'Next!' Max pointed now to the only other female member of the cast – a pretty young actress with a short blonde bob. Holly had noticed that she smiled a lot, even at tense moments.

'Nikki. Nicola if you like. I'm so pleased to be here – really excited. It's going to be great. I play Mistress Rachel – Dolores is my hand maid –' She giggled coyly. 'Especially in scene eight!' Nikki flashed a smile to all the men around the circle. Holly pulled the script from her bag and flicked through it, looking for the offending scene. She found a stage direction. 'Dolores pulls Mistress Rachel's breast from its corset and sucks hungrily on it, whilst rummaging in her own skirts in pursuit of self gratification . . .' 'It'll be fun!' Nikki insisted, seeing Holly's face blanch.

'Oh yeah, of course.' Holly was still compelled to be polite, much to Jeff's amusement.

'Loosen up will you, Hol!' He laughed. 'Come on, Max, let's get her relaxed. She needs it, I can tell. Take it from me.' Holly saw Max smile properly for the first time – a smile of complicity with Jeff. There was something between them. Suddenly she felt like she had been set up.

'Can't we just do a read-through?' she asked. Max thought for a moment. She could tell he was contemplating something, but he seemed to think the better of it and instead clapped his hands.

'Today we will be kind to ourselves. Let us look at the language of the period, at the manner, dress and so on.' He glanced at Jeff. 'When we have a handle on the world of the play, then we will explore ourselves a bit more. And this afternoon we can all go home and look at our lines. Yes?' He glared at Holly, who nodded. 'Right. Everyone on their feet!'

The cast spent the morning improvising and discussing the play. Holly was constantly aware of Jeff's presence in the room – smug and somehow mocking. She didn't like it, but wasn't about to show him that. She didn't even glance at him when they were discussing fidelity and affairs in Victorian England, although she would have loved to have given the unfaithful bastard a knowing look. But she knew that her indifference to him would get at him, and she was right. When they broke for lunch he brushed past her viciously.

'Sorry, love,' he snarled. Holly ignored him and turned to smile at Nikki who was leaning over her bag looking for her mobile.

'Wanna get some lunch, Nikki?' she asked. 'There's a lovely chippy on the sea front.' Nikki looked up, her bright blue eyes quizzical.

'Oh no, can't have fried food,' she breathed. 'I've brought a salad with me if you want to share.' Jeff let out a wry laugh.

'Holly doesn't have to diet – she eats like a horse, don't you, Hol?' Holly pointedly ignored him. 'In fact, she lets rip with all her appetites.'

'Grow up, will you,' she finally snapped, and marched out of the building into the sharp brightness of the early afternoon sun.

The pebble beach was pretty deserted except for a couple of young mums and their children running wild with kites and buckets of shells. But for the uncomfortable knot in her stomach she could almost believe that morning's confrontations with Jeff hadn't happened. What must the other actors have thought of her? She paused to pick up a particularly pretty stone, luminous and white like a huge pearl. It grew warm in her hand as she meandered along the beach.

'Holly?' She looked up to see the well-built torso of Oberon, glowing deep brown in the sun. He lay on a big red towel in a pair of green shorts, shielding his eyes from the light with his script. 'Join me. You poor thing!' He smiled warmly, patting the space on his ample towel. 'He's really got it in for you, hasn't he?'

'Seems like it.' She sat dejectedly.

'Don't worry about it! It's Jeff's problem. He'll calm down.' Oberon chuckled. 'Although I can't see what you ever saw in him. What a loser.' This even provoked a laugh from Holly. 'Must have hidden talents, eh?'

'Not really, no.' She smiled. 'One of life's big mistakes. Making a lot of those lately.'

'Like taking this job you mean?'

'We'll see.'

'Listen, if you're going to have a shit time, may as well do it by the seaside.' He grinned. 'Could be worse. Treat it like a free holiday.'

'With a bit of slow emotional torture thrown in?'

'Why not? Sounds like every family holiday I've ever been on.' They both laughed. A rogue beach ball suddenly came rolling up between them, followed timorously by a chubby five-year-old boy in a huge hat. Oberon threw it back to him. They both watched the child stumble away with it, shouting to his mum.

'I feel like a swim,' Holly declared suddenly.

'Go ahead.'

'No, I – I haven't got a costume with me.'

'No one's here – go in your pants. Go naked – nobody will notice!' Oberon was encouraging but Holly was aware of other people along the beach. 'It's sad because I can see that you want to.' She did. There was nothing she would have liked more than to swim in the cool sea, naked, washing the morning off her, and to emerge, all salty and shivering to dry off in the sun. But she couldn't.

'Listen,' Oberon took her hand warmly, 'you've had a bad morning, a bad relationship by the looks of things, and now there's this strange guy nagging you to go skinny-dipping. I'm sorry.'

'Sometimes I wish – I wish I was freer. You know? I want to be one of those girls who don't care, who swim naked, who have sex with strangers on trains. I look at

16

someone like Nikki – she looks like that type. I just think about it.'

'You do?'

'You know what I mean.'

'Well, listen, honey, this play's going to loosen you up if that's what you want. You can't have any inhibitions playing the part you are.' She looked at him doubtfully. 'And you'll do it – I can tell. You're a passionate woman.'

'Underneath?' She smiled. 'You know I haven't had a chance to read the bloody thing. That'll be tonight's little project.'

'Well, make sure you're sitting down. It's sex sex sex all the way!'

'Oh God.' She grabbed his script and flicked through the pages. 'Sex? It's all involving me too, I bet?'

'Pretty much.' He shrugged. 'You'll have to kiss Jeff. How will that be?'

'Hideous. What page?' She found it eventually and read aloud. '"Dolores is washing at the basin, soaping her naked breasts" – oh shit – "her husband Francis enters, drunk and nervous." – Jeff can do drunk all right. "He creeps up behind her and inhales loudly. She swings round, dripping." Then he says, "I can smell them on you – the other men. You could wash yourself in acid, I'd still smell them." Then "He kisses her with a desperate violence, and licks his way to her breast –" Oh my God! – "I can taste them on you" . . . Oh, I get the picture.'

'The whole play is pretty much like that.'

'If I'd have known . . .' She was flicking through the pages with some anger now. 'I could call my agent, you know. Back out of it. That would be the sane, healthy thing to do.'

'You could. You should if you want to. Only, well –' His eyes searched her face.

'What?'

'Wouldn't that be a bit like letting Jeff win? It seems

17

to me he and Max want to break you, for some ungodly reason. Why let them?'

She stared out to sea for some time, watching the sun dance off the waves, then turned to him with a wry smile. 'What if they do break me?'

'They won't.' They were silent for a while.

'Think I'll read this thing, then,' Holly said eventually. 'See what I've let myself in for.' She got to her feet, taking her white pebble with her. 'Thanks though. For the friendly ear.'

'No worries – any time.' He smiled up at her. 'I've got two, by the way, if you wear one out.'

'I'll bear that in mind.' With that, she made her way along the beach, ready to face the Briars.

As she pushed the door open and put the rusty key back into her bag, she was hit by the inviting aroma of a fry-up. Voices were coming from the Briars' kitchen, then laughter. She gently shut the door and started to creep up the stairs. She had had enough ogling for one day, and she needed to look at this script. She was half-way up when a handsome young lad emerged from the kitchen. He had shoulder-length dark-blond hair, with the same warm brown eyes as Mrs Briar. He had the air of the surfers she had seen on TV, with long toned limbs, tanned and furred with blond hair bleached by the sun. He looked at her a little awkwardly.

'Mum and Caleb want to know if you want some lunch,' he said, abruptly. 'There's lots here, they say, if you want some.'

'Caleb?'

'You know. Mum's husband. My stepdad?'

'Oh! Mr Briar?' Holly glanced up the stairs. She should work and she wanted to avoid Mr Briar at all costs, but the smell of fried bread and crispy eggs filled the landing and made her stomach churn with hunger. 'I am peckish . . .'

'Up to you.' The young man disappeared back into the kitchen again. Holly hovered on the landing, and after a few moments gave in to the demands of her body.

'There you are, darling!' Mrs Briar was already at the stove, piling a plate high with all sorts of goodies. 'Sit down and have some nice grub.'

'Is that all for me?' Holly sat down next to Mr Briar, pointedly avoiding his loaded glare.

'You smell different,' he said. 'What have you been up to?'

'Just rehearsing.' She was trying to sound casual but ended up appearing a bit short with him.

'Leave her alone, Caleb!' Mrs Briar chucked a tea towel at his head. 'Let the poor girl eat!' She placed the food in front of Holly, generously topped with tomato ketchup. 'You've met my son, Ben?' she added.

'Yes, we've . . .' Holly trailed off, smiling at the young man sitting opposite her, who seemed just as ill at ease as she was.

'He's a stunner, isn't he?' Mrs Briar continued. 'He's a good lad, too, aren't you, darling? It's his birthday next week!'

'Oh really?' Holly couldn't help but smile at Mrs Briar's obvious pride in her son. 'How old?'

'I'll be nineteen,' he said and shovelled a huge mouthful of French toast into his mouth.

'Don't!' Mrs Briar shuddered. 'It makes me feel so old, you know! I only had him when I was twenty, you see. I'm only thirty-nine.'

'Relax, woman, no one cares!' Mr Briar was his usual gruff self, but punctuated his remark with a well-aimed slap that resounded noisily on his wife's bottom.

'Caleb! Honestly.' She grinned and sat down opposite Holly, her ample body making the chair creak a little as she did so.

'Well – happy birthday, Ben.' Holly caught his eye properly for the first time, and flushed slightly as she did so. 'I hope you have a nice one.'

'Oh, he will, Caleb has some surprise in store, don't you, love? Won't even tell me what it is, will you?'

19

'No, I won't. She couldn't keep a secret if her life depended on it,' he retorted, with obvious affection.

'What must Holly think of us!' Mrs Briar shovelled a fork-full of sausage in her mouth. 'We're not always this argumentative.' Her mother had obviously never instructed her not to talk with her mouth full.

'Yes we are!' exclaimed her son softly, his eyes twinkling at Holly. 'This is a good day.' The conversation volleyed back and forth between them as Holly savoured her plateful of food, watching them in amusement. She eyed the couple with interest, having seen them in such different circumstances the night before. Then Mr Briar had been helpless and submissive, his wife a voluptuous dominatrix, and both of them apparently exhibitionistic. Now they were a squabbling couple. As they all finished their meals, Mr Briar sat back in his chair and patted his belly.

'Few more meals like that and you'll have a bit of flesh on you, too.' He grinned. 'You'll need your strength. By the looks of you these rehearsals are draining your blood.'

'He's right, dear, you looked really pale when you came in.' Mrs Briar showed concern.

'It wasn't brilliant,' Holly replied, awed at her own sense of understatement. 'Still, tomorrow is another day. I hope it'll go better.'

'Oh dear, that bad?' Even Mr Briar softened a bit. 'Bad enough for you to do a bunk?'

'Pardon?'

'You know, skive off? I've got the boat tomorrow morning, it's supposed to be a calm one out at sea. She's just a small vessel, but big enough for us. Ben's coming, aren't you, lad.'

'Too right, Caleb.'

'See, even he shows enthusiasm. Loves boats, don't you? A real sea boy.' He reached over and ruffled his stepson's hair.

'Get off!'

'It'll be lovely. Go on!' Holly considered a moment.

She had enough temptation in the form of the tall, muscular young Ben to entice her away from the grim prospect of rehearsals, but could she be that irresponsible?

'You should come,' Ben said softly. She knew she couldn't resist.

'I will then,' she declared. She almost instantly regretted her decision as she saw the look of lusty delight that passed over Mr Briar's face. He eyed her with that overfamiliar gaze and, to her amazement, placed his large firm hand on her thigh under the table.

'Well. Be down here at seven.' His fingers squeezed slightly, and she jumped up from her chair.

'I – er – I have to go and do some homework – I mean, work. On my lines and stuff. Upstairs.' They all smiled at her as she backed out of the room.

She closed her bedroom door firmly behind her, pulled her script from her bag and threw it onto the bed. In her bag the unopened letter she had received from Jeff lay mocking her. Ever since it had arrived, she had been reluctant to open it. It would have been like opening up an old wound. The writing on the envelope was sharp-edged and slanted backwards. She could guess what it said. She had had enough of him for one day, she thought. She would be happy never to see him again, and tomorrow out at sea, she would get herself used to the idea of being around him for a while. With that thought, she settled down on the bed and started flicking through the script.

Chapter Three

*S*ix thirty a.m., the green light of her radio alarm clock flashed as it came alive to some long forgotten eighties hit, still on the play list of this particular local radio station. Holly reached over in the half-light and fumbled it into silence, her mind gradually focusing on the day ahead. Before she could change her mind about the boat trip, she took herself into the shower and blasted herself with hot, refreshing water. When she made it downstairs at seven on the dot she felt awake and excited to be escaping for a day. Mr Briar and Ben were waiting in the kitchen over a cup of tea, laughing about something. When Holly came in they both looked up with very different smiles – Ben open and welcoming, Mr Briar knowing and wry.

'Hello, sleeping beauty.' He grinned. 'Got your sea legs on today?'

'Yip,' she replied shortly. 'Will I be warm enough?' She indicated the clothes she had picked out – jeans, a thick shirt and a long warm coat.

'We'll keep you warm enough.' Weary of his innuendo, Holly rolled her eyes slightly which made Ben laugh.

'Perhaps we should go?' the boy suggested, saving her from any more of it.

The three of them made their way through the thick morning air, still pink with sunrise, down to the harbour. A few other small vessels bobbed about on the water, some inhabited by men working or sitting back with a cup of hot soup or tea. The sea before them seemed calm enough.

'We're in luck,' commented Mr Briar. 'Not a wave on her today.' He nodded to another man scrubbing the deck of a boat called *Jenny*. 'All right, Simon?' The man, equally gruff, grunted in reply. Seagulls wheeled overhead, their mournful cries filling the silence.

'Which one's ours?' asked Holly. Ben pointed to a small boat attached to the jetty, with '*Delilah*' painted clumsily on its side in red letters. 'Of course.' She smiled. When they reached it Mr Briar jumped aboard as Ben held it to the jetty. He then began to lift the anchor and shift a vast pile of netting from the deck.

'Hop on,' Ben said softly when the boat was ready. Holly did so, wobbling slightly as she adjusted to the rocking of the boat. She lowered herself onto the bench that ran along the front of the vessel and moved her feet to make way for Ben to come on board. 'Actually I have to stay behind.' He apologised, glancing quickly towards the back of the boat at his stepfather for approval.

'Yes. Ben's going down the coast with some friends to do some surfing.'

'Oh!' Holly's face brightened, about to ask if perhaps she could come with him, but before the thoughts reached her mouth, Mr Briar had revved up the engine and the boat was reversing into the vast expanse of blue.

'Have a good time!' Ben waved and turned to go. Holly watched his broad back topped with lovely blond curls disappear. When she finally turned to Mr Briar he had more than a little laughter in his eyes, but said nothing. He turned the boat around and they sped out to sea for some time, leaving the coast and the other boats behind them. They travelled at speed, the boat

23

revving above the water and leaving a trail of waves behind them. The hazy sunshine flashed on the sea and clung to a faint mist that hugged the air. When their boat was surrounded only by water and no one else was in sight, Mr Briar turned off the engine and sat back, his hands behind his head. The boat rocked a little as it settled, then seemed as calm as the sea itself.

'Beautiful, isn't it?' His voice was devoid of its usual irony. Holly looked about her, feeling her tension uncurling like a fist opening.

'It really is.' She reached down and trailed her fingertips in the icy water, and for a while they sat there, forgetting where they were.

'So you want to tell me what was up with you yesterday?'

'What do you mean?' Holly looked sharply at him.

'When you came in. You were all tensed up.' He seemed, suddenly, surprisingly attractive to Holly out here, like he had found his natural environment. It seemed to fit that he was surrounded by the salty sea, out in the open. He seemed more honest and direct, and she found herself wanting to talk to him. She sighed and her green eyes flashed with gold as she took in the horizon.

'There was someone there from my past – at rehearsals.'

'I see.'

'An ex.'

'Right.' He waited for her to continue, but she felt she'd said it all. Eventually he asked: 'Had it ended badly?'

Holly laughed, her voice ringing across the water and causing a far-off sea gull to cry out in reply. 'You could say that. He left me for some young thing.'

'That old story.'

'Yip. Full-on cliché. And I was the clichéd poor victim too for a bit – you know, crying into my pillow, wearing big baggy jumpers, all that shit.' She slapped the

24

water with her hand, enjoying the splash of cold water. 'Then I realised it was the best thing he ever did leaving me.'

'Why?'

'Why?' Holly put her mind to this question, screwing up her face in thought. 'Because he's an idiot.'

Mr Briar smiled and reached into his bag pulling out a flask. 'Tea?' Holly shook her head. After he'd taken a swig he leaned forward.

'He was a fool. You are the most beautiful thing I've ever seen.' His eyes were steady on her, and his voice direct. Holly watched him, curious. Their eyes locked. Feeling suddenly nervous, she looked away. 'I want to touch you,' he continued, and put his flask casually back in his bag. She looked back at him sharply. He rose to his feet without upsetting the balance of the boat and moved towards her until he stood over her, looking down. She wrapped the thick wool of her coat around her and drew her knees protectively to her body. Mr Briar didn't react, instead he brushed a gentle finger under her chin and tilted her face up to meet his eyes. She felt a shiver where his skin touched hers and at the determined power in his eyes. She felt that she would have to do what he said, whether she liked it or not. The silence of the sea and sky seemed sharper now and lonely. He drew his fingers from her chin and down her throat, resting in the hollow at the base of it. 'Open your coat,' he said.

'No.' Her voice faltered out in a whisper. He dropped to his knees before her and gently opened it for her. She watched silently as he slipped the coat off her shoulders, his eyes taking in the curve of her breasts under her shirt. He brought his thick fingers up to the top button and slowly undid it, then moved them down to the next button.

'Don't.' Holly suddenly found her voice. He ignored her, continuing to undo the coat slowly button by button. As she leaned back in a gesture of resistance he moved forward until he was half lying on her, kneeling between her legs. He pressed against her so she could just feel the stiff shape of his erection. She tried to jerk her hips back to escape its hardness, but was pinned down by his weight. The boat began to rock a little under their silent struggle. Once he had opened her shirt to the navel, he pulled it apart exposing her powder-blue bra. Now his eyes took in her breasts, and as he carefully forced down the cups of the bra she heard him let out a breath. Her breasts were full and fleshy, topped with even cinnamon-coloured nipples, which were now hard with cold and strangely anxious to be touched. Holly gave up all resistance and melted reluctantly into the sexiness of the moment. She let her legs fall open and subtly brought her hips forward to get a harder feel of his cock against her. He felt this move and responded by slowly gyrating against her crotch, and bringing his lips down to her cleavage. He kissed along the swell of her left breast and sighed with pleasure when the nipple sprang into his mouth. He was very different now to how Holly had seen him with his wife – then he had sucked like a ravenous baby in a frenzy – now, he licked and nibbled and suckled with careful, slow, delicious precision, as if wanting to savour every moment. She bent her head to watch him, seeing with pleasure the lazy circling of his head at her breast and the way his stubbled, sun-weathered face looked against the pale smoothness of her skin. He spent a long time slowly licking the tip of her nipple, occasionally letting his tongue flutter and vibrate against it which made her feel like an electric current ran between her breast and her clitoris. He took it in his mouth and sucked it tentatively, and sometimes let his teeth softly nip at it. After what seemed like half an hour, he kissed his way across to the other breast, leaving her left nipple smarting with cold as the air hit its wetness. She groaned a little and threw her head back as he began the same attention on her right breast, and automatically wrapped her arms around his hips, grabbing his firm buttocks and pulling him into her body, grinding through their clothes to feel as much of him as she could. Surprised by this, he seemed to lose some of his control, and began licking and suckling her with more vigour, breathing hard against her. 'Oh, I can't wait to taste your pussy,' he sighed, one hand starting to grapple urgently with the buckle of her belt. Her knickers dampened with lust at the thought of it.

Suddenly a strange voice seemed to come at them across the water. Mr Briar reluctantly lifted his head, his eyes heavy with arousal.

'Shit,' he said, and hurriedly sat back on his haunches. Holly swung round and saw, in the distance, the boat *Jenny* coming towards them. It was too far away for anyone to have seen them, but the voices carried across the water and cut through the still air. Holly shakily reassembled her clothing and sat up straight. She and Mr Briar did not look at each other, but she heard him start the engine and they made their way back to shore without a word.

When they came through the front door of the house, Mrs Briar was singing in the kitchen and the sound of pans bubbling greeted them.

'I'm hungry!' Mr Briar called out, throwing his bag by the door and kicking off his boots. 'Where's the love of my life with my grub?' Mrs Briar popped her head around the door with a rounded grin on her pink face.

'Peas, mash and pie,' she said simply, as if answering an unasked question. She gave her husband a loud kiss on the lips and pulled him through to the kitchen.

'I might just go upstairs,' Holly said hurriedly, suddenly unable to look her hostess in the eye. 'Could I just have some toast or something?' Mrs Briar looked at her as if she was coming down with flu.

'Toast?' she cried in disgust. 'Oh well, if that's what you want – I'll get Caleb to bring it up when he's finished. I've got to go out.' This caused Mr Briar to look up at Holly for the first time, the ironic smirk back on his face.

'Thank you.' Holly started up the stairs, hoping she didn't look too guilty. 'I think I'll just have a nap if that's OK.'

As soon as her head hit the pillow, she felt heavy with impending sleep and unresolved frustration. The sea air had cleared her head but made her tired. Her eyes refused to stay open, and dreams came flooding quickly into her imagination. She dreamed she was lying naked in the boat *Delilah*, but it was filling with warm water. She knew she had to get out or drown, but she was pinned down by a thick, long, muscular snake, which slithered heavily up her leg until its green head reached her naked sex. It flicked its tongue out to taste her and her body sparked with pleasure. Its head pressed into her slightly, forcing her open and sliding into her wet pussy. It wriggled and writhed inside her, climbing higher and higher. When it retracted, it started to slide up her body and between her breasts, its fat body forcing her legs open even further. The water was swilling around her ears now, she was deafened by it, but her arousal and terror pinned her down. Just as the water reached her mouth, she opened her eyes and awoke.

The room was dark, the curtains drawn. She could see through the crack in them that it must be late evening, the sky a purpley black. Beside her on the dresser was a plate of cold toast. She shut her eyes and could still feel the sensation of the snake on her body. She opened them again and realised that it was no dream. Her bare legs were open under the duvet and the bed dipped under the weight of someone crouching under the covers at the foot of the bed. She felt the brush of stubble against her upper thigh and the hot trickle of her own wetness mingled with saliva run down between her legs and down the crack of her bottom. A soft, slippery tongue was tickling the lips of her pussy, tentatively opening them and searching out the hard button of her clitoris. It made soft circles around it, and the stubbly jaw roughly scratched her sensitive inner thighs. Holly sighed silently as the anonymous tongue began to probe her, lapping at her like an eager dog. His breath felt hot against her sex, and occasionally she felt him stifle a groan or swallow quietly, obviously still thinking she was asleep. She lay still, not wanting to interrupt the illicit pleasure. He tried to get her whole pussy into his mouth, sucking hungrily at her, and then forced his tongue inside her, wanting to taste as much of her as he could. The tongue flicked and curled, and she began to tremble with pleasure. Whenever its stiff tip met her clit she almost bucked with appreciation and gratitude, willing him to do it faster, but she kept her body taut and unmoving. The tongue seemed to read her mind, and increased the urgency of its licking. She felt the soft moans of a man's voice vibrating into her pussy. He licked harder and harder, faster and faster, until she felt the unmistakable urgency of a coming climax grip her. She stretched and tensed and ground against his face, still not making a sound. The tongue was sent into a frenzy against her, the head bobbing up and down wildly beneath the white covers. Holly widened her thighs and started to buck against the anonymous face. When she came, two strong hands clasped her buttocks and held her hips firmly against his mouth so he would not slip away at the wrong moment. Her body became limp again, but he could not seem to stop. Still the tongue continued in its delicious, invasive rhythm, tasting the juices of her orgasm and gently continuing to stimulate her. She smiled lazily and began to enjoy it again. She thought it must be Mr Briar crouched between her legs, but wasn't sure. It could be Ben, she mused happily, or Oberon. It could be Nathaniel, she thought, as the tongue lightly teased her clit again, or it could be Max. It could be anybody, she thought, as the tongue started to fuck her hard. She didn't really care who it was.

Again her body geared itself up for a climax, and she spread her legs as wide as they would go. The man moaned deeply at this, and continued to groan and sigh into her pussy, pulling her hips harder to his mouth, and crushing her against his face. Holly slid her hand under the covers and grabbed the back of his head, her fingers buried in his tangled curls. She urgently pulled his head even closer against her, until he was almost swallowing her. When she came this time it was hard and violent, and she almost drowned him in her juices. She cried out finally, until the waves of her orgasm subsided. Awash with pleasure, she fell back into a deep sleep and didn't even hear it when he closed the door behind him.

Chapter Four

Walking down the bramble path the next morning, Holly congratulated herself on having avoided all the Briars as she left the house. After such a long sleep the sexual adventures of last night seemed like a dream, but she was certain now that the man beneath the covers had been Mr Briar, and she just couldn't face him. Having to face Max after not turning up for rehearsals was bad enough. She braced herself for a confrontation as she went up the steps of the theatre and walked into the auditorium.

The first thing she saw was Max's face, peering down at her from over the top of his script. His eyes clouded with a thunder that she tried to match.

'So what was it, Miss Parker? Death in the family? Sudden bout of amnesia?' He glared at her as she confidently strode up to the stage. 'I am sure there is some amazing excuse for an apparently professional actress to decide to take the day off without so much as informing the company manager!' Holly didn't reply. Instead she slowly removed her jacket and carefully laid it across the back of one of the seats. She looked up to the stage and saw, for the first time, the bewildered faces of her co-stars, and the cold, drawn face of Jeff.

'Hello, everybody,' she said calmly. 'I am sorry about

31

yesterday. As you can all imagine, after our first day here, I was giving some thought as to whether or not it was worth my doing this show at all. Part of me was, I admit, saying, ' "Life's too short." ' Oberon laughed knowingly. 'But I have decided I will stay on. You all – well, most of you – seem like lovely people and the play is good, and . . .' She faltered slightly.

'Yes?' Max was glowering at her.

'And it's never been my style to give in to bullies.' This surprised him, she could tell. His mouth fell open a little. Nikki was staring at her in disbelief and looked quickly at Jeff to clock his reaction. Suddenly Jeff smiled and started a slow handclap.

'Congratulations,' he sneered. 'A very good imitation of a strong woman. Quite an actress, our Holly. Should get an Oscar for that one.' Holly, who had been standing in the auditorium, made her way coolly up the steps to the stage until she was on his level.

'You,' she said, 'are making a real fool of yourself.' Then she turned to Max. 'Shall we start or is this going to get drawn out into a Jerry Springer type thing? With punch-ups and accusations and everything? I do hope not.'

'We will start when *I* say, Miss Parker. I am still the director. Everybody sit. Sit!' Max lost his cool for a moment, and the cast all hurried to get a chair. Everyone sat in a circle, Oberon next to Holly. He winked at her and gave her thigh a supportive squeeze. She smiled warmly back. Max, seeing this, seemed to combust with anger.

'I will not have this!' he growled. 'You – you have a problem, Miss Parker. I don't know what it is yet, but I'll be damned if I'm going to let it screw up my production.'

'You can call me Holly, you know.'

'I will call you what I like!' He took a breath, and steadied himself. 'I'll tell you this much. By the time our first night comes, you are going to have to loosen up and lose the attitude. I've been doing some phoning

32

round. Adrian!' He turned and yelled for the stage manager, who hurried up within seconds, clutching a piece of paper.

'Thank you, Adrian.' Max passed Holly the paper. She unfolded it. On it was a name and address, local to the village.

'Joshua Delaney?' She was confused. 'Who's he?'

'He is a therapist. Or used to be – a famous one. Specialises in sexual problems.'

'So?' All eyes turned on Max.

'So he has agreed to see you. To help loosen you up.' Max smiled graciously. 'The company will pay, of course.'

Holly was aghast. 'I don't need a therapist, Max. You may well need one, but I don't.'

'Naturally we cannot make you go.' Max was unnervingly polite. 'Of course, if you don't you may not be up to the part of Dolores. Which would mean letting you go. Finding another – less inhibited – actress for the role. Purely in the interests of the show, you understand.' Nathaniel, who had been silent all this time, was outraged at this.

'For Christ's sake, man!' he cried. 'What is this?'

'No, don't worry, Nathaniel.' Holly smiled at him. 'I'll go. It'll be interesting. No need to fire me just yet, Max.' There was a stiff silence around the room. Nikki let out a nervous giggle, then cleared her throat.

'Right.' Max opened his script. 'Let's begin this read-through. Act one, scene one. 'Lord Hunter enters bearing a letter . . .' Continue . . .'

It was six o'clock by the time rehearsals ended and Max finally allowed the weary actors to go back to their digs. The day had been long and hard, with knotty discussions regarding the script, and Holly's head was throbbing slightly as she pulled her jacket on to leave. Oberon came and put an arm around her.

'Walk with you?' He smiled. 'My digs are up past yours, I think.'

'Yeah, that'd be nice.' They made to leave but were stopped by the sound of Max clearing his throat meaningfully behind them.

Holly looked back at him. 'Can we help you with anything?'

'A word before you leave, Miss Parker.' His face was serious. 'Oberon, you may go – learn the ravishing scene for tomorrow. We'll be doing that in the afternoon.' Holly gestured to Oberon that he should go, and soon Max and Holly were the only ones standing in the theatre.

'I like your fire,' he said unexpectedly, furrowing his bushy grey eyebrows. 'But you are too – English. You try to keep it in too much. I can see that in you is great potential.' He had an appreciation in his eyes as he appraised her. 'Great passion. But you are afraid of it. This is what you will speak to the therapist about. Yes?'

'Yes.' She couldn't argue with him – she felt she was being complimented and insulted all at once, and that he had seen right through her on both counts. Max saw the self-doubt cross her face.

'I cast you, remember. I am not stupid.' She looked quizzical. 'I wouldn't have cast you if you didn't have the fire in you to play Dolores. The sexual abandon. The spark. You have it.'

'How do you know?' she asked doubtfully.

'Call it an instinct. A scent on you. A chemical thing.' For a moment his gruff exterior seemed to be melting, but then he snapped again. 'You may go. Tomorrow you have an appointment. Eleven a.m. Be there. Then come straight here.'

'Fine.'

Max swept out of the building leaving Holly picking up her bag to go. She stood in the silent auditorium for a moment, reflecting on Max's words. Maybe talking to a therapist would be a blessing in disguise. Maybe she should be more in touch with her desires. She thought about the previous night – how she had been able to abandon herself to the pleasure only because she was

34

barely conscious. And of the boat, when she had been surprised by her own body's arousal.

Suddenly she became aware of a noise coming from the backstage area, something falling. She stopped still and listened. There it was again, a shuffling, then a whisper. She quietly climbed onto the stage and crept through the wings into the darkness. Following the noise, she found herself standing outside the open props cupboard, which was a small room crammed full of old chairs, masks, costumes, hats, goblets and weird props from previous productions. A small halogen lamp burned blue on the floor, illuminating the shape of Jeff leaning back against a bookcase. In front of him, Nikki was kneeling on the floor with her back to Holly. Her blonde head was bobbing up and down at the open fly of his crotch, her blouse was hanging off her shoulders and her mini skirt was hunched around her waist. Holly walked a few more steps and could see the familiar sight of Jeff's erect penis, with Nikki sucking and licking it for all she was worth.

'Push your arse up in the air,' he grunted. Nikki instantly arched her back, displaying her perfectly rounded bottom, barely covered by a cream G-string. Jeff took the sight in hungrily with his eyes. 'Oh!' he gasped. 'Yes, that's good.' And Nikki resumed her thorough blowjob in this new position. Holly wasn't so much jealous over Jeff, but she did envy Nikki's eager sexual openness. Jeff's strained face revealed that he was about to come, and he opened his eyes to look straight up at Holly as if he'd known she was there all along. 'That's the best,' he murmured to Nikki, and smiled at his ex smugly. 'The best I've ever had.' Nikki let out an aroused whimper at this compliment and worked harder, her hair flying about like crazy, her mouth completely full. Jeff kept eye contact with Holly as he came, thrusting at Nikki's mouth, pouring his come into it. She seemed keen to drink it all up, something that Holly had never liked, and afterwards she smiled up at Jeff with a glowing face. He looked down at her too, relieved and spent. Baulking at this, Holly rushed out into the night.

When she got through the front door of her digs, Holly made to go straight upstairs. Mr Briar spotted her from the kitchen and called out to her to come for some food. Holly knew she would have to see him at some point.

Why not, she thought, and went in. He was on his own, standing at the stove frying some fish. A pan of new potatoes boiled on the hob, and another full of peas. 'That looks nice,' she said politely.

'Delilah's favourite.' He smiled. Holly was suddenly hit by a pang of guilt. Here was a happy couple and she was allowing herself to be seduced by the husband, without a thought for the wife.

'Look,' she said, in a way that instantly made him turn to her. 'I know what happened was – well, nice, pleasant, whatever – but it has to stop.' He waited for her to elaborate. 'You're not going to make this easy for me, are you?'

'What? You mean in the boat?'

'Yes, in the boat. And in my room.' He looked at her blankly. 'For a start, I would appreciate it if you would knock before you came in . . .'

'Oh, you mean the toast?' He smiled. 'Well, I did knock, but you were out like a light. Sorry, I came in anyway, to leave it for you. Thought you might wake up hungry.' He got on with the job of frying the fish.

'Not the toast!' Holly became exasperated. 'The other thing. When you woke me up!'

'I'm sorry, miss. I really don't know what you're talking about.' His face seemed genuine. 'In the boat – I am sorry. You just looked so beautiful, and it feels so free out there in the middle of the ocean. And I did know you wanted to, deep down. But I won't approach you again, unless you ask me. How's that?'

'But you were in my room. In bed with me . . .' Holly was confused.

'Maybe someone was.' His smile was rather ironic

now. 'Maybe a certain soon-to-be nineteen-year-old I know. He's a popular boy with the girls, you know. Pretty inexperienced, but you could soon sort that out.' He winked at her. 'Up to no good, that rascal.' And he chuckled as he turned the fish over in the pan. 'Do you like peas? We're eating in five minutes.'

That night, lying in bed, Holly found sleep hard to sink into. She felt hot and awake with the memory of Jeff and Nikki, grabbing such an urgent moment in a props cupboard like sex-mad teenagers. She could never imagine herself doing that with him when they had been an item. Then her mind filled with thoughts of the night before, and the man who had gone down on her. Could it have been Ben? She flushed at the idea. Maybe he was too shy to come to her in the daylight. Maybe he would come again tonight, and relieve her of some of this frustration. She pulled off her knickers under the duvet and flung them out of the bed. If he was coming, she wanted to be ready. She realised that she really wanted him to come – even if it wasn't Ben but his stepfather. With this thought, she melted into sleep, and dreamed again of the snake winding its way up her body, slithering and sliding into all of her orifices, arousing her with its flicky tongue.

Chapter Five

Joshua Delaney's house was at the top of a hill. It stood alone, perched on a cliff edge overlooking the Atlantic Ocean. It was a modern, airy property, Holly noticed as she approached it, simple and devoid of a woman's touch, built in strong clean lines and surrounded by flowerless lawns and fields. This guy was definitely a bachelor. He was obviously a loner, too – the house was at least half a mile from the next property, and the view was endless and uncluttered. Holly wondered what had made him retire from therapy, and how he could afford to live here now. Maybe he was an old man, living off his life's earnings. She wasn't sure how she would feel opening up about her sexual neuroses in front of someone who looked like her granddad.

She rang the bell and soon saw a figure approach the frosted glass of the front door. It was opened by a tall, well-built man in his late thirties. He had a thick head of slightly scruffy chestnut hair and warm blue eyes, which smiled at her shyly. He was wearing a thick jumper and jeans, with walking boots flecked with freshly dried mud. He saw her take them in.

'Sorry. Dog,' he said. 'He needs walking whether it's raining or not.' As if to confirm this, a dog barked in a far room. 'Come in.' Holly followed him into the house.

38

It was sparsely decorated and airy verging on draughty. There was a long window, which ran from the floor up to the ceiling, and a pine staircase at the far end of the hallway leading to the second floor. The furnishings were all wood, the walls a natural white.

'Nice place,' she said, as he led her into a study room.

'Thanks, I like it.' He gestured for her to sit down in a red leather chair, which she did. Looking around, she saw that this room at least had some signs of life in it. The desk was strewn with papers and opened books, the walls lined with bookcases, certificates and a couple of abstract prints. He took a chair from behind his mahogany desk and brought it opposite her. He was on a slightly higher level than her, which made her feel even more vulnerable in this already awkward situation. She cleared her throat.

'Are you nervous?' he asked.

'No,' she lied.

'OK. Let me take your details – name, home address, all the usual stuff.' Holly answered his questions and he filled out a small card. He filed it in a cabinet behind his desk and came back to his chair.

'What do I call you anyway? Joshua? Mr Delaney?' She realised that her voice was rather confrontational.

'I would expect you to be nervous, that's OK. And Joshua is fine.' He was genuine and reassuring, not to mention handsome. There was a long silence in which they watched each other. 'Perhaps you'd like to tell me why you're here?' he suggested eventually.

'Well. I'm in a play. A play about sex. Playing a highly sexed character.' She smiled, and decided to be honest. 'Look, the director made me come. He reckons I have some hang-ups. Maybe I do, maybe I don't. You know what? If I do have hang-ups, I like them. But he wants you to loosen me up a bit. Those are his words. So,' she looked directly at him, 'here I am.'

He looked down at his pad making a quick note. 'Do you mind if we video our sessions?' he asked. 'It helps me register patient progress, it tells more than written notes . . . Would that be OK?'

'Why not? I'm an actress. Not scared of the camera.' He went to a shelf and flicked a switch on a video camera. 'How do I look?' she quipped. He didn't respond.

'Tell me a bit about your sexual history. Or how you feel about sex?' He sat back down again.

'I like it!' She smiled. 'I think I'm pretty normal in that. Don't you?'

'Do you orgasm easily?' He remained unflustered and professional.

'I don't know. What's easy? I need someone who takes their time. My last boyfriend fell a bit short of that mark.' She paused. 'Some things make me come easier than others.' He looked at her, gesturing for her to continue. 'It depends on the guy.'

'Are you happy with that?' Holly decided not to answer that question. She shifted in her seat and told him something she knew he would like.

'I've been having this dream – just since I've been in Cornwall.' He looked up, interested. 'I'm lying in a boat, it's filling with water. It's very sensuous – and this big, thick, wet snake is working its way up my body. It slides up my leg, it invades me, it slides around my – well, everywhere. It slithers all over me until the boat is almost full, then I wake up.'

'Do you come?' Holly tried to remember. The first time she had come afterwards, but only with a bit of help from the anonymous tongue.

'It's hard to say.'

'You must know that the snake is an obvious symbol for a penis.'

'And that's what I really want? Is that what you're saying?' She let out a sarcastic laugh.

'I don't know what you want.' She met his eye and felt a wave of attraction come over her. 'You tell me what you want. What comes to mind when I ask you that?'

40

'Don't ask.'

'Are you not able to answer that?' Holly became uncomfortable. She had been given a lot of male attention lately, but this man seemed oblivious to her charms. She decided to be more honest with him.

'I want to be more sexually liberated, relaxed. I make it into such a big deal.'

'Maybe it is a big deal?'

'Casual sex isn't.' She saw him write something down. 'I want to be free to act on my impulses without that voice in my head.'

'What does the voice say?'

She considered this for a moment. 'Don't let go,' she replied. He smiled for the first time in their session.

'Good. Focus on that.' He got up out of his chair. 'Excuse me a moment. I'll be right back.' He left the room, and Holly looked around her. There were rows of books and videos lining the walls, a few ornaments from foreign countries, but no photographs. She eventually noticed that he had left his notepad on the desk. Glancing at the door, she quickly got up and went to read it. It just said her name, Holly Parker. She was puzzled. She sat back down, and the door immediately opened. Joshua Delaney returned to his chair and picked up the pad. He waited for a moment, then asked, 'Why did you feel the need to look at what I had written?'

She looked startled. 'I didn't,' she protested.

'I have you on video, remember?' She felt cornered. 'Look, it's not a trick or a game. It's healthy that you looked. You are curious – curious about yourself, about me, about sex. That's a great start.'

'Very clever.'

'Do you masturbate?' he asked suddenly.

'That's a bit personal,' she replied instinctively, then caught herself. 'OK, sexually liberated answer: sometimes. Of course.'

'How?' She was looking at him blankly, and he shifted impatiently. 'Look, Holly, if I'm going to help

41

you in as little time as we have here, I need you to be open and honest with me. I won't judge you, I won't be getting off on it . . .' Holly felt a pang of disappointment at this, 'But I need to know where you are now. So tell me. How? Slowly? At leisure? Do you take your time or get it over with?'

'How?' she repeated, slowly. She felt that she had been told off a little, and was blunt in return. 'OK. With my hands. Usually before I go to sleep. Maybe once or twice a week if I'm single. I fantasise. I don't take a lot of time over it, it's just to relax me really.' She looked him deeply in the eye. 'To be honest, I prefer sex when there's someone else there.'

'OK.' He made a note on his pad. 'I want you to experiment with masturbation, Holly. Try new things on your own. Find out what really turns you on. Tease yourself, make love to yourself! If you feel your boundaries shift on your own, you are much more likely to open up with others.'

'If you say so.' Holly was doubtful, but wanted to please him. 'I'm sure I'll enjoy trying.' Laughter creased his face and his eyes lit up.

'I'm pleased to hear it.' They both rose to their feet. 'You are a healthy young woman, Holly. Remember that. I'll see you again in a few days. Here's my card with numbers and stuff. I don't do email or mobiles or anything, I'm afraid.' He handed her a tattered card, which was warm from his pocket. 'I think Mr Biemeyer said Friday at eleven is good for him.'

'Thank you.' Holly stepped into the salty air of the sea. 'Friday it is.' She felt lighter as she stepped back down the hill, unburdened. At last, somebody was on her side. And somebody very pleasing to the eye.

Chapter Six

*B*y the time she arrived at the theatre, the rest of the company were just returning from lunch. They seemed chatty and in good spirits – even Max was smiling. Holly instantly noticed that Nikki was standing next to Jeff, giggling helplessly at one of his awful jokes, occasionally giving his arm a semi-territorial squeeze.

'Ooh, shouldn't have had that second glass of wine,' Nathaniel was saying to Oberon. 'I feel quite pissed.' Oberon laughed his deep, rich laugh and noticed Holly come in.

'Hello, psychopath. Are they going to put you in a home?' he quipped, giving her a quick hug.

'No, apparently I am not a danger to society, but a normal healthy woman!' Holly declared, loud enough for Max to hear. 'But I shall be going again on Friday, just to be sure.'

They soon started work on Holly and Oberon's big scene, and the other actors went to sit in the auditorium to watch, although Nathaniel had trouble keeping his eyes open. They read it through first, Oberon reading the part of the foreign Knight Derry with great passion and authority. Holly noticed the change in him with pleasure, and in turn let herself go more, allowing her character, Dolores, to have a lusty spark and brazenness. In the scene, Derry had come to win the hand of Dolores' mistress, Rachel (played by Nikki, who was busy in the back row with Jeff). Dolores was testing him out for her. Holly was a little apprehensive about the scene, which ended with Oberon having to grope her roughly, but decided to say nothing. She wasn't going to give Max any ammunition against her today.

'Right,' Max declared when the scene had been read. 'We will start with improvisation, to get your bodies used to the sexuality of the scene. When Dolores asks you to kiss her, Oberon, so that she can report it back to her mistress, do not be too eager. This will give you somewhere to go.' Oberon nodded in agreement. 'Then, when the lust of the kiss takes over, I want to see your bodies express this. Yes?' Max glared at Holly. 'No faking.'

'She doesn't have to!' Jeff called out from the stalls, getting a light slap from Nikki.

'And I think it should be Dolores who first puts her hands on Derry. Go for his penis, Holly. You are, after all, testing him out for your mistress, and the size of this can be an important thing, no?' He was amused at his own insight into women, but Holly remained silent.

'So when does Derry lose control?' Oberon asked. 'It says he ravishes her – I'm not sure what that means.'

'Let's find out. Improvise on what you have – no words! Put your scripts down!' Max barked. Oberon and Holly obeyed, then came to face each other in the centre of the stage. Holly felt the sudden hush of an audience. She knew that Jeff would be watching this with interest.

'You may start when you feel the moment,' Max said, quieter now, and took himself into the auditorium.

Holly looked into Oberon's dark eyes, noticing for the first time how they were lined with long, thick lashes. He in turn was noticing the gold flecks in her green eyes, how her lips were fuller than they should have been on such a slender face, how they got redder as he

44

looked at them. Holly kept her hands by her side and went up onto the tips of her toes, so that her face was almost level with his. She looked up at him and slowly brought her lips to his. His mouth was fleshy and warm, but he didn't respond. She moved her lips over his, brushing and teasing them, gently parting them with the very end of her tongue, then opening her own mouth wider and kissing him harder. He instinctively started to return the kiss, opening his mouth and then allowing his tongue to caress hers. He tasted sweet and Holly felt a gasp of pleasure catch in her throat. Suddenly, she wanted to be closer to him. She wrapped her arms around his neck, her body pressed against his, moving subtly against him as his tongue became more urgent and insistent.

'Good, good,' Max called from the stalls. 'Show us that you are turned on. Show it in your body, don't just feel it.' Holly only too willingly increased her movements, widening her legs and wrapping one slightly around his thigh, her white cotton trousers affording her plenty of room for movement. There was now a slight pressure on her sex and she groaned loud enough for the audience to hear. Oberon was kissing her harder now, violently almost, in his character.

'Touch his penis, Dolores. It must be hard by now, feel it for your mistress!' Max yelled.

Holly hesitated. This crossed all the lines of professionalism and she wasn't even sure how Oberon would feel about it. She remembered her session with Joshua earlier, how he had encouraged her to be more experimental. And she had to admit, she was curious. She nervously brought her arm down from around Oberon's neck and slipped it between their hot bodies. She felt his kiss get slower and more sensuous in anticipation of her intimate touch, his tongue rolling sexily around hers. Knowing how damp her panties were getting, she was curious how hard he would be as her hand travelled down towards his crotch. Their bodies were so tight together that she had to force her hand between

45

them. He was wearing denim jeans with a thick button fly, but even so, she could feel the fat shaft of his hard cock lying upright against her. This was acting, she thought, so she didn't have to really rub it. But she had an urge to, to tease him just slightly. She moved her hand against him and he groaned.

'She's driving you too far, Derry!' Max called. 'You take control now!' Oberon was ready to do that. He had so far been passive, but now he had a fire in his belly. One hand clutched the back of Holly's head, pulling her mouth closer to his, his tongue thrusting harder into her. The other hand grasped her buttocks and forced her up against him, so that the shape of his erection rubbed against her crotch. She wrapped her left leg higher around his thigh, and fell backwards, losing balance. He fell on top of her, his hand tangled in her hair, his heavy body gyrating over her. Max let them continue for a few moments, until they both felt they were ready to explode, then clapped his hands.

'Enough!' he called. He leaped up onto the stage, and the two actors pulled away from each other blearily, their faces hot. Oberon tried to cover his modesty with his hands, which gave Max some amusement. 'That was all right,' Max said. 'Quite sexy, I admit. Now we will try it with the dialogue as well. And I want just as much passion! Not a dry cunt in the house!' Holly heard Nikki giggle at this, and turned to her. It was then that she saw Jeff, with a face as black as thunder, jealousy setting his square jaw in a stiff, sharp line. He glowered at her, then turned to Nikki and tried to smile. Holly shrugged this off. It was Jeff's problem. It was almost comforting to know she still had some hold over him, she thought, as they got into position to rehearse the scene with the dialogue.

'Take two?' Oberon smiled, as they stood face to face again.

'Action.' She smiled back.

* * *

46

By six o'clock, Holly and Oberon felt they knew the scene and each other inside out. The other actors had long since gone home, Jeff in a terrible mood, and Oberon and Holly took the walk together. The day was just yielding to the pink spread of sunset and the seagulls were calling each other to feast on the scraps of fish that had been discarded from the fishing boats. It was hard to think of anything to say after so many hours of intimate kissing and groping, and both of them felt more than a little frustrated, so they remained silent. Somewhere in her, Holly knew that Oberon was waiting for her to ask him in to her digs, to finish what they had started, and it was a tempting thought. But if she was to get anywhere with Joshua, she was going to have to at least try to take his advice and learn how to pleasure herself before she thought about letting another man do it for her. When they got to her door, she kissed Oberon on the cheek.

'See you tomorrow.' She smiled.

'Sure.' He walked a little further up the hill and turned back to her. 'Keep practising some of those moves! You're getting pretty good at them.' And he chuckled to himself as he left her.

Mr Briar was sat at the kitchen table cleaning his boots when she got in, with Ben sitting opposite him reading aloud from the local paper. Ben was looking especially handsome, with a glow in his cheeks from a new day's tanning on the beach. He beamed up at her as she came in.

'Well, if it isn't our famous actress,' Mr Briar announced.

'Evening,' she said, more to Ben than his stepfather. 'How are you? Ready for the big day?'

'What?' The boy thought for a moment. 'Oh, my birthday? Yes, thanks.'

'It's tomorrow,' Mr Briar said. 'We're going out on the boat again, if you're interested.' He gave her a loaded look.

'I told you, that can't happen again,' she said, hoping Ben wouldn't pick up on her irritation.

'Yeah, that's what you said.' Mr Briar spat on the boot and polished it vigorously. 'We'll see. Offer stays open.'

Holly decided to go to her room and start to explore new ways of pleasuring herself, as Joshua suggested. She excused herself and went upstairs.

Once in her room, with the door firmly closed behind her, Holly slowly undressed and splashed her face with cold water. She walked about her room naked, aware of the warm air on her body, awakening every nerve ending in her skin. She paused by the full-length mirror and studied herself. Her body was full and generous in all the right places, with a flat milky tummy and smooth thighs. Her nipples were small and dark pink, erect, still pert even though her breasts were heavy. She gently ran her hands over the smooth rise of her chest, feeling the firm buttons of her nipples against the palms of her hands. She caressed them lightly, her skin beginning to tingle. She followed her hands in the mirror as they moved down her torso and reached the neat triangle of auburn hair between her legs. She softly buried her hands in the hair, feeling the moist lips of her sex. She had been brought to arousal so often that day, that her sex was slippery and warm, ready for some male attention. She sighed as she pressed the fingers of her right hand harder against it, moving them in rhythm, as her left hand went back to her left breast and teased the nipple there. She took a few steps back and perched on the edge of the bed, opening her legs to see herself more clearly, how a man would see it. It was pretty, she thought, soft and inviting. She slipped a finger inside, then another, enjoying the sight of them disappearing, then re-emerging glistening with juices. She brought the wet fingers to her mouth and tasted herself – heady and musky. She anointed her breasts, her neck, her mouth, her inner thighs. She lay back, her legs hanging off the edge of the bed, and imagined a man coming to lick her scent off her, starting at her face and working his way down. Her legs fell open at the thought. She shut her eyes and let her fingers arouse her clit. Her memory flooded with the thought of Oberon's sensuous kisses, his tempting cock, how it would feel to have him on top of her. Then it was Ben on her, a young eager body. Then Mr Briar, thickset, rough, heavy, grateful to be able to finally possess her sexually. As her fingers worked harder, the image of Joshua making love to her filled her head. Her skin fizzed and her pussy poured at the thought of him panting against her breast, thrusting into her, helpless with desire, knowing he should not be inside her. As her lust mounted, she thought of Caleb Briar sitting downstairs, so keen for her to invite him up. What harm would it do? She needed a man, and he was willing and attractive, and he knew how to turn her on. She hadn't had a man inside her for so long – not since Jeff had left – maybe now was the time? She got up quickly from her bed and wrapped the bathrobe around her. In the mirror she could see that she was flushed, but she didn't care. She would go down and give him the nod. She was aroused enough to risk meeting Ben on the stairs.

When she got to the kitchen, Mr Briar was standing by the window and Ben nowhere to be seen. He turned to face her, quickly taking in her state of dress and her blushing face.

'Where's your wife?' she asked throatily.

'Away for a few hours.' He eyed her questioningly and she nodded subtly in reply. 'Come on,' he said, and took her hand, leading her back up the stairs to her room.

He closed the door behind him and turned to face her again. Holly waited before him, nervously. His eyes were dark with anticipation and lust. He roughly opened her bathrobe and slid it off her shoulders. Then he stood admiring her, taking in her body, not touching her. His eyes burned into her, and when they lingered on her pussy she felt a heat there as if he had scorched her. Eventually she reached out to him, her hand lying

49

on his muscular chest and sliding up to his shoulder. She took a step towards him, totally naked, and even before she was pressed against him felt the buzz of his body. Suddenly they were kissing, entwined, falling back onto the bed. The fact that he was fully clothed made her feel all the more naked as he lay on top of her, filling her mouth with passionate kisses, his hands all over her in a frenzy, electrifying her breasts and buttocks and thighs as they passed over them. She was willing him to touch her between the legs, where she now felt the need most, but he avoided it. Instead he struggled against her on the puffy white duvet, never taking his mouth off hers, and suddenly rolled off her. He sat on the edge of the bed, running his hand through his wild hair

'What is it?' she asked, sitting up.

'It's Ben's birthday tomorrow,' he said.

'So?'

He faced her. 'So. I am going to give him a magnificent birthday present, although God knows I want it for myself.' He ran his hand up her leg, and she suddenly realised what he was talking about.

'Me?' She couldn't believe it.

'I want to teach him to make love to a woman. He's a virgin, you see, and all kids do these days is read porn mags and talk to their mates for advice.' He looked at her directly. 'Look. I know he's not my natural son. We're more like mates, to be honest. But I want him to know how to please a woman. And a real woman, not just a local girl out for a good time on a Friday night.'

'How dare you?' She felt like slapping his face.

'Oh, come on. I've seen the way you look at him. You'd love it as much as he would.' He was right there, and at that moment she was so horny she would consider anything. 'You're a beauty. It'd probably be the best moment of his life.'

Holly glared at him. 'Well, it sounds like you've made up your mind.'

'Although I do want you so much for myself.' He

thought for a moment. 'No. Wait here.' And he got up and left the room. She rolled over onto her stomach in frustration, burying her head in the pillow. It made her nervous to think of Ben making love to her, although it was exciting. He seemed so shy, she could barely believe he would do it. A few minutes later she heard the door creak open. She could not bring herself to look up. She felt the bed dip under the weight of someone sitting next to her, then a gentle hand brushing down her spine.

'That's right, boy.' That was Mr Briar's voice, coming from just by the doorway. She turned to look and saw that it was Ben caressing her back. He was just wearing his shorts and his bare torso was sculpted and lean. He smiled down at her nervously and she melted a little. 'Touch her bottom, softly caress it,' Mr Briar suggested. Ben touched her gently. It tickled and Holly giggled involuntarily. 'No, harder than that – but take your time. You can kiss her back if you like, and her buttocks. Do it gently.' Ben bent over her and laid warm, sensuous kisses down her spine, starting at the nape of her neck and going all the way to the swell of her bottom. He knelt on the bed and showered her buttocks with little kisses, occasionally straying to her upper thighs, which made her jolt.

'Part her legs.' Mr Briar's voice was quiet but commanding. Ben obeyed, gently pulling her thighs apart, exposing her fully. His fingers tentatively brushed against her sex, dipping a little in the wetness of her. She heard him sigh.

'God, that's lovely,' he gasped, and brought his fingers back for more.

'Not yet, Ben,' his stepfather ordered. 'What about her breasts, her mouth, her toes – all of her? Don't rush it.'

'Sorry, Holly.' Ben gently pulled her over onto her back, and saw for the first time the heavy orbs of her naked breasts and her hard nipples. His eyes hungrily took it all in, glancing occasionally down her body, his eyes filled with admiration.

'She's so beautiful,' he breathed, almost to himself. 'Where do I start?'

'How about kissing her?' Mr Briar chuckled at his stepson's naivety. Holly looked at him encouragingly. She was starting to enjoy this strange situation, this mixture of innocence and experience. She reached up and stroked Ben's cheek, then hooked her hand behind his neck and pulled him lightly down to kiss her. They had an indulgent, sensuous kiss, her guiding his tongue with hers until his instincts took over and he became more forceful. He started to kiss her deeply.

'Good.' Holly was aware that Mr Briar had now moved to the foot of the bed, where he could get a better view of her. As the kiss grew more arousing, she brought her knees up and opened her legs so that the older man could see everything. She was sure she could hear his breathing quicken. 'Now kiss down to her breasts. I'm sure you've been dying to do that.' Ben anxiously obeyed, hurriedly leaving a trail of kisses until his mouth fell delightedly on one of her nipples and he began to suck urgently and hard. 'Careful! Don't hurt her!' The boy softened his mouth, sucking more gently but occasionally unable to stop himself from going at it like a hungry baby. 'Try twirling your tongue around her nipple. Try flicking it.' Ben did as he was told, moving to Holly's other breast. He sent delicious waves of lust through her with this new method, and she let her legs widen even more. She could feel the air on her sex, feel Mr Briar's eyes on it. She bent her head to see him, and she was right – his face was dark with desire. He looked at her and crept to the bed. Ben was too busy to notice as his stepfather knelt at the base of the bed, reached forward and began to tease Holly between the legs. All Ben knew was that this amazing woman underneath him suddenly arched her back with delight. Mr Briar's fingers felt magical playing around her pussy, and his face was intense with desire. The

52

pleasures of a man at her breast and a man at her pussy mingled into one uncontainable urge.

'Please,' was all she could say.

Mr Briar slipped his hand back to his side and whispered, 'She wants you to touch her between the legs. She wants you to come.' Ben looked at his stepfather for guidance. 'Gently at first. With your hand or your tongue.' Ben glanced up at Holly, his eyes shining.

'What would you like, Holly?'

'It all sounds fantastic to me,' she breathed back. 'Just hurry. I feel like I might explode.' She then stroked his blond hair and guided his head downwards, until his face hovered above her dark triangle. He inhaled and moaned at the scent of her, then nervously kissed her mound. He aimed too high to start with, planting kisses on her mount of Venus, but gradually moved his head until he hit upon her clit. She gasped and bucked a little.

'That's it, son. Now kiss her properly down there. Taste her. I'll bet she's lovely.' Ben's tongue played along the crease and swirled around her clitoris. 'Do you like it?' Mr Briar asked.

'God, yes!' came the muffled reply as his intimate kisses grew harder and more ecstatic, his mouth fixed on her, sucking and licking enthusiastically. She was caught up in his excitement and the wonderful sensation of the kiss, but his tongue missed her clit too often and she jerked herself against his face in pursuit of her orgasm.

'Hold her still, Ben. Find the button with your tongue. When you've got it, stay on it.' The boy was panting and gasping into her cunt now, trying to follow the older man's advice but losing control at the same time. He was lying on his stomach on the bed and with every lick he gave Holly, he thrust against the bed sheets chasing his own pleasure. She cried out, breathing hard, desperate to come.

'Please! Oh, don't stop!' But Ben was overwhelmed

with lust and, with his mouth still open against her, he came. He sat up, shivering, and looked down at Holly.

'Thank you! Oh, thank you!' He seemed almost to be crying. He kissed her full on the mouth, her own juices still tangy on his tongue. Mr Briar could see her gyrating, twitching pelvis and read her frustration. As Ben was French-kissing her, he knelt deftly between her legs and buried his face in her mound. He soon found her clit and with a few skilled flicks of his tongue a jerky orgasm powered through her body. She held on tight to Ben, moaning and yelping into his mouth, as Mr Briar worked his magic down below. She knew then that it had been him the other night – that tongue had had the same instinct and urgency. When the spasms had subsided, she let go of Ben and smiled at him.

'I hope there will be more lessons,' she said.

'Oh God, so do I!' He went to kiss her again, but was interrupted by his stepdad.

'Go on now, boy. That's enough. Holly'll be tired.'

'Sorry.' Ben gave her a quick, respectful peck on the cheek and hurried out of the room, doubtlessly off to his bedroom to relive the moment in his head. Holly pulled her legs together and sat up. Mr Briar was still kneeling at the foot of the bed, his mouth glistening with her moisture.

'I really want to go inside you,' he urged. 'Let me.' Holly couldn't have been more willing, still feeling frustrated and unfulfilled.

'Take your clothes off,' she said. He got up and began to carefully lay his garments on the back of her chair – T-shirt, braces, trousers, vest . . . 'Hurry up!' He looked at her, astonished. She really wanted him. Within seconds he was naked on the bed beside her. He began to kiss her neck, draw his hands over her bosoms, but she was impatient. 'Just fuck me. Please.' He saw that she wanted something rough after so much foreplay. He flipped her over onto her belly and climbed on top of her. Forcing her knees apart with his sturdy legs, he grasped his straining cock and slowly guided it into her.

She sighed with pleasure and pain as his thick shaft sank inside her. Wanting to go deeper, he pulled one of her pillows from under her face and stuffed it beneath her hips. With her pelvis higher, he could fill her up completely. Holly sweated with desire under the bulk of this man and her pussy held on tight to the large shaft of his cock. He began to thrust, hard, fast, lovelessly. He was panting and grunting into her ear, which she loved, and held tightly onto her hips so she could feel each thrust deeper.

'Yes. Yes,' she murmured, and he slipped a hand under her belly, searching out her clit with his fingers.

'I want to feel you come,' he urged, quickening his pace. 'Come for me.' His fingers danced against her pussy as his thrusts got more and more violent, until she felt a climax mounting in her loins again. She pushed her hips back to meet his and turned her face so that he could kiss her. He was moving so fast that their tongues could only collide roughly. He was losing control, his face red and sweaty. Their mouths locked together and he stifled Holly's screams as she felt a searing orgasm wrack her body. Feeling her convulsions milking his cock, he came too, his come pouring hotly into her. Their bare bodies jerked and struggled together, until finally they both became limp with exhaustion. 'I want to do that all over again,' he breathed into her ear. 'If I was ten years younger!' She laughed, the movement making him slip out of her. They lay there, catching their breath, him still half on top of her. Downstairs the grandfather clock chimed nine. He sat up.

'Is Mrs Briar coming home?' Holly asked. He got up and started to pull on his clothes.

'I've got half an hour. But I said I'd make the tea.' He grinned at her. 'I've worked up quite an appetite. Want some?' Holly was starving, but knew she couldn't face Mrs Briar, let alone Ben.

'No, thanks, Mr Briar.'

'Oh, and by the way – I think you can stop calling me that now. Caleb's the name.' And with that, he bent down to kiss her and left, slamming the door happily behind him.

Chapter Seven

*H*olly woke up early the next morning, and soon heard the clattering of breakfast dishes coming from downstairs. Mrs Briar's voice shrieked and giggled heartily at some joke her son was telling, and Holly could also make out the growling, sardonic voice of Mr Briar. As she dressed, Holly felt in surprisingly good spirits. She had expected to feel embarrassed or ashamed, but she felt great. After being called uptight all week, she felt like a sex goddess and she loved it. And now that Mr Briar had had his way, and she had admitted her attraction to him, hopefully all the innuendo and loaded looks would be out the window.

She trotted downstairs, hoping to take in a brisk morning walk before work. Her landlady heard her and came out into the hallway.

'Hello, early bird! Out to catch the worm?' she cried. 'Not on an empty stomach, I hope. Not when there's a birthday breakfast on the table!' She ushered Holly into the kitchen, where Ben sat with a huge smile on his face, looking more tanned and gorgeous than ever. He had a pile of gifts before him, wrapping paper everywhere.

'Hi, Holly.' He couldn't quite meet her eye. He obviously had a lot to learn about keeping up appearances from his stepfather, who gave her a perfunctory wave and smile as if nothing had ever happened between them.

'Morning, Ben. Mr Briar.'

'It's Caleb, I told you!' he exclaimed, in mock exasperation. 'God, woman, what are these London types like?' He smiled at his wife and pulled her big bottom down onto his lap.

'She's just got nice manners, is all.' Mrs Briar beamed at Holly. 'Sorry I haven't been around much, dear. It's been a nightmare down the leisure centre this week, everyone's off sick.'

'You better not get it,' her husband goaded. 'You're the only one bringing in the bread! And someone's got to pay for that boy's present.' Ben glanced at Holly.

'What was your favourite gift?' Holly asked him, knowingly. He blushed and leaned back in his chair.

'Oh, it's all right, I know,' Mrs Briar sighed. 'Out with it!' Everyone looked at her sharply. 'Oh, there's no secrets in this house!' Even Mr Briar looked a little worried. Mrs Briar turned to confide in Holly. 'He doesn't want to offend me. I got him underwear and boring mum presents like that. Caleb got him a new surfboard! It's all right, Ben dear, I don't mind. No need to hide how chuffed you are with your gift from Caleb.'

'Too right he is,' Mr Briar muttered.

'Well, I hope you get good use out of your presents,' Holly said. 'I will have to think of something for you. Let me know if *you* can think of anything!' And with that she got up to go. 'Anything at all.' Ben's face was a picture of gratitude as Holly left for work. This was going to be a good day, she could tell.

The morning passed without an outburst from Max, partly because of Holly's positive attitude. Everyone picked up on it, especially Jeff who seemed to find it rather disturbing. Things seemed to have soured between him and Nikki – she looked pale and tight-lipped. When the cast broke for lunch, he strode over to Holly.

'You seem very happy today,' he sneered.

'You don't,' she replied lightly, pulling on her jacket. 'This week's blonde dumped you or something?' He glanced over at Nikki who was tucking into a bowl of salad in the corner, reading a magazine.

'*I* always do the dumping. You should know that.' His voice was hard and his face set in a mask of bitterness. Holly suddenly saw how he had changed – he had not always been this way. Once they had had fun, he had been witty and charming. Yes, he had had a possessive streak, and a temper, but now his whole personality seemed to have screwed up into a ball of anger. He saw her concerned expression and lashed out. 'What? What the hell are you looking at me like that for?'

'I was just wondering what happened to you, Jeff. How you got like this?'

'Maybe it was you, sweetie,' he spat. 'Maybe you drove me to this. And how you clung onto me when I wanted to leave you, it was sickening. You still haven't let me go. You'll always want me, Holly, and you can't bear to see me happy with someone else.'

'Well, that's a joke but if it makes you feel better, go ahead and think it.' Her calmness aggravated him further.

'You sad bitch,' was all he said, venom on his lips. 'You don't even know your own mind. No wonder Max has had to send you to a shrink.'

'Is that everything?' Holly picked up her bag and called to Oberon who was waiting for her by the door. 'Let's go, Oby. I'm starved.'

They found a grubby little seaside café, with auto-graphed pictures of years' worth of D-list celebrities who had visited the theatre lining the flaking walls. Outside, the pebble beach gave way to sand as the tide was completely out, the sea just a distant streak on the horizon. This was obviously a hang-out for the teenagers of the area – there was an amusement arcade and pool hall next door – and the menu was basic.

They sat on tall stools at a bar that ran along the front of the café, with a window out to sea. Oberon picked up the menu and stroked his chin like a restaurant critic in some trendy London hot spot.

'Hmmm. Shall I go for the burger with fries and onion rings, or the potato skins with assorted dips?' he mused, in his most cut-glass of accents.

'I hear their chicken nuggets are superb,' Holly reposted.

'And to drink? Cola or Orangeade?'

'Cola.'

'Obviously. Ah, here comes our fine waitress.' An enormous woman with a pink tabard on waddled over to their table and scribbled their orders on her pad.

When it came, the food was surprisingly delicious. Holly was just about to ask Oberon what he thought of Jeff, when they spotted him walking along the promenade.

'Isn't that your lovely ex?' Oberon asked.

'Yeah. Looks miserable, doesn't he?' He was walking with his head bent, kicking stones as he went. Holly almost felt sorry for him.

'Not a happy man,' Oberon agreed. 'What's the deal with him and Nikki? They seem very touchy feely?' Holly told him what she had seen in the store cupboard, and he laughed loudly.

'It's not funny!' Holly tried not to laugh with him. 'It's not nice seeing your ex getting his end away like that.'

'Oh, sorry. It's just that, when I told one of my mates that I was working with Nikki, he said he had done a job with her too – and what she was famous for was sucking everyone's cock!' He started laughing again. 'I didn't think he was serious!' Holly looked out and saw Jeff further along the strand, sitting chucking stones at a tin can.

'Well, from the look on his face, it's all stopped,' she wondered aloud.

'Do you care?' Oberon looked at her meaningfully.

'What? You're as bad as he is.' She took a large gulp of her drink. 'He reckons I'm still in love with him and will "never get over him".'

'And are you?'

'No!' She shouted this so defiantly that the waitress looked up at them. 'No. It's just him being so fucking arrogant. And the fact I'm not seeing anyone makes him still feel he's the man in my heart.'

'Well, we could soon rectify that, if it bothers you,' Oberon said enigmatically, and took a large bite of his burger. Tomato ketchup spurted out all over the table.

'Oh, that's nice,' Holly commented. 'And what are you talking about?'

'Well, he's a sucker, Jeff. And he needs to be taught a lesson or two. And you want him off your back. So – why don't we play a little game with him?'

'Such as?'

'Just a practical joke, nothing serious. For a start, he could overhear you talking to a mate – saying you've met someone else.'

'He'd never fall for that!'

'He will if you're specific enough. Say this new guy is the best you ever had. Say all the things that'll drive Jeff mad. Say – say his dick is enormous.'

Holly laughed. 'And who would this well-endowed stranger be? You I suppose?'

'Why not? I seem to fit the bill.'

'He'd know I was lying.'

'OK. Say you have to go, 'cause you're meeting this wonderful handsome guy, a special rendezvous. That'll get him curious.' Oberon put his fork down as the final coup de théâtre came to him. 'Let him follow you to the beach – where I will be waiting, looking stunning! And then we'll – you know.'

'Oh, I see.' Holly couldn't believe his cheek. 'This is just an elaborate way for you to get your oats.'

61

'Don't flatter yourself. We don't have to really do it. We're both actors.' And he flashed her a cheesy grin. 'We can make believe instead of making love.' They laughed and Holly continued to eat as she considered the plan. It would certainly feel good to turn the tables on Jeff, to get him off her back once and for all. If he thought she was with Oberon, he would leave her alone, she was sure. He had always been a coward, and Oberon was bigger than him for a start. And Jeff had been quite sadistic so far. He deserved a little teasing.

'OK. Why not,' she agreed. And they sat there for the rest of their lunch hour, formulating a watertight plan, like two kids playing at war games in a schoolyard.

At six o'clock that evening, the actors were released as usual and Oberon suggested they all go for a drink.

'We've not been out as a company,' he said. 'There's a great little village pub down by the cliffs.' Before anyone could agree, Holly falteringly spoke up.

'I – I can't, I'm afraid.' Her face was a picture of guilt. 'I've got . . . things to do.'

'What? What things?' Jeff sneered, disbelievingly.

'Just – oh, you all go. I'm just going to stay here and make a phone call. Maybe I'll catch you up.' Her tone implied that she knew she wouldn't. Jeff's interest was sparked. She slipped away, in a conspicuously surreptitious manner, and crouched in the props cupboard where she had seen Jeff and Nikki a few nights before. She heard the other actors disappearing, saying their goodbyes. Hoping that Jeff had stayed behind, she got her mobile from her bag and turned the ring down in case it went off.

'Hi! Katie!' she said loudly into the dead phone. 'Thank God you're home, I've got so much to tell you.' She left a gap for her friend to supposedly answer. She had chosen her mate Katie because she knew that Jeff had always been intimidated by her – she was sassy, sharp and unforgiving, and she had always maintained that Holly could do better than Jeff. 'Yeah, I need some

advice. Yes, it is about a bloke, how did you know . . .?'
There was a slight creak of a floorboard as Jeff crept
across the stage. He was coming! 'Oh, Katie, he's gorgeous – just so handsome. I knew from the moment I
saw him I was in trouble.' Maybe Jeff would think she
was talking about him – that would make the trick all
the sweeter, Holly thought. 'I know you shouldn't get
involved with people you work with, but how can I
ignore my feelings? Yes, I know it's a recipe for disaster
. . . yes, I have learnt my lesson, but, Katie . . .' She
lowered her voice to an emphatic whisper. 'He's the
best I've ever had!' She could hear Jeff breathing outside
the door. Maybe he still thought she talking about him.
'He really knows how to make love to a woman. You
know how rare that is . . . Oh yes, *much* better than Jeff.
What did I ever see in him?' She was sure she heard
him take a sharp breath. 'And, Katie, he's really big. His
cock is a dream – enormous!' She stifled a giggle. 'So,
do I have your blessing? Are you sure?' She paused,
and then changed her tone of voice. 'Oh, shit – sorry, I
have to go. I'm supposed to meet him in five minutes
. . . Yeah, I know, lucky me! I'll call you soon. Bye!' She
heard Jeff scurry from the door as she got up to go, and
pretended not to see him as she marched out of the
theatre, although glimpsing him wrapped up in the
stage curtains, she felt his hiding skills left a lot to be
desired.

She walked briskly along the beach, her lungs filling
with fresh sea air. She could feel Jeff's presence behind
her, his eyes burning into her back. She stopped suddenly at one point, pretending to do up a shoelace, and
glimpsed him loitering behind a bus stop.

'Pathetic,' she muttered. She eventually came to the
rockier part of the beach, where pebbles and sand gave
way to cliffs and alcoves. She climbed deftly over some
slippery rocks, jumped over some large boulders, and
finally arrived at the place she and Oberon had chosen
for their rendezvous. He was lying in a secluded spot,
spread out on a green satin throw, wearing just his

shorts. He did look very inviting. He glanced behind her and tried not to smile as he spotted Jeff's face peering out over the top of some large boulders.

'At last,' he said. 'I couldn't have waited another minute.'

'Oh, me neither.' She sank to her knees and kissed him full on the lips. This was nothing new – she had done it a hundred times in rehearsal – but here it felt strange, exciting, with the breeze brushing against her and seagulls crying overhead. They melted down onto the blanket and rolled around a little, their legs wrapping around each other. 'Oh, God I want you!' she exclaimed dramatically.

'Don't overdo it.' He chuckled into her ear, under the pretence of nibbling it. She giggled, and wriggled underneath him, feeling a little as if she were being wrestled. His big hands started to explore her body, slipping under her white blouse and effortlessly unhooking the front fastening of her bra.

'Nice move!' she whispered, scratching her way down his back leaving pale trails down his spine.

'Oh!' He groaned loudly with pleasure. 'Ow!' he muttered to her, privately. He fumbled at the fly of her combat trousers, growing impatient. 'What kind of chastity belt is this?' he hissed.

'Let me.' He rolled off her and she stood up, with her back to Jeff and facing Oberon. She slowly pulled her blouse over her head. Her bra, already undone, slipped easily off her shoulders. Oberon's arousal at the sight of her bare breasts was genuine. She stepped out of her shoes, then smiled, undid her trousers provocatively, and slid them down her legs, kicking them off her feet so they flew into Oberon's face. She was left wearing only her knickers – a black thong which accentuated the white rounded orbs of her buttocks. She bent over Oberon, knowing that Jeff would get an eyeful of her behind, and kissed him. The kiss was a little more sexual this time. She took her mouth away and leaned over his face, so that her breasts dangled at his lips.

'What are you trying to do to me?' he breathed, taking in a nipple and sucking it, then the other. Before he could get stuck in, Holly was kissing down the length of his body, gradually arriving at his shorts. She nuzzled into his crotch like a cat, hooking them under her fingers and forcing them down till they stuck at his knees, acting like a constraint around his legs. He was erect, and as well endowed as she had suspected. Bigger than Jeff, she noted, shifting to one side so that she knew Jeff could see how adequately sized his rival in fact was. She caressed the dark shaft as she pondered on whether to go further. It would be so easy to take it in her mouth, to turn the tables on Jeff completely. And seeing Oberon like that did make her horny. He was getting harder and harder at her touch, she noticed, enjoying the power. She let one hand gently stroke his balls, the other pulled gently on the tightly curled hairs around his penis. She swung one leg over him and sat straddling him, her crotch directly over his, delighting in the sensation. His face was expectant, questioning. What was she going to do? She leaned over his body, rotating her hips so that the pleasure began to mount and whispered into his ear.

'I want to do it to you for real.'

'Please do!' he gasped back.

'I can't.' She gave him a lingering kiss, her tongue invading his mouth. 'I would be using you to get at him,' she murmured eventually. 'Just like he was with Nikki.' His face was disappointed.

'You're already using me, Hol. And at this point in time, I don't mind!' He grasped her hips and answered her gyrations with his own, harder and more insistent. She could feel the moisture of arousal dripping from his cock.

'But I do,' she breathed. 'I'm being cruel to be kind.'

He laughed ironically. 'OK, then. Begging isn't my style.' He slipped one hand between her legs and pushed the flimsy material of her thong to one side, exposing her pussy. 'But let's at least put on a convincing show!' He pretended to guide himself into her, but actually his cock was trapped between their bodies. Holly began to move her pelvis as if fucking him, measured at first. The muscular shape of his cock was perfectly positioned against her clitoris as she moved, and she became slippery against him. It would be so easy to slide him inside, she thought, to feel that weapon inside her. His face registered his own pleasure at the friction between them. His eyes were half closed, and he was biting his full lips as if to control himself. 'God, I think this is harder for me than it is for him,' he whispered.

'Sorry,' she said, and quickened her movements, thrusting against him, her juices mingling with his sweat. She leaned forward on her hands and dropped her head as if in ecstasy. She squinted behind her and could see Jeff clearly now, white as a sheet, standing behind the rock. His face was fixed on her bottom as it rose and sank against Oberon. Feeling the power she was having over both men, she let her hips go wild, jerking and pushing with a violent speed.

'Shit.' Oberon suddenly began to come at this new rhythm. 'Don't stop.' She obeyed, and soon felt the hot splash of his come on her belly. As she did, she pretended to climax too, throwing her head back, her mouth open, letting out a single cry. She looked warmly down at Oberon who was smiling contentedly.

'Thanks,' she mouthed.

'No problem,' he whispered. 'Aren't you going to tell me that I'm the best?' And he nodded subtly towards Jeff, who was standing, rigid in every way, behind her.

'Oh, baby! You are the best!' she cried. 'I never knew it could be like this!' Oberon was looking past her.

'He's gone,' he said after a few minutes. 'Mission accomplished.' Holly climbed off him and rearranged her panties. Oberon grimaced at the mess on his stomach, and saw that it was on hers too.

'Shit!'

'Oh, wait.' Holly got some tissues out of her bag and

she wiped them both down. 'That was fun,' she said as she pulled her clothes on.

'You bet.' He got to his feet and brushed the sand off his legs. 'And I tell you what – I *am* the best. If you ever want to try me out!'

'I believe you.' Holly kissed him. They climbed over the rocks and out of the private alcove, finally reaching the open beach where children were playing with kites in the wind. It was odd that people had been so close by for their little performance. Oberon walked her to her door and kissed her lightly on the cheek.

'Well,' he said. 'Tomorrow we shall see how Jeff took that. I think he'll leave you alone from now on.'

'I hope so.' Holly grinned. 'I wonder what my therapist will make of this little escapade.' Somehow she was really looking forward to telling him.

Chapter Eight

Joshua Delaney answered the door with his usual formality and ushered Holly in. Once again she noted the clinical, pristine quality of his house and wondered what it said about him.

'I thought you said you've got a dog?' she said, as he made his way to the study.

'Yes.'

'Where is he? Where's his toys, his blankets . . . ?' Joshua knew what she was getting at.

'He lives in the back of the house. This area is for my work and receiving guests. He has the run of the kitchen and my leisure quarters.'

'Leisure quarters?' She let out a little laugh. 'And you don't mix up those parts of your world at all?'

'No. No I don't.' He appeared mildly defensive. They went into his study and Holly went straight to the red chair. 'I wanted to talk to you about something.' He seemed awkward, slowly going to turn on his video camera.

'Yes?'

'It's just a clarification, actually. I know that Mr Biemeyer has requested these sessions and he is fully aware of my – my credentials, if you like, my history. But it occurred to me after our last meeting that you may not know, and I'm not sure if that's ethical.' He stood stiffly in front of his desk, speaking quickly. 'I *was* a qualified and practising psychotherapist, specialising in sexual matters. But now, I don't call myself that. I don't practise in the same way, partly because I became disillusioned with the process and partly because – well, there were lots of reasons.' Holly was intrigued.

'Like what?'

'Well, nothing we need to go into.' He waved his hand dismissively. 'I just wanted you to be aware of the situation. As far as I'm concerned, you are coming to me to talk out any problems, and I am being paid on the understanding that I am no longer registered as a psychotherapist.' It was obviously a huge relief to get this off his chest and he sat down. Holly sensed that there was something to tell here, but decided not to push it. Instead she leaned back in her chair and grinned.

'Enough about you, Josh, let's talk about me.'

'Quite. How have you been.'

'Fucking fantastic.' He raised an eyebrow. 'I have decided to face a few demons, and it felt great.'

'Yes, that's always a release.'

'I would recommend it. If your demons are bothering you.' She eyed him, pointedly.

'How did the masturbation therapy go?' he asked quickly.

'Ah.' She was aware that she had failed at this. 'I have to admit that I didn't make it. I went back home and started to explore – like you said – but it all got a bit much and I . . . didn't feel able to fulfil myself.'

'I see.'

'Maybe I'm just doing it wrong. Maybe you can help me?' She leaned back in her chair. She had carefully chosen her clothes that day, wearing a tight-fitting black sweater with no bra underneath, and a tartan mini skirt. Her bare legs were lightly tanned from the summer, and her strappy black sandals flattered their shape. She had tied her hair back in a loose bun, to accentuate her pretty features. She could see he admired her on some level, even if he couldn't admit it to himself.

'What do you mean?' he said nervously. 'I mean, tell me what you have tried and what you feel went wrong.'

'Well.' She took a deep breath. 'The other night after I saw you, I went home and stripped naked in my room. I looked at myself in the mirror and watched myself touching myself. It was . . . nice.'

'Go on.'

'I sat on the edge of the bed and opened my legs and touched myself there, and watched myself, and I was getting really turned on.' He nodded, professionally. 'But, it just made me want a man, Joshua. I was rubbing myself gently like this.' She put her hand between her legs over her skirt and gently massaged herself. 'And my other hand was stimulating my nipples, which I love, like this.' She brought her other hand to her breasts over her jumper, and pinched both nipples in turn to attention. 'And it was lovely!'

'Holly –' He began to protest as she opened her legs a little further.

'I need you to help me. How can I excite myself the way that a man can?'

'Miss Parker, please stop that!' She innocently took her hands away. 'Please.' There was a silence, in which he wrote something on his pad. Holly was sure this was just a distraction tactic. She noticed that he had crossed his legs – maybe he wasn't as indifferent to her as he would have her believe.

'Sorry, Joshua.' She leaned forward again. 'I became so aroused, the other night, and I so wanted to feel a man's touch, that I let the guy who rents me a room fuck me. Is that bad?'

'Did you feel bad?'

'God no, I came and came. His son was there too. Ben.' This sparked his interest. 'We taught him how to pleasure a woman. He wasn't that great at it, but he will be one day.'

'You mean, they both had sex with you?' His face

70

wasn't shocked, but the crack in his voice gave him away.

'No. The boy just felt me up and went down on me. His stepdad did most of the hard work. I thought I had died and gone to heaven.'

'I see.'

'So I'm not the repressed little English rose Max would have you believe.' She looked into his eyes, which were, she noticed, a vivid shade of blue.

'And does this bother you?' he asked. 'Would you like to be an English rose, as you put it?' She grew impatient at his probing questions, and decided to hot things up a bit.

'Joshua, do you think one can love sex too much?' she asked, leadingly. He shifted uncomfortably. Sensing his arousal she let her legs fall open, leaning back in the red leather chair.

'Is that what you want to talk about?' he asked.

'I don't want to talk at all.' She hooked a leg over the arm of the chair and saw his eyes linger between her legs. 'If I had wanted to talk I would have worn underwear.' For a moment he stared, transfixed. If she had set out to shock him, she had succeeded. She let him look, feeling her naked sex open up like a flower under his gaze.

'Holly, I . . .' He looked down. 'This can't happen. I'm sorry.'

'Why not?' His resistance only served to titillate her. 'You would love it, and so would I.'

'That's not the issue, I'm afraid.' She brought her legs back together again. 'Look, let's go out with the dog and get some air. I find that walking and talking can be the best thing when things get – stuck. OK?'

'If you say so.' She was a little hurt at this rejection, but put on a brave face. The past few days had got her used to a level of male adoration and attention that she had never encountered before – perhaps it had made her arrogant. 'Don't you find me attractive?' she asked.

He saw the coy, provocative woman give way to the insecure girl and smiled.

'Holly, come on. Let's get some air.'

She was glad to see that his 'leisure quarters' as he called them were indeed messier and more lived in than the rest of the house. Newspapers, tennis rackets, CDs and books littered his large pine kitchen table, and in the corner sat a tatty old dog basket. The beautiful golden retriever in it barked as they came in, his tail thumping noisily against his blankets.

'Be quiet, Freud!' Joshua tutted, clipping on the dog's lead.

'Freud?' Holly was amused. 'It's not like you to call your dog that!'

'And why not?' Joshua knew that she meant he was stiff and serious.

'Well – it's just, it's like a pun on your whole profession.' She bent down and cupped the dog's face in her hands, his black eyes shining back at her. 'I mean, don't get me wrong. I love the name. You just surprise me, that's all.'

'Yes, well,' Joshua opened the back door and they stepped into the sunlight, 'it's mutual.' She laughed and they started a brisk stroll across the fields. Soon they had reached the cliff edge and strode along the coast path there, and when they had safely left a few fields of sheep behind them, Freud was let off the lead to run about. He sprang off, looking for rabbit holes and exciting smells.

'Oh to be a dog,' Holly sighed.

'You were right, by the way,' Joshua said. 'I didn't name him. He was a gift, actually. Came already named.'

'Perhaps I should be the therapist?' She laughed, and chased Freud for a bit, who had found a stick he was rather proud of. The air was cooler up on the cliff tops, and she was aware of her nakedness beneath her skirt. She was sure Joshua could not have forgotten about it either. She bent over to take the stick from the dog's mouth and throw it, and she glimpsed Joshua behind her, his eyes gravitating instinctively to her bare bottom. She was pleased. 'Look,' she said, jogging back to him a little out of breath. 'I'm sorry I was a bit naughty in there. Don't know what came over me.'

'Why did you do it?'

'I don't know, I just said!' She was exasperated. 'I want you to like me I suppose.' She looked up at his face as they walked, and he looked back at her, his hair blowing softly into his blue eyes.

'I do like you,' he said simply. 'You don't have to turn a man on to make him appreciate you, Holly.'

'Ah! So I *did* turn you on!' she cried, stroking his arm briefly. Something in his face shut off, and he became serious again. He looked out across the bay, unsmiling.

'For our next session, I want you to try to liberate yourself more, but not for the approval of a man – think about your fantasies, what turns *you* on.' He didn't look at her as he spoke. 'Continue with the masturbation therapy.'

'Calling it that doesn't help to make it any more erotic,' Holly quipped.

'We'd better go back.' Joshua whistled to Freud who eagerly bounded towards them. 'I'll see you again on Sunday. Nine o'clock, in the evening. That way you won't have to take off work.'

'Thanks.' The air had chilled between them and they walked back to the house in silence. When they arrived, Holly got her bags together as quickly as she could. As soon as they were at the front door, she remembered that they hadn't discussed Jeff. 'Oh. I played a weird trick on my ex. I wanted to run it by you. He's been pestering me, you see . . .'

'Next time,' Joshua interrupted her, curtly. His eyes seemed weary of her now, and she felt crushed as she walked back down the hill to her digs. She looked back at one point, expecting to see him watch her leave, but he had gone straight back into the house.

Chapter Nine

*H*olly arrived at rehearsals refreshed after a shower at her digs. The sun had grown stronger during the early afternoon and she had changed into a loose summer dress, with a slim belt around her waist. She decided to forget about Joshua's coolness for the time being, and get on with enjoying rehearsals. She was still feeling positive about the work, especially now Jeff had been put in his place.

Just as she walked through the doors of the theatre she was aware of a stilted atmosphere in the room. She looked from face to face to discover the source of the tension, but everyone seemed equally drawn. Oberon caught her eye and was about to come up to her and say something but was interrupted.

'Right. Come on,' Max snapped. 'Act one scene seven. Dolores and her husband Francis.' Jeff flashed a sour look at Holly. 'Come on. On your feet. Now!' They got onto the stage and looked icily at each other. Jeff's demeanour showed that last night's joke had not gone down at all well. Maybe he had been making trouble with Oberon, she thought. Max asked them to walk through the scene for lines, and the actors began. It was the scene Oberon had shown her that first day on the beach, with Dolores' husband finding her soaping her naked breasts at the sink and accusing her of being loose with other men. As they went through it, Jeff's anger seemed real enough. He constantly manhandled her, pulling her hair and grasping her face painfully in his hard hands. She almost made it to the end of the scene, but broke off when he roughly grasped her breasts.

'Sorry,' she said. 'Max. This is ridiculous.' Max slowly came up onto the stage, taking deliberate steps. She was shaking from the violence Jeff had shown her, and couldn't believe it when Max laid into her.

'I thought we were over this little girl prissiness, Miss Parker?' he growled. 'Didn't I say I want this for real?'

'But Max . . .' she protested, glancing at the other actors in the auditorium for support. 'I'll be covered in bruises.'

'Good,' Jeff spat.

'You're an actress, Miss Parker. You are privileged to play this role. So do it!' Max jumped back down into the stalls. 'Again!' Holly saw Oberon shrug at her helplessly. Obviously the whole day had been like this.

'OK, I'm an actress. But he's supposedly an actor. Tell him to act it.' She pointed furiously at Jeff. 'He doesn't have to do it for real.'

'Whine whine whine,' Max muttered. 'Hurry up. Come on!' Holly edged back into position and the scene started again. Jeff now enjoyed the power he had over her, the power that Max had given him. His aggression now came out in a sexual way, groping her intimately and burying his head in her cleavage. At one point in the scene, he forced Holly's head down his body and pressed her face against his crotch.

'OK, stop!' she yelled, trying not to lose it. Max came back onto the stage, his eyes black with impatience. Holly was sure she saw him give Jeff the nod. A secret look definitely passed between them.

'Look, Max,' Jeff protested. 'I can't work with this. She's all frigid and uptight on stage! I need someone who'll give as good as they get.'

75

'Oh, I can match you all right, Jeff. Just don't bloody push me around!' Holly spat back.

'But you're all prim and cold, Holly. You haven't got a passionate bone in your body.' Jeff was enjoying this. Holly opened her mouth to argue, but was interrupted.

'No, he's right,' Max snapped suddenly. 'You are the centre of this, Holly. It all depends on you. If you aren't open to sex, if you're not constantly turned on, it simply won't work.'

'But, Max,' Holly was pleading now, 'you said the other day that you cast me because I did have passion. You said I had that "spark"!'

'It's not enough to have it buried somewhere deep down,' he countered. 'You have to be able to let go at a moment's notice. You have to be always open to the erotic. I want to be able to put my hand to your pussy at any time and feel it dripping like honey, you understand? I want you to eat, sleep and dream sex. You're very ... English. You hold yourself so upright. Relax!' Holly instantly tensed up at the very word. Max fixed on an idea. 'Right. I want everybody on stage. I want no talking. I need a scarf. Now!' Adrian, the hassled stage manager, started to scramble around at Max's request. Everyone shifted nervously, not least of all Holly.

'What do I do?' she asked.

'Nothing, my dear. Absolutely nothing. You stand still – totally still. There. Now ...' He was handed the scarf, which he proceeded to tie tightly around her eyes. 'Just a little trust game, don't worry. We'll all play.' The blindfold cut out all but the faintest of shapes and figures, and no one appeared to be talking. Holly vaguely heard Max whisper something and the sound of floor creak around her.

'What's happening?'

'Quiet!' Max's voice was thick and secretive. She felt a hand on the back of her neck – very gently caressing the nape under her auburn hair in small circles. Then someone took her hand and began to kiss her palm softly.

76

'Get off me.' She was ignored and another hand deftly unbuckled her belt. She heard it fall to the floor. Her dress felt loose and flimsy against her skin, and she shivered slightly.

'Good,' Max whispered. The kisses on her palm were warm and wet, and the mouth made its way along her fingers, sucking occasionally at the tips, nipping her gently. She tried to pull her hand away, but was held fast by another person.

'Who's that?' she asked. She heard a muffled whisper and the hand at her neck became bolder, pulling at her hair. Another joined it, cupping her chin and her throat. She let out an involuntary gasp as she was pulled off-balance by the force of it, finding herself leaning back against the firm torso of a male body. She could feel his breath on her ear. He blew softly and lowered his lips to the side of her neck. His moist, hot kisses travelled up to her ear, and she felt a tongue dart inside. Holly had never been able to resist this and her knees buckled. The tongue became more probing, filling her ear with thunder. Suddenly she felt her hands being bound before her by the belt, which had been discarded. She struggled, but was rendered weak with it all. The belt was pulled tight around her wrists with a grunt, and suddenly her bare legs were grasped from in front. These hands swept up her legs slowly, lingering at the backs of her knees, tickling slightly. She jerked and the caresses rose higher, climbing up her skirt.

'Stop it,' she breathed. The hands paused on her buttocks, stroking the smooth skin there, and her knees weakened slightly. She was suddenly aware of how wet she had become, and how short her breaths were. The tongue playing with her ears and the nibbling at her throat had taken her breath away. Now everything seemed to stop. The silence became electric. Her ears strained to hear people move near her. The kissing had stopped. She felt the man behind her reach around her body and slowly undo the buttons of her dress starting at the top and working his way down until her bra was exposed. He pulled the dress firmly down her arms and unhooked her bra, exposing her heavy breasts and taut nipples to the room. She felt the cool air on them and her mouth fell open.

Someone's fingers tenderly pinched at each nipple, rolling and stroking them until they were as hard as bullets. At the same time the hands beneath her skirt began to climb again, the fingers hooking under the elastic of her panties and pulling them down slowly. A cry of protest whimpered in her throat, sounding more like a sigh of pleasure. Her feet were lifted one by one as her panties were removed, leaving her feeling utterly exposed. The fingers on her breasts continued to flicker gently over her nipples, and the kisses returned to the nape of her neck. She felt a thick, rough hand cup her moist sex, the palm pressing against her swollen clitoris in slow, measured movements. She instinctively opened her legs as she felt herself melting into this man's insistent hand. Reading her desire, he slipped one finger inside her, then brought it out and rubbed her juices around her swollen vulva, before burying two fingers back inside her, deeper this time, moving them slowly in and out, sending waves of need up through her body. The fingers were thick but she wanted more. She squirmed a little against the hand until three and then four fingers were plunged into her, more roughly this time. Without removing his hand from her sex, the man rose to his feet before her. He continued to work his fingers inside her, his palm moving tantalisingly against her bud, but from this angle he was able to get deeper. Each sensation was acute. Even beneath her blindfold, her eyes were now shut so as to better concentrate on each touch. Hot breath lingered on her naked breasts, and suddenly she felt one nipple being taken into a mouth. She leaned her weight back fully on the man behind her now as the man in front fucked her harder with his hand and sucked at her tingling nipple. The man behind reached around her and his hand joined the first one between her legs, finding her clit and vibrating against it fast. Both hands squelched and pulsated between her legs, the wet noise betraying her loss of control. She could hear the breath of both men getting harder and was thrilled to feel against her buttock the burgeoning erection of the man behind. It was thick and steely hard, and would fill her to the hilt. She moaned aloud at the thought of it as the hands and tongues and lips smothered her and invaded her with their persistent demands. The fingers between her legs increased the pressure and pace and those inside her vibrated madly. She moaned again, her wrists jerking against the belt, unable to stop herself, and opened her legs as wide as she could, no longer caring who was touching her or whether they knew she was loving it. The men let out their own groans as they concentrated on bringing her to orgasm. Her wet cunt contracted hard against the fingers as she began to spasm wildly, jerking and screaming with pleasure. She was being totally supported by the man behind as her body weakened in climax, flailing against him, her legs losing all their strength.

When the orgasm subsided, Holly remained where she was, shell-shocked. The alien hand inside her, her exposed breasts, the anonymous men who held her up, all felt suddenly unreal and deeply humiliating. The men did not move, but she heard a laugh coming from one of them.

'Get off me,' she hissed, unflinching. 'Get. Off!' One hand slipped casually from her and was followed by the fingers, that had a few moments before felt the intimate workings of her orgasm. As they were removed, Holly felt the wetness of her own pleasure escaping down her leg. She came shakily to her feet.

'Untie me. Please.' She tried to iron the shake out of her voice. Someone slowly released her hands. With as much dignity as she could muster she brushed her dress down and did her bra up before pulling off the blindfold. She was pleased to see that almost everyone had left, but her stomach churned when she saw that Max had been in front of her and Jeff behind. Everyone else had gone. 'How dare you?' Her fingers fumbled at her buttons as she glared at the men. 'Pigs!'

'You loved it, my dear.' Max's voice was mellifluous with smugness. 'Still, I can see that your sexuality troubles you, despite your sessions with Mr Delaney. You will need more work. Although, as I said, you loved it – despite yourself.' He held up four fingers glistening with her juices as proof, bringing them to her cheek so she could smell the musky sweetness of her own desire.

'I could always make you come, Hol,' Jeff chipped in. 'I still fantasise about it. She could come over and over again, Max. Honestly. She especially loves the tongue – anywhere. In her ears, her mouth, on her toes, but especially on her lovely little pussy. She likes it fast. She goes wild for that, don't you, Hol?'

'Dream on.' She grabbed her panties and attempted to put them on without shaking or falling over, much to the men's amusement. 'You were never the Casanova you thought you were.'

'Well, I hope we'll see some of that fire on stage,' Max interrupted. 'Because if we don't – well, we'll have to find more ways to get it out of you.' Max jumped down off the stage and into the darkened auditorium. 'I think this has been a useful acting exercise – don't you?'

'Really?' Holly's voice was heavy with sarcasm as she saw Max was still labouring under the burden of quite an impressive erection. 'Am I allowed to go then?'

'Yes, see you on Monday morning, my dear.' Max pulled on his jacket and shuffled his script. 'Learn your lines over the weekend, there's a good girl.' Holly grabbed her bag and rushed out of the stage door and into the early evening sun.

When the light hit her she stopped in her tracks, dropped her bag and gulped back a sob that rose in her throat. She had betrayed herself, she had let them humiliate her – and she had even enjoyed it. Shame reddened her cheeks. She collected herself, not wanting to be caught in tears by Jeff as he left the building, and walked hurriedly along the shore towards her lodgings.

As she got to the bramble path, she hesitated. She didn't have the energy to face Mr Briar and Ben after her experience with Max and Jeff. Instead she found herself walking toward the cliffs where Joshua Delaney lived. She climbed the hill and walked along the cliff top until she came to his house. She hadn't realised that she had been crying, but now in the cool wind she was suddenly aware of the wet streaks on her face. She looked down at herself and saw that her dress was not buttoned up right and gaped open at the front. Her wrists were still red from the tightness of the belt. She was a mess. Instead of ringing Joshua's bell, she kept walking. She didn't want him to see her like this. She hiked over the hills, climbing higher and higher, until she had a staggering view of the sea and the whole of the village. She finally stopped, panting with the climb and with emotion. Below her, the ocean rolled into the rocks of the shore, foaming and breaking. She could see the small shape of the theatre in the distance, so insignificant and humble compared to the vast expanse of the Atlantic. She breathed deeply and felt calmness return to her body. Slowly she made her way back down the hill, glimpsing Joshua briefly through a window as she passed his house.

He was sitting at the desk in his study, apparently watching TV. He was in a dark navy bathrobe, his hair wet from a shower. He seemed intent on what he was watching. Holly was curious. She sidled up to the window, keeping behind him so he could not see her. On his desk sat the video camera, and at the other end of the room was a monitor. Holly could see the image of a young woman on the monitor. She crept closer to the glass to get a better look. He rewound a section and watched it again. Holly suddenly realised that the woman on the film was her. She was sitting in that red chair wearing her tartan skirt – it must have been the footage from that morning's session. On the monitor she hitched her knee over the side of the chair and flashed a full, unadulterated view of her dark triangle to the camera. Holly glanced at Joshua's face as he watched, but couldn't read his reaction. Surely he didn't need to see this bit for professional reasons? He rewound it again and watched it, leaning forward. She could see that his robe was tenting at the front. So he did have human emotions after all! All at once, he turned to the window, as if he had seen her shadow across it. Holly crept away from the house and back down towards the village.

It was Friday night, and all the village youths were getting ready for a night out, such as could be had in such a small place. Boys on bikes and mopeds sped around the harbour, and groups of teenage girls in high heels and strappy dresses giggled outside the fish and chip shop. Loud music blared from somebody's car, and the pubs all had their doors open to welcome the evening's first revellers. The energy of the place lifted Holly's spirits, and she decided to get herself a bottle of wine on the way home. She was going to celebrate the end of a bloody difficult week. She slipped into the off-licence and slammed a tenner onto the counter.

'Bottle of your best sparkling wine, please.' She grinned.

At home, she was relieved to find that all the lights were out and the house empty. She grabbed a large wine glass, a bottle opener and a bag of crisps from the kitchen and made upstairs with them. Her room felt like a little den now, her haven. She settled down on the bed and poured herself a full glass, watching with satisfaction as the bubbles danced about.

'Here's to an interesting week,' she toasted, 'and to the fact it's over.' She gulped down the first glass without any trouble. The bubbles went quickly to her head and she suddenly remembered Jeff's letter. It had come three weeks ago now, and she had to admit, she was curious. She rolled off the bed and rummaged for it in her travelling bag, eventually finding it stuffed inside a book. She bounced back on to the bed and poured herself another glass before ripping it open. His weird, slanting hand was scrawled across two pages. She took a sip and started to read:

Holly,
The last time we spoke you were very upset and irrational. I hope you are over it now and realise that it wasn't working out between us.

Holly let out a hiss of laughter and drank a little harder.

Mandy, my new girlfriend, is everything I wanted you to be – sweet, accommodating and feminine. We had a great time in the play, and an even better time in our digs. Still, I don't want to make you jealous again. It doesn't suit you. I was writing to let you know that, despite your behaviour, I've recommended you for a part to our director, Max Biemeyer, for a play he's doing in the summer. He's a great guy, quite big on the Continent. You don't have to thank me, and I'm sure you won't.

Holly read more avidly now, putting her glass down on her bedside table. So all this had been Jeff's doing?

The thing is, Max owes me a few favours. Well, a lot of favours actually. To put it bluntly, he's under my thumb. You don't need to know the details. It's quite pathetic, actually, and is a pretty funny story – the old man is quite a fool in a lot of ways – but he directs well. I put your name forward for this summer job because I'd like to do something nice for you. Even after all the horrible things you said to me when I met Mandy, I still care for you and think you deserve a break.

83

Holly couldn't believe her eyes. Jeff certainly had a talent for twisting the facts and absolving himself of blame. He was also incredibly patronising.

So, if you still think I owe you one, that's your payment. As I said before, this isn't the end for us. I know we'll see each other soon. And when we do, I know it's going to be a lot of fun in whatever way. I hope you are over your angry phase – that was pretty ugly.

Till next time.

Jeff

Holly collapsed back on the bed in amazement. She couldn't believe Jeff's audacity, to criticise her behaviour when he had been the unfaithful one. But something else hovered in the mind and bothered her even more – Max's alleged debt to Jeff. What on earth could that be? *He's under my thumb*, Jeff had written. Whatever the story was, it had to be pretty powerful. Max seemed to do everything Jeff wanted. She drained her glass, her mind racing through the facts. It had to be something that had happened in his job, or around that time. It had to be pretty sordid, or damaging to Max's career – or illegal. And it had to explain why Jeff and Max were thick as thieves. Holly couldn't help thinking that, if she could get in on the information, she could make life a lot easier for herself around both of them.

Holly jumped off the bed and grabbed her filofax. She was still on speaking terms with some of Jeff's mates – perhaps they could shed some light on the matter. She flicked through the pages, sobered up by the excitement. Seeing the name Darren Carpenter, she decided to call him. He wasn't an actor, just an ordinary bloke that Jeff often confided in. She grabbed her mobile and dialled his number. An answerphone clicked on.

'Damn,' Holly muttered and continued to trawl through the address pages. Most of Jeff's friends weren't all that trustworthy – even if Jeff had confided in them, she didn't dare phone them. They would tell Jeff instantly that Holly had been sniffing around, and she felt safer if he didn't know. Mark, Steve, Sanjay – they were all blabbermouths. She was about to shut the filofax, when she suddenly spotted an address in Jeff's writing. She remembered he had written it in there when they split up. It had been his forwarding address at Mandy's flat in North London. Next to it he had scrawled: 'Please forward ALL male.' She snickered at his appalling spelling. She studied the address for a while: Mandy Marks. Obviously a stage name, Holly thought – and if Jeff's behaviour with Nikki was anything to go by, obviously an ex. She contemplated phoning her. It would be a lot like conferring with the enemy. Holly had managed to avoid meeting Mandy all along, not wanting to do the showdown thing with her. She had sounded like a shallow, ignorant type – but she had been close to Jeff at the time, and she knew Max. Holly had no choice but to call her. She dialled slowly and, as the phone rang, she poured herself another generous helping of alcohol. She needed it. Just as Holly was about to give up, someone answered.

'Hello?' It was a girl's voice.

'Hi. Um – is that Mandy?'

'Yes. Who's this?' The accent had a northern lilt to it.

'It's Holly.' There was a long pause as the name sunk in. 'Holly Parker.'

'What's happened?' Mandy's first reaction was to think Jeff had been in an accident. Maybe it was wishful thinking.

'Nothing. Nothing bad. I just . . .' Holly took a gulp from her glass. 'I need to speak to you about something.'

'What?' Holly didn't know how to put it. Mandy was getting impatient. 'Look, I'm going out soon.'

'Sorry. I need to know about Max Biemeyer. I need to know about him and Jeff.' She heard Mandy sigh wearily on the end of the line.

'Look, I don't mean to be rude, but why should I help you, or even talk to you?' she said. 'It's history with Jeff and, let's face it, you and me never even met.' Holly felt like pointing out that she hadn't ever done anything to hurt Mandy, but knew she had to keep the peace.

'I know.' She was desperate. 'Let's just say it would be one woman helping another woman out.'

Mandy considered this. 'Right. OK.' She was terse. 'Come over here tomorrow afternoon. We'll talk then. But I wouldn't mention to Jeff that I'm seeing you.'

'Oh, don't worry! I won't,' Holly answered, and they ended the call. She sat back, feeling both heady and alert. She would get a train up to London tomorrow. It would be nice to spend Saturday night in her own bed, and she was aching to know what Mandy had to say for herself. She would easily be back in time for her session with Joshua on Sunday night. It was all falling into place.

Holly drunkenly threw some things in her overnight bag for the next day's trip up to London. Her head was buzzing. She was going to make Max suffer now. It felt a little like revenge, but more like justice. By ten o'clock, Holly had crashed out on the bed, an empty bottle of wine beside her and her things ready to leave first thing. She didn't even hear the knock on her door at eleven, when Ben had come home early from his night out to see her. He pushed the door open and saw her sleeping heavily, still half dressed. He approached her, pulled a blanket over her and turned off her bedside light. He would have to come back for another lesson some other time, he could see. Regretfully, he went back to his own room, leaving Holly to her vivid dreams of snakes, frantic chases, espionage and the other woman.

Chapter Ten

*L*ondon on a Saturday afternoon was a flurry of activity and noise, especially after the space and peace of a Cornish village. Holly battled her way through the crowds at Paddington Station, hopping onto the circle line to Kings Cross. She took a squashed ride on the Victoria line up to Highbury and Islington underground station, the closest tube to Mandy Mark's flat. By the time she got there, Holly had been travelling for five hours in all, and she didn't look her best. She glimpsed her reflection in the window of a charity shop and saw a dishevelled, manic woman with a large bag. She paused in the street to brush her hair and apply some lipstick. She was not going to look a state in front of Mandy.

She soon found Mandy's flat. It was in a trendy, up-market road but her flat had a shabby exterior that looked vaguely out of place. The other properties were period houses converted into flats, with steps up to the front doors and large bay windows at the front. Mandy's building was in the seventies style, square and new, built from brown brick. Holly rang the buzzer and recognised Mandy's voice over the intercom.

'Yeah?'

'It's me. Holly.' After a second the door buzzed and

clicked, and Holly gave it a shove. She found herself in a neon-lit hallway, with bikes leaning against the walls. She climbed the stairs and soon came across flat 4, Mandy's apartment. The door was off the latch and slightly ajar. Holly could hear the stereo playing inside, some cheesy new boy band massacring a decent song. Mandy was humming along in there. Holly followed the voice and went in.

It was a small flat, but cosy. The walls were painted bright colours and the furnishings were all draped with printed fabrics and scarves. The living room was separated from the kitchenette only by a work surface. Mandy was standing at the sink, making tea.

'Are you herbal or normal?' she asked, barely turning round.

'Normal, please. Black,' Holly replied. Mandy turned and passed her a mug. She was even younger looking than Holly expected, small and slight with fine fair hair pulled back in a ponytail. She had a bright, clear face – not a wrinkle in sight, Holly noticed – but she was far from beautiful. She was observing Holly in return, masking her curiosity with a feigned indifference.

'Wanna seat?' She gestured to the living room. Holly smiled and sat herself down on the sofa – it was low and uncomfortable, and the springs protruded through the material. Mandy came and sat cross-legged on the floor in front of her, sipping her tea. 'Did you find it OK?' she asked politely.

'Yes.' Holly drank her tea too, suddenly feeling thirsty. 'Look, I know it's a bit odd me coming here. I wouldn't if it wasn't important. Important to me at any rate.' Mandy looked at her questioningly.

'You're not going to ask me about my relationship with Jeff, are you?' she asked directly. 'Because that's all over now, and I don't see the point.' Against her wishes, Holly liked this girl – she was down to earth.

'No. I don't care about all that.' She took Jeff's letter out of her bag. 'I got this a few weeks ago. Read it.'

Mandy obviously recognised the script and took it.

She read slowly and carefully, lingering momentarily over the section about herself. When she had finished it she gave it back to Holly.

'Sweet and accommodating?' She smiled wryly. 'Christ, makes me sound like a right wimp.'

'I think he was just trying to wind me up to be honest,' Holly replied. 'He likes to do that.'

'I'm sure. Got a real thing about you. You really got under his skin.' For the first time a hint of bitterness clouded her voice. 'So you're doing that job with Max down in the West Country, are you?' Holly nodded. 'How's it going?'

Holly wasn't sure how much to tell. 'It's difficult.'

'I bet. Glad I'm not doing it now.'

'Were you going to?' Holly was curious.

'Oh yeah. I was all set to go when Max recast it. Same day as Jeff dumped me. Funny that, eh?' She looked knowingly at Holly. So Mandy had been going to play Nikki's role – and then Jeff had obviously decided to get rid of her.

'That must have pissed you off?' Holly hoped Mandy was angry enough to tell her everything about Max and Jeff. She was lucky.

'I hate the bastards,' Mandy said simply. 'Jeff's just a waste of space and Max is a mess – got a real problem with women.'

'I'd noticed.' Holly decided to get to the point. 'In the letter Jeff talks about Max owing him favours. What's that about?'

'Oh, the famous "debt of gratitude" Jeff was always on about?' Mandy laughed ironically. 'It all happened when we were doing our show up in Northampton. I'm not really supposed to tell anyone . . .' She hesitated for a moment. 'What the hell. Well, do you know about Max's little addiction?'

'No.' Holly sat forward, intrigued.

'Oh, he's got this big thing for girls on the game. It's like a compulsion. And not anyone over twenty-two, either, they have to look . . . virginal.'

'Really?'

'Jeff thinks it's got something to do with him wanting to make his mark on the world – you know, taking a virginity and all that.' She took a gulp of tea. 'Anyway, when we were in Northampton he got into a bit of trouble.'

'With the police?'

'Not quite. He found this girl he liked walking the streets – they've got quite a few up there – and she was really young and pretty and stuff, so he went back with her to her place for sex. She leads him into this room and tells him to get naked, which he does. She goes down on him, says she loves to suck his cock, gets him all riled up. She says she's got to go and get her condoms from the next room, so she leaves and closes the door behind her. So he waits and waits, ten minutes go by, and he's getting suspicious. He gets up and tries the door – it's locked.'

'Shit.'

'That's what he thinks. So he starts calling out and banging on the door, with his tackle out and everything. And these two enormous lads burst in – her brothers. One guys pins him against the wall, beating the crap out of him, the other takes his wallet, his watch, everything. He threatens to go to the police.' She paused for effect. '*Then* they tell him that their sister is only fifteen years old. They're going to lock him in there and get the police themselves!'

'How did he get out of that one?' Holly was enjoying this.

'Well, Jeff had been with him earlier and had seen the guys running into the flat. He knew there was trouble. So he ran in after him and got him out.'

'But Jeff's a coward. He's a wimp!' Holly interjected.

'I know.' Mandy laughed. 'But he had this strange thing with Max. He'd keep an eye out for him. And he acted without thinking.'

'What happened?'

'Jeff grabbed Max's clothes and they legged it down

the road. Max had to get himself decent in a doorway.'
Mandy chuckled. 'Max swore Jeff to secrecy, but Jeff
couldn't resist telling me – to show what a big man he
was, you know.'

'Have a bit of a boast.' Holly could well imagine. 'So
this was the "debt of gratitude"?'

'That's what Jeff called it. And Max has done everything Jeff says ever since.' Mandy raised her eyebrows.
'Including firing me!'

'And hiring me,' Holly thought aloud. 'But why? Just
so he could then make my life a misery?'

'Oh, I wouldn't be surprised. Is that what they've
been doing?' Mandy was intrigued. 'Jeff has this big
thing about you, Holly. He needed to get his revenge
on you.'

'But I never did anything to him!' Holly cried. 'He
was the one who . . .' She stopped herself, tapering off.

'Just the fact you got on with your life was bad
enough for him. I hate to say this, but when me and Jeff
got together, I soon realised it was just a way to get at
you. He thought he was losing you and wanted to bail
out first. He thought you'd crumble and beg to have
him back. You didn't. That pissed him off.' Mandy got
up and moved into the kitchen. Her CD had finished
but she hummed on regardless, leaving Holly alone
with her thoughts on the couch. She began to rinse some
dishes on the drier, scrubbing hard at a pan. It was
coming clearer to Holly now: the looks between Jeff and
Max, the power games, even the therapy she was forced
to take, all of them were Jeff's way of getting back at
her. Jeff was obviously determined to break her down.
Where would it all have ended, had Mandy not revealed
all?

'Thanks, Mandy,' Holly said. Mandy didn't reply. 'I
won't tell Jeff I saw you, if you'd rather.'

'I couldn't care less.' She continued scrubbing. 'Have
you met Max's wife yet?'

'He's married?'

'Oh yeah. Meet her and you'll see why he needs to go

91

to a pro.' Mandy chuckled to herself. 'I think he fell in love with the fact she was English aristocracy. Lady Eleanor. When you started out as a poor immigrant like he did that title's pretty appealing.'

'I bet. So is she rich?' Holly came up to the kitchen area and took a tea towel to help Mandy dry.

'Bloody loaded! She produces all his stuff. But,' Mandy fixed her with a naughty glare, 'you've never met a more stuck-up, frigid, uptight little cow in all your life!' And she laughed. The words echoed in Holly's head – they were all words Max had levelled at her in rehearsal.

'God. I think he takes all that out on me,' she muttered.

'Well, he needs to take it out on someone,' Mandy remarked. 'And I doubt you get many perky young prostitutes in your Cornish fishing village, now, do you?'

It was dark by the time Holly arrived at her own flat in Hammersmith that night. She was instantly comforted by the familiarity of it all – her own kitchen, her own bed. Holly took the pile of post lying on the doormat to her sofa and opened it. It was mostly bills, with a couple of party invites and some junk mail. She flicked on the TV, put on some table lamps and made herself some pasta. Her life in Cornwall with the Briars seemed like a dream now. She didn't even recognise herself as the woman who let both Ben and Mr Briar make love to her. With a plate of hot spaghetti on her lap, she called her friend Katie and indulgently recounted all the events of the past week. Katie was intrigued, shocked and amused all at once.

'You're fighting them off, Hol,' she teased.

'Hardly.'

'Well, it's obvious to me that this Oberon guy is in love with you.'

'Don't be silly.'

'But it's no good if you're so in love with the dashing doctor.'

'What are you talking about?'

'Joshua Delaney! Oh, come on, don't try to deny it!' Holly made some noises of derision, but Katie would not let her get away with it. 'It's obvious, Hol. But be careful. He sounds like he's got some kind of weird history.'

Sleeping in her own bed that night was a luxury, and she was happy to awake the next day without any crazy dreams winding around her mind. As she was leaving, she noticed a letter which had slipped under her door-mat. She hadn't seen it last night. She picked it up and saw that it had a Plymouth postmark. She quickly ripped it open and pulled out a tatty single sheet of lined paper. In neat, black capitals was written: I HATE YOU in the centre of the page. There was no other mark on the paper. She scoured the envelope for clues, but saw only the neutral writing of the address. Disturbed, she stuffed the envelope in her jacket pocket. There was a beep from her road, and she saw that the taxi had arrived. She locked the door behind her and ran down to meet it.

'Paddington, please,' she said. She watched the houses of West London pass outside her window as she combed her mind for clues as to who could send her such a spiteful letter. Jeff was the first to come into her head, but somehow she didn't feel it was him, although he did know her home address. It was a bit childish for Max. It didn't seem like Mandy's style either. She read it again and shivered. She decided to not let it bother her – whoever had sent it was an immature idiot. She ripped it to shreds and stuffed it in the bin of the cab. She felt better for that and as she got on the train her spirits lifted slightly. Home was nice, but tonight she would be seeing Joshua – her heart beat faster at the thought. Maybe Katie had a point about him, she thought, and smiled to herself. Katie was usually right.

Chapter Eleven

*I*t was turning dark when Holly reached the top of Joshua's hill, the sun sinking behind the cliffs that curved around the far side of the bay. The light glowing warmly from his windows gave the house a welcoming feel. Despite having caught Joshua avidly watching the video of her, Holly had decided to dress demurely tonight – a simple long black jersey dress that clung to her figure, and knee boots. And underwear. Joshua answered the door and seemed pleased to see her.

'Hello there,' he said. 'Come in.' They walked automatically to his study and Holly dutifully resumed her place in the red chair, sitting back with her legs crossed, her hands in her lap. He looked at her and took up his pad again. 'How have you been?'

'Good.' She replied simply, as if that was the end of the conversation. They smiled at each other.

'Good.' He shifted his weight. 'Last time we talked about exploring your fantasies. Are you ready to do that?'

'Are you?' She couldn't resist that, half expecting him to recoil as he usually did whenever she tried to flirt with him.

'Yes. That's what I'm here for – to listen.'

'And watch?' He looked puzzled. 'Never mind. You

forgot to put the video on.' He nodded in realisation, quickly getting up and flicking the switch. Holly leaned forward into the lens and grinned. 'Hi, Joshua.'

'Tell me.' He resumed his position on the desk in front of her. 'What would you say turns you on?'

'What or who?'

'Let's start with what.' Holly realised she couldn't evade his questions any longer. She was actually a bit reluctant to reveal all her innermost desires to a man on whom she hoped one day to exercise them.

'Right.' She thought for a while. Her mind was blank.

'Anything that comes to mind.' He waited for her.

'Well, it's not a fantasy – it's something that happened to me when I was eighteen.' Holly's mind instantly shot back to this one incident. She didn't want to share it particularly – it had been shameful and humiliating. And completely out of character which is why she found it so erotic.

'Yes, often early experiences are more potent.' He nodded for her to continue.

'OK, when I was eighteen I took a temping job in London – in Euston. It was a boring filing job. I worked in the back office of some firm. It was summer – I remember that, because it was so hot I couldn't wear very much.' She glanced at him. His face was neutral. 'This one time I just had on this short white dress. So, I was on a crowded rush hour tube home – I mean, awful. We were all crammed up against each other in eighty-degree heat– me and all the other poor bastards, all the men wearing suits.'

'Yes?'

'And the train was rocking and we were all jiggling up against each other. I didn't have anything to hold on to, so I kind of leaned against this guy in front of me. He was facing me and I leaned slightly against his chest – didn't even look at his face. The train was shaking so much and I never wore a bra in those days. And the more I brushed against him, the harder my nipples got. I shut my eyes and began to enjoy the closeness of it.

95

And he must have read my mind, because he reached down with the hand that wasn't hanging on to the rail and I felt him press against my – well, between my legs. I didn't open my eyes, but I leaned into him a little harder – to let him know it was all right, that I liked it. He reached down and slipped his hand up my skirt and inside my knickers. I wasn't quite ready for that – mentally or physically – I mean I wasn't wet yet or anything, but it was so naughty that I started to gush at his sheer cheek. Meanwhile all the other commuters were bouncing against us, all crushed up against each other. I didn't dare look up, but I was getting really turned on –and hotter even than I was before. He suddenly pushed me backwards into the carriage a little – we had stopped at a station. Oxford Circus. Loads of people crowded on, and we were pushed even closer together. I think he knew I might get cold feet and pull away at any minute. He became a bit rough, but I was into it so I didn't mind. His other hand was kneading at my breasts, quite nastily. It hurt a bit. Part of me was scared, but the other part really wanted it. The train slowed down for the next station – it was Green Park. He said in my ear, 'Let's get off here.' And kind of pulled me off. He didn't let go of my hand – we raced up the escalator. I could only see the back of his head – he was slightly greying, but he had a fit body, nice broad back. He pulled me into the toilets at the station – the men's toilets, no less. There were a couple of guys there having a pee. He ignored them and dragged me into a cubicle. We faced each other and I saw his face for the first time. About forty, good-looking, very groomed, sort of rich-looking. He yanked up my dress, ripped off my panties – literally, I mean tore them off – and hitched me up against the wall. I was powerless against him really, my legs just wrapped around him to steady myself, and he was inside me. He pushed hard. I yelped with pain. He didn't hang around. Then he started to thrust straight away – hard, almost angry. I clung on for dear life, feeling him push me open and

force his way inside me. It burned. But then he kept
thrusting and his body was right up against me, and I
started to get into the rhythm. The burning became
pleasure. And the fact that this stranger was fucking me
in a station toilet started to really turn me on. My tits
were bouncing around – oh God, he couldn't take his
eyes off them – and my legs were stretched out in
pleasure – my feet were pressing against the wall of the
cubicle, my high-heeled sandals coming off the heels. I
was trying to be quiet. I didn't want us to get arrested
or anything, but I couldn't stop panting and whimpering. He got more and more aggressive, and I felt him
about to come. I wasn't there yet. And I was breathing
in his ear, 'Wait. Don't come. Don't stop!' But he did.
He came for what seemed like ages. I felt so hot I didn't
know what to do with myself. My pussy was soaked
and fluttering like a bird. He pulled out of me. I said,
'Don't go! Make me come!' I just wanted him to touch
me or go down on me. But he didn't. He zipped up and
walked out, leaving me in that men's toilet with my
panties in shreds on the floor and his come running
down my thighs. I came out and was greeted by leering
looks from two blokes in there. I was stumbling a bit,
he'd been so rough. I felt really used. I felt like a whore.
I couldn't believe I'd done it. But I still think it's one of
the sexiest things that's ever happened to me, and when
I think about it – God, I get all hot and sticky and I wish
I could do it again.'

'But this time, you'd come, right?'

'Oh yes.' Holly uncrossed her legs and sat back,
titillated by the memory. She was amazed how easy it
had been to recount it to Joshua. He seemed unfazed by
it, she noticed sadly.

'Have you had other experiences of anonymous sex?'
Holly instantly thought of that night at the Briars', when
someone had gone down on her under the covers. She
told the story to Joshua, adding that she still wasn't sure
who had been the culprit.

'I think it was Caleb, the father. He had that experienced tongue.' Holly felt restless. 'How can you sit around and talk about sex all day and never do it?' she demanded. 'Isn't it tempting just to get into bed with a client and get it on?'

He shook his head. 'That way lies all sorts of misery,' he said. 'And this is about you, not me.'

'Couldn't it be about both of us?'

Joshua took a deep breath of utter patience and leaned forward. 'You had a dream about a snake. A sexual dream?' She nodded. 'Has it recurred?' So he wanted to keep himself out of it. Holly sighed.

'I can't remember.' She wracked her brains. 'No – I think it left me over the weekend.' She couldn't remember dreaming about it again, that thick-trunked snake slipping up her body.

'What happened over the weekend?'

'I went home. I sorted out some stuff.'

'What kind of stuff?' Holly wondered how much to tell him. She didn't want to sound like a scheming woman.

'Stuff about my ex. I met up with the woman he left me for. Well, girl, I should say. She wasn't much more than twenty.' Holly tutted. 'Poor thing, didn't know what a snake she'd fallen for. Well, she knows now.'

Joshua smiled. 'Well, I think we've identified the snake!' he said. 'Good. Obviously wasn't the classic penis envy dream we thought.' Holly didn't like to say that she had never thought it was that. If there was one thing in life not to be envious of, it was a penis. They were indiscreet appendages, stiffening when they shouldn't, needy things wanting constant attention, pretty ugly too in their flaccid state.

He looked back at some notes. 'You were going to drown in this boat – the snake was pinning you down, sexually invading you. But you were enjoying it. Would you agree that there's an element of masochism in you, Holly? That you like men to have power over you? Like the man at the station?'

'Look, I don't know.' She felt irritated at him now,

telling her what was wrong with her. 'In bed, maybe.'
Joshua suddenly flashed a look at the window as if he
had heard a noise. Holly looked at it – nobody was
there. It was the same window she had spied him
through the other night. 'What is it?'

'Oh, nothing – I keep thinking I hear someone out
there.' He smiled. 'Just going mad. Freud would be
barking his head off if some stranger was prowling
outside, anyway.'

'Living alone can make you jumpy.' Holly knew the
feeling, and felt a pang of guilt that she had probably
precipitated Joshua's paranoia by prowling around
herself.

'Sorry, back to you.' He gathered himself, brushing
his hair out of his eyes in his usual way. 'We were
talking about anonymity and power.'

'Were we?' Holly was amused.

'Yes. I think it all goes back to the fact you are
searching for what your own desires may be.'

'I am?'

'This is the impression you gave me.'

'I think I know what I want, Joshua. I'm getting surer
of that by the minute.' She looked him straight in the
eye. 'But, while I'm waiting around to get it, I have to
keep myself occupied.' He fixed her with his deep blue
eyes for a moment, then got up.

'Do you want a piece of cake? It's my birthday.'

She nodded eagerly, surprised. 'Of course! Happy
birthday!' She got up and gave him a tentative hug.
'Joshua, you should have said. I'd have got you
something.'

He moved to the door. 'No, glad you didn't. I decided
a while ago never to accept gifts from people I am
treating.' He opened it. 'It never works out.'

'Oh Christ, *do* relax!' Holly laughed at him, and
followed him through to the kitchen. Freud leaped up
and gave her a warm welcome, his tail beating against
her leg. A chocolate cake sat on the table with smarties
on the top. A good half had already disappeared.

'Me and Freud have already pigged out.' Joshua saw her sizing up the missing piece. 'But I'm always ready for more.'

'Well, that's good to know.' Holly smirked, dipping her finger in the icing and tasting it. It was delicious. 'And you bake? You're just too good to be true, aren't you?'

They sat eating the cake and chatting as Freud begged for scraps at their feet. Holly was soon full and noticed that she had been there for over two hours. She got up.

'It's eleven o'clock!' she said. Joshua rose to his feet too. 'I should go.'

'If you like.' Holly looked at him to gauge what he was saying. 'I mean, if you don't want any more therapy tonight.' She looked into his eyes. Everything he said seemed to have two meanings. 'I mean, if you've said all you want to say about fantasies.' She smiled ruefully.

'Can I have my cake and eat it?' she asked.

'Probably not,' he answered. The air was taut with meaning. 'But you can take a piece home with you if you like.' He grinned, and cut her a slice. He wrapped it in foil and gave it to her.

'Well, that'll have to do for now.' Holly went to the door. Outside the evening had turned to moonless night. The air was black – only the twinkling of the harbour lights below and the light spilling from Joshua's windows would guide her way down the hill.

'Will you be all right on your own?' He was concerned.

'Yes, fine.' She smiled at him. 'And you?'

'I'll manage.'

'Happy birthday.' Holly stood on tiptoe and planted a gentle kiss on his cheek. His eyes were warm and he looked more relaxed than he had ever been in her company. 'I see that chocolate cake agrees with you. I will have to remember that.' Holly made her way back down to the village, feeling light and heady. That man had an effect on her. She whistled to herself, pausing only to greet a woman who was walking across the cliffs with a bunch of wild flowers. The woman smiled, recognising the glow that Holly had that night, and listened as Holly's whistle grew fainter in the distance.

Chapter Twelve

*A*s Holly was walking through the bramble path the next morning, she was surprised by the sound of running behind her. She swung round to see Oberon bounding up to her. He had broken into a sweat, the droplets glistening on his shaved head and trickling into his dark eyes. He slowed to her pace, brushing his hand across his forehead.

'I've been shouting your name for about five minutes!' There was a friendly accusation in his voice.

'Sorry, daydreaming.' Holly realised that Katie might be right about Oberon – he seemed awfully pleased to see her.

'I wanted to know you were OK – you know, after Friday.'

'Oh, you mean the "trust game"?' She sneered, the memory filling her with hatred for Max and Jeff. 'Where did you all go?'

'God, he'd had it arranged all day. He had told us when we had to leave – our cue was when the belt went round your wrists.' Oberon looked concerned. 'I tried to warn you but I never got the chance. Max was mental that day – really steamed up.'

'Well, don't worry about it.' Holly smiled to herself. 'That kind of thing won't be happening again.'

* * *

Nikki and Jeff seemed to have made things up, Holly noticed as she came into the theatre. Jeff was whispering something into her ear. It must have been hilarious, because she couldn't stop giggling. He glanced up at Holly and Oberon as they came in, and muttered something else to Nikki, who gasped and turned to Holly. Obviously he had told her that Holly was seeing Oberon, or perhaps that she had come all over Max's hand on Friday. Either way, Holly didn't care. She flashed a warm smile at Nikki.

'Hi, how are you?' she said casually. 'I like your hair like that.' This confused the young actress, whose natural desire to be liked compelled her to smile back.

'Thanks. Had it cut over the weekend.' She fluffed her fingers through the cropped curls. Nathaniel arrived, dumping his bag at the door.

'Sorry I'm late, everybody. Can't blame the bloody tubes down here, can you?' He came up to Holly as she was taking off her jacket and took her arm in a fatherly way. 'Look, Holly. I felt dreadful about leaving you here with those two cads on Friday. I hope they didn't do anything they shouldn't?'

'Oh, don't worry.' Holly gave him a reassuring hug. 'I can look after myself.'

'Maybe. But you shouldn't have to, my dear.' He shook his head. 'There's something amiss with that director of ours, I can tell you. But if he ever gives you any more trouble, please come to me. I'll have a word.'

'Oh, that's sweet.' Holly kissed him on the cheek. His eyes lit up.

Max walked in and sneered slightly at this happy little scene. He slammed his script down on the table and cleared his throat. All the actors, and Adrian the stage manager, looked up at him expectantly. His mood seemed slightly brighter than on Friday. When he was sure he had everybody's undivided attention, he gave a deliberate smile.

'Well. Today is the day we've all been looking forward to,' he said, rubbing his hands together.

103

'He's resigning?' Oberon murmured to Holly, who let out a short snort of laughter.

'Today, we will be exploring the sexual scenes between Mistress Rachel and her handmaid, Dolores.' He grinned in an openly lascivious manner. 'And, ladies, as we have said before, there must be no coyness, no faking and no prudishness. Understood, Miss Parker?' Holly was now immune to being singled out by him and shrugged it off.

The stage was set with a dressing table and a large four-poster bed, which had just arrived from the scenery workshop. Max pranced about the stage, eyeing it proudly. He called his two actresses up onto the stage and indicated for them to sit on the bed.

'Now, this is the central relationship of the play, ladies. Get this right and everything else will follow. Yes?' They nodded, Nikki rather more eagerly than Holly. 'Mistress Rachel has all the *social* advantage – status, money, position. But Dolores has the real power in their relationship – she tests her mistress's suitors for her, she arranges her life, she seduces her and, in the end, we see that she has swindled her of all her wealth. Dolores is the one in charge. The dominatrix, if you like.'

'Sounds good,' Nikki simpered.

'We have one scene where Dolores sexually counsels her frustrated mistress. I think Miss Parker may find this difficult.' He raised an eyebrow at Holly.

'I think we should just get on with it, Max,' she replied curtly. 'Let's not be all talk, eh?' She heard Nathaniel chuckle at this. Her knowledge of Max's misdemeanours had suddenly given her the advantage over him, even if he didn't know it yet. 'Are we going to improvise it first, like I did with Jeff and Oberon?'

'Yes, yes we are. But without words to start with. Nicola, lie on the bed, please.' Nikki obeyed, stretching out on her back with her head downstage, closest to the audience. She glanced at Jeff for approval and saw he had risen to his feet. 'Holly, you can start by massaging her if you like. Have you ever made love to a woman before?' Holly declined to answer that question – she didn't want to give Max the satisfaction of knowing she hadn't. Instead, she pushed Nikki onto her stomach. She ran her fingers lightly over Nikki's body. It felt extremely soft and yielding, lacking the muscular resistance of a man's. Holly slowly untied the bow of Nikki's pink halter-neck top, and tickled the creamy skin around her neck and shoulders. The top zipped at the back, she noticed. She gradually slid the zip down and the top fell open. Nikki had a lovely, fleshy body, Holly thought, with a straight spine and high hips. Holly straddled her and began to gently massage her back, kneading out the knots on either side of her spine, and occasionally letting her hands stroke out to Nikki's sides. The auditorium was hushed. Holly peered up through her hair and saw that Jeff had stepped closer to the stage. Oberon was still sitting at the back and Nathaniel was staring intently at their actions from an upstairs box, where he had a wonderful bird's-eye view. Max had seated himself down on a chair on stage. Holly's hands moved to Nikki's sides, working their way round to the round orbs of her breasts.

'That's right. Get to know her body,' Max murmured. Holly sat to one side and slowly untied the wraparound skirt around Nikki's waist. Once it was open it unfolded out onto the bed. Nikki was now naked from the back except for a rather sweet pair of knickers, which said 'Monday' on them in childish letters. She had a small, rounded bottom and dancer's legs. Holly rubbed her buttocks, letting her fingers graze the crack of her bottom lightly, and swept her hands down Nikki's legs. She crouched at her feet and lightly took a toe in her mouth, sucking it gently and wetly. To her surprise, this elicited a deep moan of pleasure from Nikki. Holly's mouth moved to the next toe – more moaning. She never thought she could give another woman pleasure so easily. Encouraged, she kissed her way up Nikki's legs and began to trail her tongue lazily up her spine, circling occasionally, and sometimes giving a bite. Nikki began to squirm a little, but Holly wasn't sure if this was in enjoyment or irritation. When Holly reached Nikki's neck, she gave her a big juicy love bite. She grabbed a handful of her blonde hair and pulled it so that Nikki raised her head off the bed giving Holly access to her throat. Holly kissed her way round, leaving smaller love bites as she did so. She noticed a woman's skin marked easier than a man's. She wondered if it had hurt – the marks grew more livid and red by the minute.

'Turn her over,' Max ordered. Holly obeyed, and saw Nikki's face for the first time – she was blushing furiously. Was this embarrassment or a sexual flush? Holly pulled the top away and flung it to the ground, leaving her colleague bare-chested. Her breasts were small but upright, topped by sweet pink nipples. In the spirit of curiosity, Holly popped one in her mouth and teased it as she liked to be teased – sucking and swirling it on her tongue. She kissed her way to the other breast and tried again there. Nikki was wriggling under her. Holly almost felt jealous of the erotic pleasure she was giving. She moved up the bed until she was level with Nikki's head and turned, so that she was facing Nikki's feet. She unbuttoned her shirt and took it off, and removed her bra. Now they were both bare-breasted, and Holly was going to have some fun, too. Holly leaned forward on her arms so that her face was over Nikki's nipples and her own breasts were hanging over Nikki's mouth. Nikki smiled and took a breast in her small hand, guiding it to her lips. As she started to suckle, Holly returned the favour, coming round to the pleasure.

'It's like a mini sixty-niner!' Jeff mumbled to himself, his hand busy down the front of his trousers. Nikki clasped Holly's auburn hair and encouraged her head to go lower, towards her crotch. Holly began to resist but was aware of Max watching her. She wasn't going to be the first to say no. She crawled down Nikki's body until her face was level with Nikki's panties. The word

'Monday' loomed in her face. Holly wanted to giggle as she remained there, poised for action. She could smell Nikki's intimate scent. She paused.

'Stop!' Max shouted. Holly quickly crawled off the bed and covered her naked breasts with her shirt. Nikki didn't move, but lay sprawled on the bed with just her knickers on. 'I think these girls need help, don't you?' he said to the men in the auditorium, all of whom had faces drawn with excitement. 'Jeff, come up here.' Jeff gladly came up on stage. 'Show Miss Parker how to look like you want to lick out a woman! Because, believe me, you don't always want to – but you better make it *look* like you do.' Jeff eagerly got onto the bed and crouched between Nikki's legs. Holly stepped away, not enjoying this proximity with her ex.

'Remember this, Hol?' He grinned as he lowered his head over Nikki's privates. He inhaled dramatically and sighed with pleasure. 'First, you have to love the smell. Then, the first taste.' He hooked her panties to one side and dipped the tip of his tongue into her scanty bush, giving a couple of light licks. 'You start off tentatively, slowly. You taste her. Then you find the bud.' He reapplied his tongue, letting it explore for longer this time. Nikki writhed under him and jolted as he obviously discovered her clitoris. He glanced up at her as he gave it some attention, proud of her appreciative reaction. 'Then,' he continued, pulling a hair from his teeth, 'you let passion take over.' And he buried his face down there again, but this time with a vigour that made Holly's pussy trickle with envy. Wet slurping noises filled the otherwise hushed stage. His head moved in circles as he licked, and occasionally jerked up and down. 'That's tongue-fucking!' he cried into Nikki's cunt. She kept on wriggling and writhing under him, her face a deep shade of raspberry. Her breath started to come in jerky, jagged peaks. 'Then you come back out and . . .' he came up for breath, 'and go for the final onslaught – clit only.' He returned to his administrations, the licking sounds going at quite a pace. Nikki's

107

mouth was wide open now, her lips deep red. She was holding her breath, her tummy taut, her legs splayed. 'And she's coming,' Jeff cried into her pussy, and right on cue, Nikki let out a trembling, quivering sigh. Jeff grinned smugly as he pulled his head up and shared the wet smile with the rest of the guys in the house. Nikki was exhausted and sweaty on the bed, but she sat up.

'You know, Max,' she said huskily, 'if Dolores has the power, it's Rachel who should go down on *her*.' Max considered this. 'That's the submissive position, isn't it? And besides, I'd like to try it.' Holly was apprehensive. She didn't feel like performing cunnilingus on another woman, but she didn't know how she felt about receiving it either. 'I wouldn't be as good at it as Jeff, but I could try.' Holly saw Jeff acknowledge this as a compliment and baulked.

'You'll probably be a lot better, Nikki. Sex by formula isn't ever very exciting, is it?' She let her shirt drop to the floor and took off her trousers. 'Shall we start the impro again?' Max nodded and Jeff sat back down on the stage. Oberon's curiosity got the better of him. He came up to the stage too and crouched at the foot of the bed. Holly kept her panties on, and straddled Nikki on the bed.

'Use some of the lines from the play if you want to,' Max suggested. Holly was so nervous, she thought that this would help. She switched into character.

'*Mistress Rachel, you're so pretty,*' she began, sitting on Nikki's crotch and slowly gyrating her hips. Their two pairs of damp panties stuck together as she did so. '*But you need to be more forceful with these admirers of yours.*' She bent her head down and licked lovingly at a nipple. '*Half of them don't deserve you!*' Nikki lifted her hands above her head.

'*Don't be silly, Dolores. You must never be forceful with a man.*' She arched her back so that her ripe little breast rose fully into Holly's mouth. '*Only with a woman.*'

'*No, mistress – that's where you're wrong. They sometimes*

want a virgin who will lick eagerly at their pricks, but mostly they want a she-cat who might scratch out their eyes!' With that, Holly wriggled slowly up Nikki's body. She was aware of all the men watching them with enormous erections. Jeff looked like he was in pain it was so stretched. In his box, she saw Nathaniel's hand working up and down. Her pussy was over Nikki's chest – Holly rubbed herself against the breasts as if they were pillows to masturbate with. Both women sighed. *'Do I need to show you how to scare a man by making him weak?'* Her throat was almost too dry to get out the words – it was like all the moisture in her body had rushed to her pussy. She moved further up Nikki's body until she was straddling her throat. Nikki was truly in a weak position. Her hands were stuck above her head. She tried to wriggle free but she couldn't. *'And by making him weak, make him love you?'* Holly continued. She lifted her hips and Nikki brought her hands back down. Holly hovered with her crotch over Nikki's face – did Nikki really want to do this, she wondered. As if in reply, Nikki yanked Holly's panties down so that they were stretched tightly down her thighs. Holly leaned to one side and kicked the material off one leg so that it did not constrict her. Naked now, she looked around the room. Oberon was staring open-mouthed at her dripping pussy. Jeff was masturbating furiously. She lowered herself onto Nikki's face and felt the lizard-like flash of a tongue against her cunt lips. It was sharper and thinner than a man's tongue – it darted in and out of her, fluttered and flickered against her, lightly explored where a man's tongue would burgeon. She kept herself supported on her hands as Nikki continued to lick and kiss her slippery slit lightly. *'And by making him love you . . .'* she continued hoarsely, *'make him pleasure you.'* She leaned a bit harder on Nikki's mouth, feeling the actress moan into her hungrily. Holly felt the bed dip behind her and turned to see Max crawl between Nikki's legs, roughly pulling the panties from her body. He forced her legs apart and buried his face

109

in her bush. As soon as Max's tongue-strokes kicked in, Nikki's mouth became more ardent. But Holly couldn't relax – she glanced round again and saw Nikki wrap her slender legs around Max's big curly head, eagerly inviting him to dine on her, while she feasted in turn on Holly. Holly shut her eyes and heard the sound of her own wet juices as well as Nikki's fill the room. Nikki bucked and jerked under the weight of two people, moaning continuously, but was held firm by Max and by Holly's tingling pussy. Holly kept turning round, transfixed by the sight of Max 's mouth working hard against the blonde bush, his pink tongue probing and his nostrils flared. She was staggered at how enthusiastically Nikki welcomed his sexual touch, a touch she would find repulsive. Max was obviously pretty good – Nikki sounded like she was on the brink of coming again. She kept gulping down Holly's juices and groaning in ecstasy. Holly started to wriggle about on Nikki's face, chasing her own pleasure. But Nikki was overcome before Holly even got close, and she ground herself into Max's face. Holly's pussy muffled the shrill noise of Nikki's climax, which came in long agonising waves. Severely frustrated, Holly stomped off the bed and began to dress herself. Max continued to gently lap at Nikki, as if to nurse her through the afterglow.

'Good girl,' he murmured. 'Good girl. You came beautifully.'

'Thanks, Max!' she panted, her legs still spread wide and welcoming his attention. Holly suddenly felt jealous of all the attention Nikki was getting.

'You taste so sweet,' Max breathed, still buried in her bush, still lapping hypnotically at her. 'I could taste you all afternoon.' Nikki beamed at this, looking down at him.

'Oh yes.' She was barely audible.

'Would you like to let an old man give you pleasure like this for hours on end?' he said, starting to lick more definitely again now. 'I could look after all your needs.'

'Oh yes!' The excitement was returning to her cheeks.

The girl was insatiable. Max's head started to bob up and down in the pool of her previous orgasms. 'Oh yes!'

'Let Uncle Max give your little pussy a day to remember,' he growled into her, stepping up the pace.

'Oh yes!' Everyone watched in awe as Nikki seemed to be turning her trademark crimson again.

'Let Uncle Max make you come with his mouth . . .'

'Yes.'

'With his hands . . .'

'Yes!'

'With his big cock in your tight little pussy.'

'Oh yes! Yes please!' Her legs were now clamped needily around his head. He strained to look up over the top of the bed.

'Go on! Get out!' he yelled to the room in general, his face drenched in Nikki's come. Everyone started nervously for the door. 'Everyone in at eleven. Holly, Nathaniel, come back tomorrow at ten – we'll read the uncle/niece scene.' He stared wantonly into Nikki's willing young cunt. 'That'll be my favourite.' He groaned and continued to lick her as everybody made their escape.

Holly was still frustrated after her episode on the bed with Nikki, and was bizarrely jealous that Max had turned his attentions to the younger actress. She seemed grumpy to Oberon as all the actors spilled out into the street.

'You OK?' he asked. She squinted into the sun.

'I'm great.' She tried to sound light and airy, but her voice was tight. Nathaniel and Jeff were behind her, awkwardly avoiding the subject of what had just happened.

'Pub anyone?' Nathaniel asked. 'Need a stiff one. So to speak!'

'Yeah, me too,' Oberon agreed.

'I'm going back to my digs – need a shower,' Holly said, marching off down the road. 'Bye!' She called behind her, not wishing to seem rude. Joshua wanted her to masturbate – that's what she was going to do. All afternoon if that's what it would take for her to feel better. In her mind the image of Nikki's endless orgasms taunted her. Max certainly had the knack to make her come. Holly wondered if that had made Jeff jealous. She was striding down the bramble path when she heard running footsteps behind her, just as she had that morning. She swung round expecting to see Oberon's perspiring face again, but was instead confronted by the twisted, intense features of Jeff. He grabbed her arm and pressed her against the wire mesh fence of the alleyway, her hair caught in the thick brambles that spilled over it. His face was inches away from hers, his body forced against her.

'I know you want it,' he breathed. His erection was iron hard against her thigh. 'I saw your face watching Nikki and Max. You want to be fucked.'

'No,' she protested, struggling to free herself. He was too strong. He grasped both her arms painfully, pulling them behind her back so that her large bosoms were thrust out before her.

'Oh, Holly!' Jeff's eyes widened as he studied her body. 'Let me be inside you again. Let me!' He angrily fumbled with her fly, holding both her wrists with his left hand. He quickly forced his hand down her panties, discovering with obvious gratitude how slippery she was. 'I can feel how much you want it,' he hissed, inexpertly masturbating her with his hand. His knees were buckling with lust and Holly took the opportunity to break free. She ran wildly down the path, seeing the opening onto the road before her. Jeff had caught up with her, though, and now he was livid. 'Fuck me, you little bitch.' He grimaced, pulling her trousers down over her hips and unzipping his fly. Holly's legs instinctively kicked out at him, but this just gave him the chance to get between them, the head of his cock straining impatiently at her sex.

'Get off me!' she screamed, still struggling. Suddenly he was pulled backwards by somebody. Holly saw that

Joshua was hauling Jeff away from her by the scruff of his neck. Jeff turned and swung out to punch Joshua clean on the jaw, but Joshua anticipated it. He moved into the punch so that Jeff's fist flew behind his head, then he tackled Jeff, sending him flying into the bushes. The two were involved in a violent tussle, Joshua landing a few heartfelt blows to Jeff's stomach. Finally, when he had overcome Holly's attacker, he stood over him, a boot at his throat.

'Don't you ever touch her again.' Joshua's anger was simple and clear. 'Got it?' Jeff panted helplessly. Joshua pushed his boot harder against Jeff's throat. 'Got it?'

Jeff nodded fast, half choking. Joshua took his foot away and kicked Jeff up onto his feet. Jeff fled, his nose streaming blood. Josh turned to Holly. She had started to tremble uncontrollably with shock.

'I'm OK.' She tried to smile, her voice shivering. He went to her and gathered her in his arms, feeling her body shake against his.

'Who was that?' His voice was full of quiet thunder.

'Just my ex.' Josh held her tighter. 'Thank you.' He rocked her in his arms, his face pressed against her hair. She turned her head so that their cheeks were touching. She could feel his warm, quick breaths against her skin, and the soft brush of his eyelashes on her brow.

'Holly,' he murmured. 'Holly.' His voice melted into her ear. She was hardly trembling now, there was a calmness in her breathing. 'Holly.' She brought her face round to his, subtly, so that their lips were inches away from each other. She looked up, her green eyes locked into his blue eyes, with the hair flopping into them as always. She brought a hand up and tenderly brushed the hair away from his brow, her hand lingering to cup his cheek. There was a small, deep cut on his eyebrow. Her thumb wiped away a smudge of blood. He winced slightly.

'Sorry,' she whispered. A hint of a smile glittered in his eyes. He lowered his face and brushed his lips warmly against hers. She released herself instantly to the kiss, dreamily pressing her mouth to his, her hand still touching his cheek. He wrapped his arms tighter around her, his kiss brimming with emotion. She sighed, and opened her mouth invitingly, her tongue seeking his. His hands were starting to explore her body tenderly, stroking her throat and caressing her ears. Holly couldn't believe she had finally got him to give in to her – and not through exposing herself, being witty or being flirty. All that effort for nothing! She finally had something to thank Jeff for, she thought, as her hands moved to Joshua's chest, feeling the broad firm size of him. His fingers caught in her hair as he began to kiss her harder, his tongue probing her and exciting all the nerve endings in her mouth, making her imagine with explicit joy how it would feel to be filled up by him. She opened her legs to feel the pressure of his body against her where she wanted it most. In reply, he leaned into her, making her moan softly with pleasure and drop her hands to his hips. Joshua suddenly pulled away. It was as if the sound she made had pulled him out of a reverie. His face was troubled.

'No. No, I can't do this.' He backed away. 'I'm sorry.'

'Why?' Holly started to follow him. 'Don't go.'

'I'm sorry.' He turned to go. 'Please. We'll forget this ever happened.'

'Joshua!' He was turning his collar up as he walked away. 'Wait!' He turned to her, his eyes filled with regret.

'Look. I can't see a patient, that's the end of it. I'm sorry. This is all my fault.'

Holly shut her eyes, leaning back against the fence. She couldn't believe this. The whole day had been a mix of sexual tension and sexual disappointment, but this was the worst. She knew now that Joshua did have feelings for her – deep ones if the kiss was anything to go by – but all she had to show for it was a wet pussy.

She kicked the ground and set off again, striding with new purpose towards her lodgings. She was determined to get this sexual frustration out of her system. She unlocked the door stealthily and went into the kitchen. Caleb Briar was sitting at the table smoking a pipe, playing cards with Ben. She went up to him and took the pipe out of his mouth.

'Where's your wife?' she asked.

'In the bath.' He eyed her. 'You look fired up.'

'I am.' Holly went to the door and closed it. Mr Briar stood up.

'She'll be down in twenty minutes...' He started nervously, but was interrupted by Holly pushing his chair aside and throwing the cards petulantly to the floor. He restrained her, his arms locked around her waist. She lashed out, turning in his grip and unbuckling his trousers. Ben rose to his feet and joined the tussle, holding her arms down. She struggled free of Mr Briar's grip and fell on Ben, straddling him, loving the fight. Her body ached to be satisfied, and she rocked on top of the boy to relieve herself. Caleb Briar grabbed her from behind and pulled her off, his hands roughly grabbing her waist. He pulled her against him, her back pressed to his torso, shoving his hands up her shirt, down her trousers, biting her neck like a tomcat mating in the heat of summer. Ben knelt before her, undoing her trousers and yanking them down, her panties with them. He pulled off her shoes and trousers, leaving her lower half exposed. Mr Briar's hands roamed freely to her crotch now, sinking into the slippery warmth of her pussy.

'Christ, you're wet,' he breathed. Ben watched in awe as his stepfather's fingers danced in and out of her, and she strained against him like a bitch on heat. Holly had had enough foreplay today – she wanted fucking. She pushed his fingers away and bent over the kitchen table, presenting herself to the men like a prize cow being shown to a bull about to mount her. 'If that's how you want it.' The cool hard surface of the table bruised her cheek as she felt Mr Briar enter her from behind. The head of his prick was large and bulbous, sobering her with pain. He eased it inside her well-lubricated sex, then pushed further until he filled her entirely. She grasped onto the table for leverage, pushing her bottom back into his hips to get as much of him inside her as she could. She had ached to be filled by a man all day, and with every thrust, this cock was doing it for her. She felt his hands creeping round to her cunt, seeking out her clitoris. Delilah obviously had him well trained for he found it straight away, pressing against her with a flat palm as he pumped like a piston inside her. She started to groan as images of the day flashed before her – of Nikki's red face, Max slurping away like a dog between her legs (God, they were probably still at it, she thought, sending a fresh gush of excitement to her groin), of Jeff trying to force himself on her, of Joshua . . . She started to climax at the thought of Joshua. What if it was him fucking her, she imagined, his hand so skilfully teasing her clit. But they wouldn't do it like this, like animals, she thought as Caleb Briar grunted like a horse about to come, his cock swollen to a comparable size. She widened her legs, wanting to be completely filled with him. He grabbed a handful of her hair with his free hand, pulling her head back. Her mouth and eyes were stretched open as her head came up, and the room came sharply into focus. He was still thrusting, his pace so fast she was sure he was about to climax. His hand went like crazy between her legs. She abandoned herself to the sensation, and felt an orgasm start deep inside her. From upstairs the faint sound of Mrs Briar emptying her bath could be heard, then her humming on the landing. Mr Briar was banging Holly wildly now, as the top stair creaked under Mrs Briar's weight. Holly erupted helplessly into a gooey, silent climax, pressing back on her lover's huge cock as far as she could. He instantly came at this, shooting inside her vigorously. Mrs Briar was nearly at the bottom of the stairs. Ben stood nervously by the door. Mr Briar fell back onto his chair and hurriedly readjusted his clothes. Ben chucked Holly her knickers which she pulled on, and she was just picking up her trousers when the door began to open. She leaped to the sink and ran them under the tap.

Mrs Briar came in all pink and glowing from her bath, a towel wrapped round her head. Holly turned round, smiling, her hair only a little out of place.

'Hi,' she said, glancing around the kitchen. There was an empty can of lager on the table. 'Got beer all down these trousers. Like an idiot!'

'Oh dear.' Mrs Briar's sympathy was genuine. 'Sorry I took so long in the bathroom, love, or you could have run them under the tap in private – without these two jokers leering at you!'

'No worries.' Holly could feel that her panties weren't as straight as they could have been: they were twisted slightly at the back, fully exposing one buttock. At the front she knew they were stained with her juices and Mr Briar's come. She took her trousers out of the sink and held them in front of her crotch as she backed out of the room. 'You know, I will go upstairs,' she smiled. Ben winked at her. 'Just to preserve my modesty.' Caleb Briar let himself snicker slightly at this last statement, considering the spectacle she had just made of herself.

'Caleb!' Holly heard his wife chastise him as she slipped upstairs. 'You sarcy old man, you.'

Holly stepped in a steaming hot shower and got naked into her bed, slipping back into the memory of all the day's events. Her mind was still stuck on the kiss Josh had given her, and the compulsive way that Max had stimulated Nikki on that four-poster, but at least now Holly was sated. Her body began to rest, even if her mind wouldn't, and she slid into a light sleep. After a few minutes, or it could have been hours, she heard a tapping on the door.

'Yes?' Ben came in, bearing a cup of tea, holding it before him like a tribal peace offering.

'Thought you might like this.' He put it on the bedside table and sat on the edge of the bed, looking at her respectfully. 'I came up to say – you had a message earlier. A guy came over.' Holly was intrigued.

'Who?'

'Joshua somebody.' Ben saw her face blanch. 'It's OK, he just said he didn't have your number so can you call him to fix a time for a session. That's all.' Holly fell back on to the pillow, suddenly tense again. He must have been coming back from there when he had seen her and Jeff in the alley, she thought. He had probably been starting to miss her, and she had blown it by kissing him. Or had he kissed her? She couldn't remember. 'You seem stressed,' Ben said quietly.

'That's an understatement, Ben.' She smiled. His golden crown of hair framed his chiselled face as he looked down at her.

'I was wondering. To relax you . . .' He looked down, shyly.

'Yes?'

'I was just wondering if I could touch you – touch your breasts.' He smiled. 'I can't forget them, you see. How lovely they are.' Holly was reluctant. The day had already been a mess of erotic entanglements.

'I don't know,' she said.

'I'll be ever so gentle.' Ben softly pulled back her duvet to reveal her breasts. 'Please.' He cupped one softly. 'To help you sleep.' His hand was so smooth on her, so undemanding, that she didn't see the harm.

'OK,' she whispered. His face illuminated at her permission. He slipped to his knees on the floor, leaning across the bed so that his face was over her chest. Her breasts looked generous and womanly in the late afternoon light, her cinnamon nipples were large and soft. He kissed each nipple quietly and cupping both breasts in his hands began to lovingly lick and suckle on their teats. He remained tantalisingly gentle, his mouth brushing softly over her. She began to tingle, her breasts flattered by their avid admirer, her back arching subtly to meet his lips. This was sexual healing, she thought after the dark emotions of the day, the domination, the jealousy, the addiction, the fear. Ben's mouth was a warm, comforting presence at her breast. Holly took one of his hands and guided it under the covers. She let it brush over her flat belly, sending butterflies through her, then eased it into the downy hair of her pussy. Ben's face was intense with concentration as he gently began to caress her under the sheets, tentatively exploring her sex, parting the lips, dipping his fingers between them.

'Don't stop kissing my breasts,' Holly whispered, eyes half closed. Ben returned to her bosom, the rhythm of his tongue a mirror of the rhythm of his fingers. Holly let her eyes close, listening to the barely audible sounds of her own growing wetness, Ben's mouth suckling her nipple and the rustling of the sheets, with a rhythm like the sea. She drifted off, her body making its own response to his touch. After a while, he felt like his hand was in a honey-pot, she was so sweet and sticky, and his tongue started to flicker over her nipple as his stepfather had taught him to do. In her sleep, Holly let out a sigh of longing. Ben was encouraged. He caressed her swollen clit lightly but relentlessly, still using his tongue on her breast. He never grew impatient, watching her cheeks blush and her breasts swell as her body welcomed his attentions. Holly began to breathe faster in her dreaming state, her body arching and stretching under his touch. He carried on, hearing her sigh and whimper in her sleep, her legs apart, her pussy opening up to him. His hand moved quickly against her and she shuddered in climax, undulating unconsciously. As he felt her come, he pushed two long fingers inside her. He could feel her inner muscles pull and clasp at him, trying to swallow him up. It was the most exciting thing he had ever felt, even if she was still dreaming as it happened. One day, he knew, he would feel that pressure on his penis when it was inside a woman. He hoped that the woman would be Holly.

119

Chapter Thirteen

*I*t wasn't that Holly didn't find Nathaniel attractive, she thought as she brushed her teeth the next morning, it was just that she wanted a day off from all the so-called impros Max was so fond of. She had been pretty intimate with all of her co-stars now, and was sure she would have to be with Nathaniel, but not today. She knew that their scene involved his character Lord Hunter having a good old grope at his (admittedly willing) niece, Dolores. She could imagine what a field day Max would have with that, especially after all that 'Uncle Max' stuff yesterday with Nikki. And she would enjoy it too – another day. She spat and rinsed.

Ben cornered her on her way out. He was looking perky, she thought, only vaguely recollecting the sensation of his hands stimulating her under the covers. He was obviously out for a surf. He was wearing a rolled-down wetsuit with a baggy T-shirt over the top which read 'It's Up!!!' and was emblazoned with a surfboard insignia. Holly had seen these faux-scruffy surfing T-shirts in the local shops, and knew now that they were actually designer items in the surf world, with designer prices. They sure looked good on Ben, though.

'Hey, Holly.' He smiled.

'Hey,' she replied.

'I just wanted to make sure you knew about the dance on Friday night? Down at the old barn.' It was obviously important to him that she came.

'Oh. No I didn't.'

'I've got a spare ticket.' He pulled it out of his rucksack. 'It'll be fun.' Ben handed Holly the scrunched-up ticket, which she dutifully slipped into her wallet.

'Then I'll be there!' she said, and left for work.

She met Nathaniel having a cigarette at the entrance to the theatre. From his nervous face she could see he was as reluctant to be sucked into another day of sexual exploration as she was.

'I think we should go on sex strike,' she said. 'Like in the Lysistra or whatever it was.' He nodded.

'Except that was just the women going on sex strike, Holly,' he said. 'It's not a very manly thing to do.' He took a deep drag of his fag and put it out against the wall.

'Well, I don't think anyone should be required to be that manly on a Tuesday morning.' She smiled. They linked arms and went in.

Max didn't seem to be there yet, the stage manager said apologetically, so Nathaniel and Holly took it upon themselves to read through their scene over a cup of tea in the green room. When they had finished, Nathaniel leaned back in the grubby old armchair and sighed.

'This is what rehearsals should be about! Cup of tea, few lines, sitting down, no aggro.' Holly held her mug up as if to toast that statement. It was the cleanest one she could find, although it still had black, greasy thumb-prints on it.

'No shagging, no nudity, no director getting his end away with the juvenile lead!' she added.

'Oh, no, I'm afraid the director *always* does that,' Nathaniel replied ruefully. Holly laughed. 'Shall we read through the scene again, my dear? It's such a relief to do a bit of acting!'

* * *

When Max did arrive, it was nearly eleven. Holly spotted him through the window. Nikki was on his arm, seemingly still in the throes of some sexual flush. Adrian came to collect Holly and Nathaniel from the green room and they went up onto the stage. Max was sitting in a big ornate chair on stage, with Nikki curled in his lap. She was fondling his chest hairs through his shirt. His hands looked big and gnarled on the small peach of her round bottom. She was wearing tight white shorts and a vest top – all very virginal, Holly noted.

'Yes, we are late and we are sorry,' he announced with absolutely no apology in his voice. 'If you must know, we were rehearsing the Dolores/Lord Hunter scene in our own way and – well, we got some ideas.' Nikki beamed. Obviously the ideas had been to her satisfaction. Holly saw Max's hand drift from Nikki's bum and slip between her legs a little. He paddled his fingers against her crotch as he spoke. 'We will not go through it now. But you will end up in this position – all very cosy, yes? And it will be a quiet scene, not a bawdy farce.' Nikki wriggled a little, her thighs clamping around Max's hand. 'Don't, my darling. Or we will have to send everyone home again.' It was obvious that these two had been at it constantly since Holly had left them on the bed.

'Well, we've done a couple of read-throughs.' Nathaniel valiantly ignored the fact that Max's fingers were now rhythmically stroking his young lover's crotch. Nikki flung her thigh across Max's lap so that her legs were open.

'Marvellous,' Max said, either to Nathaniel or to Nikki. Nikki writhed into him a bit, demanding attention. It was like she had been drugged or hypnotised into a constant state of arousal that only Max's fingers could relieve. 'Yes, my little one,' he whispered into her hair, slipping his hand down her shorts. 'Excuse me, please.' This was to Nathaniel and Holly, who didn't know where to look as Max fondled Nikki to a quick climax on his lap. Right on cue, Jeff walked in just as

Nikki was panting her last 'I'm coming!' He seemed disturbed by this – maybe he was jealous. He dropped his bags and coat on the floor.

'Are we ever going to get any fucking rehearsing done in this shit hole?' he muttered.

'Here here,' Nathaniel agreed. 'Except without the expletives, of course.' Max slipped his hand out of Nikki's shorts, licked his fingers and pushed her off his lap. He got up, apparently oblivious to the erection pressing against his fly.

'I think we have done a lot of the sexual groundwork, yes. I think we have opened up to each other.' He gave Nikki a dirty look as he said this. 'I think for the next few days we will consolidate the work we have done, block the moves, do the boring nuts and bolts of staging.'

'Hooray,' Nathaniel interjected quietly.

'And, when we feel you two are ready,' Max looked at him meanly, 'we will do the scene between you and Holly.' Oberon arrived, running in a few minutes late.

'Sorry!' He was out of breath. 'Met a girl!' It wasn't the traditional excuse but it pleased Max.

'No problem.' It was only when Oberon saw the look of surprise on Jeff's face that he realised he had blown his cover as Holly's new man.

'Shit,' he said under his breath.

'Never mind,' Holly mouthed at him. As Max was setting the stage for act one, scene one, she filled Oberon in. 'We are going to start doing some actual work today.'

'What, no gratuitous groping?'

'Well, there probably will be. Nikki and Max can't keep their hands off each other.'

Oberon grinned. 'There's a lot of it about.' He had obviously got lucky. Holly was filled with curiosity. 'I'll tell you at lunchtime,' Oberon said, seeing her face.

'I look forward to that.'

* * *

123

Oberon and Holly made for their usual cheap seaside café after the morning's work. Holly left her bag pointedly in the theatre as Oberon had offered to treat her to lunch in a rare fit of generosity. The play was shaping up surprisingly well, they agreed, reluctantly acknowledging that there may have been some method in Max's madness. Holly could see a difference in Oberon. He had stopped giving her quite so much care and attention, for one thing, which she tried to accept as healthy. He had a swagger in his walk and a smile constantly curled around his lips.

'OK, tell me about her,' Holly sighed, finally, as their food arrived. 'You are clearly smitten.'

'Don't talk crap.' Oberon ate in big mouthfuls, managing to talk fluently as he did so. 'No, it was just yesterday, all that action in rehearsals, it was doing my head in.'

'What, turning you on or turning you off?'

'Both, to be honest. So when we left, you and Jeff disappeared and me and Nat went to get a drink down the Feathers. Trying to calm down.' He grinned. 'Didn't work. It was OK for him – just made him sleepy. But I got hornier and hornier. Anyway, the barmaid had her eye on me. I ignored it at first – you know, token black man in Cornish pub, trophy lay and all that. But after a few jars, I began to notice how sexy she was.'

'Nothing to do with the alcohol?' Holly didn't try to hide her amusement.

'No, she still looked pretty hot this morning.'

'Ah, so I know where this story ends up.'

'Yeah, but it goes via a strange old route.' He stole a chip from her plate. 'Can I carry on telling my story?'

'Please do.' She took an onion ring from his.

'OK, so it gets to closing time. By now we are undressing each other with our eyes type thing. She's wearing this tight red vest top, no bra, and her nipples are pointing at me like bullets in a loaded gun. She's got these tight blue jeans on – too tight for her really – and she's a fleshy girl. She's got this cute belly spilling out

124

over the top of them, and a belly button ring. I can't keep my eyes off that.' This sent him into a reverie for a minute.

'And Nathaniel?'

'Oh, he'd long gone. He's besotted with you by the way – sang your praises all night.' Holly was chuffed.

'Of course. Carry on. Serving wench with big tits and tummy . . .'

'Her name's Julie. Julie Simonds.'

'Lovely name.'

'She comes over to clear my table, says she's got to close up. Could I wait behind? She's very forward. I say, of course. By eleven thirty the place is dark, everyone out, just me sitting there wondering what's going to happen next. She was very much in charge.'

'Sounds like a strong woman!'

'Wait for it.' He gulped at his water. 'She comes over to me in the dark. Says she's been watching me all night. I say, I noticed. Close up she smells of beer and smoke, but under there somewhere is a perfume – a cheap one . . .'

'You're really selling her to me, Oby.' Holly laughed.

'No, cheap but sexy. She stands over me, legs apart and leans her chest into my face. I get a nose full of it. It's like a drug. And her tits are big, swinging free in that red top, really mountainous. A man could lose himself in those tits and it would take a helicopter to pull him out. And they're right in my face, you know? So I have to look. It's only polite.'

'Naturally.'

'So I brush my face against the left one and stare at the right one. And then I see it. A weird shape, a sharp bulge under there.' Holly's stomach turned.

'Is this going to be gross?' She put her burger down.

'No! I slip down the material, and there before me is a huge, white breast, a big juicy nipple and a shiny silver nipple stud!'

'You said this wasn't gross.'

'Come on, it's sexy. It feels funny in your mouth, all

125

that soft skin and fat flesh, then this sharp piece of metal. She seemed to get extra sensation from it, I don't know.'

'So did you do it in this empty pub?'

'No. We started to. We got down to it. She was pretty full on. Not afraid to take the initiative.' His smile was smug. 'She had a tongue stud as well. Made me nervous at first, but I got to enjoy that.'

'Are we talking blowjobs here?' Holly enquired.

'We are. On the bar. Me sitting up on it, her leaning against it. Her mouth was really big and wet and eager. What she lacked in skill she certainly made up for in enthusiasm.'

'Sounds like a school report!'

'Well, it's true. She seemed to be getting off on it as much as I was – she'd pinned one of my legs between hers and was kind of rubbing up against me while she was performing. I thought she was going to come before I did. I stopped her before I lost control. I realised I didn't even know her name.'

'You're so old-fashioned,' Holly mocked.

'So we had a chat. Turns out she loves to suck guys off after hours. She's had whole football teams in there and given them all a show.'

'So she's not choosy then?'

Oberon tutted at her. 'Are you jealous?' This made Holly laugh. 'No, she's just amazingly sexual. Holly, can you take this much detail? Because it gets better!' Holly nodded blithely. 'She asked if I was open-minded. I said I liked to think so. She pulled her top back on and said, 'Come with me then!' and dragged me out. She had a motorbike outside, quite a big one, a Harley, no less. She got on it and told me to hang on at the back. We revved up and she drove me for about fifteen minutes, top speed, till we ended up I don't know where. It was on the edge of some woods, a big field with a campfire in the middle. Motorbikes everywhere. Blokes in leathers and lots of hair, girls in pvc and no bras. People milling about, smoking joints. They all seemed to know her. A couple of the guys grabbed her and French-kissed her, but it was all OK. I got it quite quickly – this was one of those free love deals. We walked towards the fire and I could see the moving shapes of couples making out in amongst other people just chilling. God, there were some hot women. Some were just snogging, but some were there rutting away. One girl was completely naked except these long black boots, hanging over the shoulders of the guy doing her. She was hot! She was coming and screaming, but others were taking it easier. There were two guys at it in a sixty-nine – that's something I've never seen before. They wore the leathers with style, I'll say that for them. One lucky guy had one woman bouncing around on his face and one squirming about on his dick. Julie says he's there all the time with the same two girls in the same position. I don't bloody blame him. There was one really old biker – long grey hair, big walrus moustache – and he'd managed to pull this foxy young chick in a tiny rubber dress. She was riding on top of him like all her birthdays had come at once. Julie said he was like the alpha male of the group – all the women wanted him 'cause of his status. Apparently this old bloke gets laid by a different chick every night! He's known as "granddaddy". He's their leader. And it's a real honour if he chooses you.'

'Has Julie ever been chosen?'

'Well, I asked that same question. She said that he doesn't fuck her, because he's best mates with her real granddad who runs the pub and it wouldn't feel right. But he loves to suck her pussy. And she loves to go down on him too.' Oberon was telling this story as if it were an adventure, full of wonder and energy. 'She told me all this with no coyness or anything – just straight down the middle. So we were in the middle of all these heaving couples and the noise was pretty sexy – it sounded like a leper colony or something, all the groans and sighs and screams . . .'

'Sexy!' Holly smirked.

'So she asked if I wanted to make out. I said, of course. She took her jeans off – she didn't have any knickers on. That got me for a start. Her pussy was amazing, really bushy, really black hair, especially as her skin was so white. There was a motorbike behind her, and she sat back on it and opened her legs. And there was this flash of silver. She opened herself up to me, and I saw she'd had her clit pierced. It was incredible.'

'Oh my God!' Holly was awestruck. 'That must hurt so much.'

'No, apparently it wasn't too bad. And she told me later it had made her come much more and much faster. She says she can be sitting on a bus now, or a moving bike, and she just has orgasm after orgasm.'

'How tiring.' Holly felt the envy creep into her knickers.

'In a good way. She got onto the motorbike and straddled the saddle of it. I know it's a porn calendar cliché, but God that's sexy! To see her naked bush slipping all over the leather. And she knows how to turn it on – arching her back so her tits looked pneumatic. She pulled her vest top off and there she was, naked, writhing about on a bike just to give me a hard-on. Which I had had for at least an hour by this point, anyway. This girl just by my feet suddenly let rip with this huge orgasm. She was being fucked by this fat biker. That did it. I pulled Julie off the bike and turned her round. And the rest is history.'

'Well,' Holly said eventually, 'I don't need to know any more details, but surely the girl deserved a bit more foreplay than just being "turned round"?'

Oberon grinned. 'Oh, there was foreplay.' Holly decided not to ask for details. She thought about the amazing pockets of communities you could find in one place. Even in this sleepy Cornish village there was a seething set of horny bikers. She was instantly tempted to go and join them for a night. She loved the idea of hedonism, of uncomplicated sex. She'd never really achieved it. But she knew she wouldn't fit in, with her summer dresses and nice shoes. She would have to pick up some rubber before she could really blend in. She would have to feel totally disguised, masked, in character. Perhaps she would just go and observe one night. She knew this was only a fantasy, but it made her pelvis quiver with anticipation.

'What are you thinking?' Oberon asked.

'Oh, nothing.' Holly's voice was light. 'Just how lucky you got. Are you going to see her again?'

'No question.' He threw down his knife and fork and wiped his mouth with a paper napkin, then drooled in his best Barry White impression: 'Gotta get me some more of that biker love!'

Chapter Fourteen

'Hi. Is that Joshua?' Holly hung nervously on her mobile. She knew that Joshua might have a problem with seeing her, but she missed him. She had decided she would rather see him as a therapist than never see him at all. A couple of days had passed since he'd come to her rescue in the alleyway, and he had played constantly on her mind since then, but she was determined to play her feelings down. He wanted her to be appropriate with him, and she would be. But she had to see him.

'Hello.' It was Josh's voice, thick and warm, honey in her ear. Oh God, she was in trouble with this guy.

'It's Holly. Holly Parker.'

'I know.' There was a pause. 'How are you?' he asked.

'I'm great,' she responded, a little too breezily. 'Just checking in to see when we could set up another session?' She could imagine his face as he paused, that troubled look, the hair flopping in his eyes.

'Is that a good idea?' he asked eventually.

'Why not? Look, as you said, let's forget what happened. I can if you can?' She so hoped he couldn't. 'I still think Max would be happier if I was seeing you. I've got a lot of stuff to talk about. I think it's really helped me.' She sounded desperate, she knew. She heard Freud give a bark in the background. 'Someone's ready for their walk,' she said.

'Yes. All right. Look, Holly, strictly professional, OK?'

'Yes. Knickers on,' she said, military fashion. Did she hear him laugh?

'Tomorrow morning. Ten o'clock.' The phone clicked off. Holly lay back on her bed, laying the phone on her chest. Tomorrow was Friday. It had been a long week without seeing him, and it would be a long session if she wasn't even allowed to flirt. She had begun to feel lonely now that Oberon's focus was firmly aimed at the Feathers pub and the daughter of the house, Julie Simonds. Even Max and Nikki's mutual involvement made Holly feel inadequate. Only Jeff and Nathaniel were left to flirt with at work, and her ex was obviously no candidate. Ever since the episode up the bramble path they had carefully avoided each other. Nathaniel was comforting in a fatherly way, but she couldn't tell him about her feelings for Josh. She didn't think he'd approve. She was almost beginning to look forward to rehearsing their scene in Max's now infamously sexual style – at least that way she would feel cherished and desired by someone, and perhaps she would get the same younger-woman kick out of it as Nikki was obviously getting with Max.

Holly decided to call Katie for a chat. She wasn't at home; maybe she was at her boyfriend, Mark's. Holly reached in her bag for her filofax and flipped it open. A piece of paper flew out onto the floor. Holly reached for it and picked it up. It was just a piece of scrap – old rubbish. She was about to throw it away when she saw, at the very bottom in tiny red letters, the message: 'I'M WATCHING YOU.' Holly's heart froze. The note hit her veins like poison. She recognised the neutral, neat hand from the hate mail she had received at home in London. Through the post was one thing, but for someone to take her bag and her personal diary ... it had to be someone very close to her. Jeff was the obvious candidate.

A fire in her belly, Holly got up from the bed and wrapped a thick cardigan around her shoulders. That bastard was not going to intimidate her. She stormed down the stairs and slammed the front door behind her. It was getting dark, but she confidently strode through the bramble path to get to Jeff's digs the quicker. She didn't want to lose this energy. This energy was anger and it was stopping her from crying.

Holly recognised the house Jeff was staying in. It was right opposite the theatre and had his beat-up old Metro parked outside. She knocked loudly on the door. An old woman answered, her hunched frailty taking the edge slightly off Holly's tough attitude.

'Is Jeff here? Jeff Mansfield?' Holly peered up behind the old lady's head, seeing a burgundy-carpeted staircase. The house smelled sickly sweet.

'It's Jeff you want?' Was she deaf or just vague?

'Yes. Please.' Holly clutched the paper in her hand.

'Jeff?' The woman craned forward. 'I think he went down the Feathers, dear.'

Holly turned on her heel and made for the pub. As soon as she went in the thick air of smoke hit her. It was a man's pub, all darts and pool and pints. The only woman she could see was the infamous Julie Simonds serving buxomly behind the bar, nose ring glinting. Then she saw Jeff. He was playing pool with some local boys. They were beating him, by the sour look on his face. Good.

'What the fuck is this?' She slammed the paper down on the pool table, sending balls flying across the baize.

'Hey!' one of the boys protested.

'Explain it, Jeff. You fucking baby.' She was slightly disarmed by the genuine look of bafflement on Jeff's face. He was shocked by her emotion, then confused by the paper.

'What? What are you talking about?' He picked it up. 'It's blank.'

'It was in my filofax, damn it. In my bag!' The shakes

132

came to get her now. She stabbed her finger at the small lettering.

'What's this? "I'm watching you"?'

'Are you OK?' One of the boys brought her a chair. She felt like she was going to be sick.

'Nothing to do with me, Holly.' Jeff gave it back to her. She found herself disappointed that she believed him. At least if it was him she would know what she was dealing with.

'Holly?' Warm hands held her shoulders still. Their firmness calmed her.

'Josh?' She swung round hopefully. He really was her knight in shining armour. It was Ben.

'What's up? You look white as a sheet.' He stood behind her, his face furrowed with worry.

'I . . . I had some weird note in my bag, that's all.' She screwed it up. 'And some weird letter in London. Sorry.' She got unsteadily to her feet. 'Sorry, Jeff.'

'I'll take you home.' Ben was strong, she could really lean on him. They didn't speak on the way back. He was lovely, but they had nothing in common, Holly thought, her head nuzzling his wide shoulder. She used the excuse of her shock to keep silent.

When they got in, Ben took her into the kitchen. Caleb Briar obviously sensed her distress, and he steered clear of a suggestive remark for once. Ben explained what had happened, and Delilah brewed up a strong sweet tea.

'Who'd do such a thing?' she muttered to herself, putting a tin of biscuits on the table. 'It's so mean.'

'Well, it's not a bloke, I'll tell you that,' Mr Briar said. 'A bloke's not that devious.'

'Oh, don't be ridiculous, Caleb,' His wife retorted sharply.

'My money's on a woman.' He drew on his pipe. 'A bloke might shout and even play a trick on a girl, but he wouldn't leave nasty little notes like that all around the place.'

'Don't listen to him.' Holly wondered why Mrs Briar

was so adamant that the culprit might be a man. Would it be paranoid to suspect her landlady? After all, Holly had bedded her husband and got pretty intimate with her son too. What woman wouldn't be angry at that?

'If it is a woman,' Holly said deliberately, 'I think she should realise I've got the message, and stop. It's just plain evil.' She watched Delilah's face as she sipped her tea. She was still the picture of sympathy.

'I hope this won't stop you coming to the harvest dance tomorrow night?' Ben asked, expectantly. 'It'll take your mind off it.' He'd lifted this line directly from his mother's lexicon of comforting clichés.

'Oh yes, it's always a grand affair.' Mrs Briar beamed.

'I haven't got anything to wear.' It was a lame excuse but it was all she had.

'Then wear nothing. You'll be popular.' Mr Briar returned to form.

'Is it formal? Or a barn dance type thing?'

'Oh, it's country dancing, with a lot of cider thrown in.' Mrs Briar looked Holly up and down. 'I might have something for you if you don't have a nice dress. Full skirts, tight bodice, old-fashioned?'

'I do not possess such an item,' Holly said, all mock-haughty.

'Well, come up, we'll have a look.' They got up and went to Mrs Briar's bedroom.

Holly heard Caleb quip in the kitchen: 'If anything of Delilah's doesn't hang of that skinny girl like a tent, I'll eat my hat.'

'There is such a thing as a belt, you know,' his wife yelled back. 'Honestly, Holly, he can be so rude.' She seemed genuinely hurt, and Holly felt for her.

They went into the Briars' bedroom. Holly hadn't seen it since that first night. In the full beam of an overhead light, it didn't seem quite such a den of sleaze, but was still obviously designed for sex. The bed was large like a giant puffy playpen and the bedstead lent itself to tying people up. It dominated the room. The wardrobe was swung open and Delilah laid out an array of dresses for Holly to try. In the end they chose a red polka-dot dress that Mrs Briar had not been able to squeeze into for years.

'You can have it, sweetheart. My bosoms are never going to squash into that bodice again.' Holly didn't like to point out that it was Mrs Briar's waist, not her chest, which had outgrown the garment. It was designed for the hourglass figure. Holly's breasts spilled out over top of the sleeveless bustier and the cotton clung to her narrow waist. The skirt was flared to just below the knee, swinging lightly as she moved. It would be great to dance in. Holly thanked her landlady, kissing her on the cheek.

'Oh, I wish I'd had a daughter.' She smiled. 'Caleb can't, you see. Ben was my first husband's. So I had to settle for just the one.' She was getting tearful. 'Oh, stop it.' She tutted to herself. 'It's not like Ben isn't a big enough handful.' Holly mused that Mrs Briar didn't know how right she was.

Chapter Fifteen

'*I* was thinking about what you said. About anonymity,' she said. Joshua nodded sagely. Holly sat, perfectly behaved in her usual chair. She hadn't flirted. She hadn't joked. She hadn't even looked him in the eye. But it felt so good to even be in the same room as him. 'I know you're right. I think it's a romantic thing. If I don't know who the guy is, maybe he'll turn out to be the man of my dreams. If he starts out faceless, maybe he'll turn out to have the loveliest face.' Josh had a distinctive scent, she noticed. Woody, warm, with a touch of sea. She crossed her legs, still looking down. 'But then, not all of my fantasies are like that. Of course.' She was staring at her hands. 'I have a lot of them, actually. I think – because I've been single for a while – a few months . . . and even before that, with Jeff, I had to fantasise. To come. Is that an awful admission?' Without being able to look him in the eye, she felt unable to read his reaction. Was she making herself sound like an awful lay?

'No. It's very common.' His voice, pure honey, dripping straight into her knickers. 'It's usual, I would say.'

'Well. I think it was a lot to do with us – me and him, I mean – not having the right chemistry. With somebody else . . .' Everything she said was like treading on eggshells. In her mind it all pertained to Joshua – did he feel that too? She glanced up at him. He let nothing show. 'It would probably be different.'

'Which fantasies would make you come?'

'Well, probably the usual ones. Being molested by a rugby team at a wild party, that sort of thing!' She was deflecting with humour. He didn't laugh. 'OK,' she conceded. 'Well. Don't take the piss, but when I was young I saw *The Thorn Birds* on TV – you know, where the priest meets the girl when she's a child and they are in love all her life. But it's forbidden. And one day they can't stand it any more so they just make love. I thought that was the sexiest thing. Ever since I've had fantasies on that theme – the forbidden man in authority.'

'Like?'

'Well, being fucked over my school desk by a teacher. Or being punished for not wearing regulation school uniform.'

'Punished?'

'Yes. In one, he – my headmaster – pulls me up on the stage in assembly and licks me out in front of all my friends. I come and come, while he's telling me how bad I am, how my skirt's too short, my shirt too tight for my breasts. Sometimes another teacher is whipping my bottom while he's doing it. It sounds ridiculous when you say it cold like this . . .' Holly was embarrassed to feel her hands shaking in her lap. She was nervous.

'It's not ridiculous.'

'Or, the priest figure is very sexy. He can't have you but you turn him on so much, he takes you on the altar, or makes you suck his cock under his robes.'

'With all these men, you find your own power – by being irresistible? Would that be fair?'

Holly thought about this. 'In a way. I disempower them, because they want to fuck me so damn much. Teachers, priests, doctors . . .'

'Doctors?'

'Yeah. That's a classic. I used to use that when Jeff

137

would go down on me – a doctor putting my legs in stirrups, examining me, finding me so gorgeous he just can't help but taste me. We both know it's wrong, but that just makes it all the sweeter.'

'Don't you think that's interesting?'

'What?' She raised her eyes to his for the first time that day.

'Well, you have found me attractive – I am one of these powerful men, men in authority, men who are taboo.'

'You are? Aren't you just Joshua Delaney?' She smiled.

'You know I'm not just that. If I was just that we could go upstairs to my bedroom right now and make love till the sun goes down.' Holly's face lit up at the thought. 'If we so wanted,' Josh added, a little belatedly. 'But if it was allowed, would you still be interested? Isn't it just the forbidden you're after?'

'In fantasies, yes.' She was stumped. His argument sounded so convincing. But looking at him, she didn't feel that he was right. She loved the broad block of his shoulders, his bear-like body, his sensitive eyes, his humour. 'Your hair keeps flopping into your eyes,' she said softly. 'I like that.' He sat back. She had lost him again. 'I'm sorry but it's true. And you make me laugh. I like that. And Freud. The way you have this big lumbering warm dog named after an Austrian psychotherapist, I love that! He reminds me of you. It's in the detail, Josh. Love is in the detail.'

'Love?'

'I'm not saying I'm in love with you.' She corrected herself, quickly. 'I'm just saying you can't apply general rules to attraction.' He sighed. 'After you left me on Monday, do you know what I did? I went back to my digs and practically begged my landlord to fuck me. I bent over the table and opened myself to him. It was a physical need. I couldn't get it hard enough. I just wanted to feel something. And it was rough and dirty and horny. But for a moment, you flashed into my head and my whole body changed gear.' He wasn't looking up. His hands were pressed firmly in his lap. Holly saw, with satisfaction, that he had hardened at her words. 'Now, I'm not waxing all lyrical and declaring my love for you and all that, because you don't want that and I respect you enough to go by what you want. But please, Josh. Please don't belittle my feelings just so they can fit into some psychological pattern you've invented. This isn't fantasy. It's real life.' Her voice was calm, her face cool. Speaking truthfully had steadied her. She could see that he was the one suffering now.

'You made love straight after I left you?'

'I got laid.' There was a long silence.

'This isn't easy for me either,' he said quietly. He put his head in his hands. For one awful moment Holly thought she had made him cry, but when he brought his face up, his eyes were clear and lucid. 'I had a patient once.' His voice was so grave that it made Holly hold her breath. 'She fixated on me – that's what we call it. Transference. You would probably say she loved me, that I shouldn't try to fit her into some psychological pattern. And you'd probably be right.' He stopped and got up, pouring himself a large whisky. 'Want one?'

'Think I'd better.' He handed her a glass. She deliberately brushed against his fingers as she took it off him, just to connect for one second. It didn't go unnoticed.

'I was weaker then. Younger.' He took a swig. 'And she was beautiful. She had a lot of problems. I wanted to help her. My desire to help her professionally somehow spilled into my personal life.'

'Do you mean you fell in love?'

'No. I didn't.' He took a swig. 'Well, maybe I did. At least I thought perhaps that I did.'

'So?'

'Well, it was a disaster. All kinds of shit hit the fan. I couldn't practise any more.' His jaw was clenched, his voice tight. 'I can cope with that. But her life was ruined by it.' Holly got up and went to him. Her eyes searched his face for answers.

'How? What happened?'

'It doesn't matter what happened, Holly,' he snapped. 'What matters is that it doesn't ever go that way again.' He meant it, she could see that. She was wasting her time.

'Shall I go?'

'Maybe you should.' Her eyes welled up. She hated it when they did that. They tended to do it especially at moments when she was trying to appear strong and stable such as now. They went to the door. Freud gave a whine from the kitchen. 'He can smell you,' Josh said, curtly. 'Wants to say hello.'

'I'd like that.' Holly wanted a friendly face, and there was none so friendly as Freud's.

'OK. Just for a moment.' He reluctantly led her into his kitchen. Freud jumped up on her and wagged his tail gaily. She got down on her knees and hugged him, whispering sweet nothings into his fur. He kissed her and nuzzled into her face, full of love. It made her cry.

'Sorry,' she said. 'I'm not usually this mental. Must be PMT or something.'

'It's because he's all give and no take. It's enough to make you weep at the best of times.' Joshua tried to make her feel better. 'You can borrow him any time for a cuddle, if you like. He can't get enough of those. Cuddles, walks and big meals are all he lives for.'

'Sounds like he's found the meaning of life.' Holly laughed, wiping her face.

'I reckon he has.' Josh saw her off. The air was heavy between them. 'Call me if you want another session.'

'Really?'

'Of course.' He smiled. She was doubtful as she meandered thoughtfully down the hill. A sad song wound around her heart. It was full of longing and pain. It was only when she reached the village that she wondered if she had imagined the song, or if a woman's voice had been carried to her on the sea wind. It rang in her ears as if she had really heard it, and it didn't leave her all day.

140

Chapter Sixteen

*T*his was a country dance of *Oklahoma!* proportions, Holly mused as she and Ben walked up the field that led to the village barn. All around them other couples, old and young, in their Sunday best were hurrying excitedly to the event, walking arm in arm up the slope with the blushing twilight sky providing a true MGM backdrop. She almost expected to see horse-and-carriages parked up outside the barn doors and men in Stetsons singing 'The Farmer and the Cowboy Should Be Friends'. Ben had the proud glow of a man with the woman of his dreams on his arm. It was sweet really. They had given up all attempts at conversation, although Holly had listened at length to some of his surfing anecdotes, including one where his mate Twig had thought he had seen a shark off the coast at Bude. The sighting was never backed up by any actual casualties, but it still made an animated tale, with Ben's hands amply demonstrating the size of the alleged shark's dorsal fin. He had lovely hands, Holly noticed with a prick of lust, big and veiny, tanned, brushed with blond hair. They had been inside her, she thought wondrously. Maybe again tonight.

Once inside the barn, Holly was greeted by the sight of yet more couples. The older ones were cosily drunk, the younger ones already sucking addictively on each other's faces. The musicians were setting up, occasionally blasting the PA with a heavily accented 'one, two' or guitar riff. There was a fiddle, guitar, accordion and drum all waiting to be played, which hinted at the sort of music they were going to be enjoying for the night. Ben put his arm protectively around Holly as a group of his friends turned up.

'Hi, guys.' He grinned. They eyed her in a way that made it obvious that they knew something, if not everything, about her. The two boys were as tall as Ben, but darker. One was obviously a little older – he shook her hand.

'I'm George,' he said. Ben's grip tightened. 'This is my little brother Roland.' Roland looked almost as if he was about to curtsy. 'And this is Roland's girlfriend Maxine.' She got a pretty frosty look from Maxine who was a size-eight girl with a big perm.

'You look nice.' Holly disarmed her immediately, but the suspicion in her eyes remained. Obviously she thought Roland was too much of a catch for Holly not to have a go.

'I'll get you a drink,' Ben said, the perfect gentleman. Holly wanted to avoid being left alone with a group of teenagers.

'I'll come too.' She smiled.

Three jars of cider later, the band got into full swing. There was a caller who shouted out all the moves and some of the old-timers were pretty expert at the whole thing. Holly let herself go, twirling and kicking with the best of them, falling occasionally against Ben and quite enjoying the sensation. The cider certainly had got her in the mood. After a particularly strenuous number, Ben dragged her outside for some air. They fell out through the door laughing and gasping.

'I am officially too old for this,' Holly panted.

'You're not.' Ben took her in his arms and danced her around. 'You're lovely.' He smiled. She tipped her head

142

back and let him sway her around the field. The velvet black sky above was infinite with stars. You didn't get stars like that in London, Holly thought; all the artificial light made the sky too orange to see them. But here, it was like the sharp sea air polished them up just for her delectation. *'Starry starry night . . .'* she began to sing, dizzily. *'Paint your palate blue and grey.'* Her voice was stopped by Ben's hungry mouth over hers. They kissed giddily, still dancing, the music swelling out into the atmosphere. He planted kiss after kiss on her face, neck, throat and eyes. They were sweet with cider and adoration. Soon he fell back onto the grass.

'If you want me to stop singing, just say so.' Holly fell on him. 'No need to stop my mouth so presump-tisly-tiously.' They cackled at her stutter, Ben rolling on top of her and giving her a good old-fashioned grope. The grass was already gathering dew for the next morning, wetting her back. It tickled against her bare shoulders and gathered in her hair. He kissed her hard, his weight pinning her down, his prick evident against her belly. She lifted her knees and wrapped them around him encouragingly, his mother's dress catching under his knee. There would be grass stains to explain in the morning. Holly was actually beginning to feel like a teenager now, indulging in intense tonguey kisses with this boy, the stars filling her eyes. She moaned. This small noise of approval sent him into a new paroxysm of ardour, his hands greedily roaming her chest, popping her out of her bodice. Holly liked Ben, she decided, grinding against him happily. He wasn't all complicated and full of rules like that stupid therapist. He wasn't all leery like his dad. He was like a human version of Freud, she thought, just nice and grateful for her attention. She flipped him onto his back, straddling him, her tongue still colliding with his. She was going to give him one big thank-you. One he wouldn't forget for a long time.

'What are you doing?' he half protested as she slid down his body.

'Nice things,' she whispered. 'Shhh.' And she unbuckled his best trousers, his fantastic cock springing immediately through the slit in his boxers, practically slapping her in the face. She took it in one hand, the smooth skin taut and clean. He was well endowed, she noticed, licking the tip with a soft tongue. She swirled her tongue around the head, concentrating on the tender underside. Ben was almost too overwhelmed to moan – his breath was caught in his diaphragm. His stomach was flat, tense, waiting. Holly fondled his balls as she continued to caress him with her mouth. She saw that his hands were grasping the grass, white-knuckled. He couldn't shut his eyes – that would be too much like dreaming – he kept them wide open, glancing from the wide open sky to her wide open mouth, taking in the reality of it all. He was awed to see her head bobbing obediently at his crotch, her pretty lips wrapped around him. Holly could hear the voices from inside. Could anyone see them? She hurried a little. He was big enough to be a mouthful, and she was careful not to close her jaw at all. She wouldn't want to give him a nasty nip. The soft wet haven of her mouth squelched as he began to fuck it, gently thrusting his hips upward. She took her mouth away for a moment.

'I like that,' she whispered huskily. 'Carry on. Grab my hair.' He willingly obeyed, clutching her hair at the back and fucking her mouth more confidently. She felt dirty now, sucking off this guy in a field, letting him use her. Her pussy foamed at the mouth. He began to groan, low, urgent noises. His hips sped up. He was going to come. Holly cupped his balls and pressed gently just behind them. He gasped, pumping quicker, his voice catching on his pleasure. Holly knew he was going to come. She was proud of herself, willingly gulping it down. She was the first woman to give him that honour. The salty splash of it warmed her throat. After he had finished, she stayed down there, gently nursing him, kissing the shaft lovingly. The night and the cider had made her feel temporarily in love. Josh

144

didn't know what he was missing. She kissed his balls and slipped his pants up, dressing him again. She hoped that she wasn't being too motherly. She looked up at Ben. He looked like he had been shot, so relaxed he was dead, his eyes glazed wide open. She laughed.

'It wasn't *that* amazing.'

'It was,' he mouthed. 'Thank you.' She lay beside him and he cuddled her, slowly coming back to life. Soon he was kissing her again, his tongue invading her mouth with more confidence now. It was more of a man's kiss. Holly was pleased – Jeff had never deigned to kiss her after she gave him a blowjob. In fact, he had sometimes brushed his teeth even after he licked her out. Ben showed none of his squeamishness, happily tasting himself on Holly's breath. Ben murmured something into her cheek. She didn't know what, but it sounded like 'I love you.' She knew what he meant. She was being pretty great tonight.

'I look forward to our next lesson.' She smiled, readjusting her clothes. She got up. 'I want to dance again,' she said.

'I want more cider.' He sprang up too, a little unsteady on his feet.

The party was hotting up inside. The oldies had mostly retired to the chairs at the sides of the room, and now the younger ones were drunkenly staggering their way through the dances. It seemed mostly an excuse to feel each other up, Holly noticed, probably as it had been for generations. Ben was in incredibly good spirits. She saw him laugh when George pointed out the grass stain on his shirt. She went to the toilets and corrected her dress, brushing her hair out and reapplying the red smudge of lipstick that had wandered across her face. The music was quieter in the ladies' room, and Holly could hear something outside – the revving growl of motorbikes. A light flashed across the window. She was like a moth to it.

She slipped outside and round the back of the building. A massive group of bikers had turned up, smoking and laughing. They were starting to dance grotesquely across the grass, taking the piss, aping a barn dance. Some were so stoned that they just lay on the ground, sucking at drugs. Holly looked for Oberon among them. He didn't seem to be there, but she saw Julie. She was leaning against an old guy – Holly recognised him as the main man from Oberon's description, the 'granddaddy'. He was sitting on his bike. Julie had her back against him. His gnarled old hand was idly fondling her nipple over her T-shirt as they chatted to some people in front of them. He had a big grey moustache, which he used occasionally to tickle her cheek. She liked that, Holly could see. They were still in conversation with someone when 'granddaddy' hitched up Julie's top. She didn't seem to care or notice. She laughed at someone's joke while the man fondled her plump naked breasts. She was passed a joint. She closed her eyes when she dragged on it. It seemed to tune her in to the sensation in her breasts. She turned to the man and he began to suck at her nipples. She had the joint in her mouth, her head tipped back as he went at it. Holly could just she the big moustache twitching every time he moved his mouth. Other couples were forming, Holly saw. Their actions were slow, automatic. One woman was lying on her back necking a bottle of beer while her partner licked away at her cunt. She was naked from the waist down. Holly noticed that her cunt was clean-shaven. It made it easier to see the pink tongue dart in and out, in and out. Granddaddy had his hand down Julie's trousers now, still attached to her nipple like a starving infant. She jigged about dreamily on his hand, sucking hard on the spliff. When she came it was like a slow convulsion.

'Oh look, it's a prom queen!' a leery voice called out from the crowd. Holly looked around, suddenly realising that he was pointing at her. Heads turned. The bloke got up, a can of strong brew clutched in his hand. He was clad in leather.

'Hello, little Miss Moffat.' They laughed at her. Julie turned her head but she was too out of her face to recognise Holly. Holly turned to go, but the man caught up with her. He flicked the bottom of her dress.

'Come as a toadstool have we?' He snickered, dragging her back to the group.

'It's one of *them*.' A woman sighed contemptuously to the man with his hand strumming her crotch. 'All dressed up.'

'You shall go to the ball,' the first man sneered. Holly realised she must look pretty outdated and girlish to this crowd. She'd felt attractive in the hall, but out here surrounded by leathers and oil she was ridiculous. The man put his hands up her skirt, lifting the material so everyone could see. 'Pretty frilly knickers.' He spat, having a quick grope.

'Fuck off.' She turned on her heel and marched away. The bikers all mocked her with a loud 'Ooooooo!'

Ben noticed how flushed she was when she got back in.

'Ready for lesson three?' he asked hopefully. He whispered in her ear, 'I'm ready to lick you again. I want to make you come this time.' He was sweet but the sheen had faded from the evening for her. He saw her edgy look. 'I don't mean to pressure you,' he apologised.

'No, I'm flattered.' But she was obviously distracted. 'I think I'll go home.' She smiled. George overheard.

'But you haven't danced with me,' he said. He clearly thought he was a young charmer. He had Italian looks with a shirt unbuttoned, a well-cut jacket.

'No,' Ben said, hurriedly 'If you want to go, we can go.' He ushered her out and they started to walk down the hill.

'You know,' she said to him, 'you're much better looking than that George guy. You're a better catch. Don't forget that.' He stopped and kissed her gratefully. His lips were tender. They walked a little more until they came to the bramble path.

'Don't go through this normally at night,' he advised, all concern, 'But it's OK now, 'cos you're with me.' They went through. It was pitch black, you couldn't even see the ground in front of you. They slowed and slowed, each step tentative. He stopped her with his hand. She could just see the glint of his eyes in the darkness. He positioned her against the wall, gently urging her to lean back. Then he dropped to his knees before her, his head up her skirt. Her knickers came down.

'Ben,' she protested softly. His tongue was warm on her in the cold night air. All she could feel was the parts he touched with his mouth, the rest of her grew numb. Maybe he thought he had to do this, to 'return the favour'. She felt cold, unemotional, but the wet pressure against her pussy melted her.

'I love the taste of you,' he murmured into her. 'I'll never forget this taste.' Her knickers twisted around her ankles like subtle bondage. His tongue was tireless and supple inside her. 'You're so wet!' It was running down her legs. The shape of his head bulged under the wide skirts of her dress. She knew she wouldn't come. She still felt too tense from her encounter with the bikers. They had seen through her. Where they had accepted Oberon, they had sneered at her. She wondered what 'granddaddy's' tongue felt like. His moustache would tickle, she thought. If he accepted you, the others would. Ben was lapping patiently away. She was hot there now. She burned for something. She gently pushed his head away.

'Sorry, Ben. I'm too tired,' she said. He looked up at her with disappointment. Her eyes were adjusting to the light and to how good-looking he really was. One day he'd make some girl deliriously happy.

'Am I really bad at it?' He was worried. She dropped to her knees before him and kissed him full on the lips.

'No. You're fucking brilliant at it,' she said. 'Now let's go home.'

* * *

In bed that night, she dreamed of the biker set. She was in the middle of a ring, naked, legs outstretched. The women were rubbing her body with crude oil. The men were leering. She was being prepared for something. The men were on their knees, peering at her private parts. One man started to lick her, but Granddaddy objected.

'Just fucking,' he ordered.

'I think she'll take twenty of us,' one man said.

'She'll take fifty,' another argued. The fat guy was the first. He crawled on her and pumped away. His prick was small and he came quickly. Her vagina tried to grasp it but he pulled out.

'Don't worry, there's plenty more for you,' Granddaddy said. They were all queuing up to fuck her. 'I'll go last.' Someone pushed her mouth full of cock. Ten men fucked her before she came, but once she'd started, the orgasms kept taking her over. She was getting sore, but it was compulsive. Granddaddy was coming towards her. She was coming and coming like someone in the grip of a fit. She woke up.

It was 3 a.m., the green lights said. She sighed and rolled over. She was damp between the legs. She considered slipping into Ben's room for some satisfaction. But she wanted something else. The group of bikers must have numbered at least fifty outside the dance, she thought. It's easy to lose yourself in a group of fifty. She needed to see more. She wanted to watch close up as they fucked and sucked each other. She needed them to accept her. She wouldn't join in, but she needed that abandon. She'd looked for something meaningful with Joshua and that had fallen flat. Perhaps it was time for something meaningless.

Chapter Seventeen

'OK, Oberon. This is going to sound weird.' She had offered to treat him to Saturday lunch at their usual eaterie. He had asked if she didn't see enough of him in the week. She had been insistent.

'Surprise me.'

'Are you seeing Julie tonight?'

He looked wary. 'Yeees.' He waited. 'Are you spending three pounds fifty on me just to find that out?'

'No.' She went all shy. 'Are you meeting up with the gang?'

'Yeah. There's some kind of party in the larch wood.'

'Party?'

'Yeah.' He looked vague. 'God knows what, I mean every night is a party with that lot. But Julie says it's "dress bizarre". I mean, what's that about?'

'In the larch wood?' Holly wondered if she needed to tell him that she was thinking of going. 'Where's that?'

'God knows. I get a lift on a bike, remember.' He grinned broadly. 'Are you thinking of becoming a biker for the night, Miss Parker?'

'Christ, no.' She thought quickly. 'I'm just concerned for you. I mean you don't know anything about these people.'

'Yes, Mum.' Oberon dripped sarcasm.

'I'm serious.' She warmed to her theme. 'I mean, who are they? Are they safe? Do you wear a helmet?'

He burst out laughing. 'Is this what you brought me here for?'

'Yes!' She almost convinced herself. 'Just – be careful.'

After lunch she went shopping. There were lingerie shops, boutiques, knitwear shops but, not surprisingly, no shops with rubber dresses and thigh boots in the windows. In desperation, Holly went into a joke shop on the promenade. There were some pretty ridiculous wigs, but nothing that made her look sexy. There was a Superman outfit, a Batman outfit, a Joker outfit ... all useless. She was just about to leave when the shopkeeper cornered her. He was the cobwebby sort, dusty white hair, moth-eaten beige cardigan.

'Anything I can help you with?'

'No. It's for a girl. This is all a bit ...'

'Naturally.' He dragged a mini stepladder from the store cupboard and rummaged around on the top shelf. 'We have a fairy costume, years 9–11?'

'Oh, no, she's older than that.' Holly smiled. 'Look, thanks for all your trouble ...'

'How about a witch's costume? She could use it for Halloween!'

'No, really.'

'Catwoman?' She looked blankly at him. 'Catwoman. Part of the Batman range. Ages 14–16.' Holly considered. It would plainly be too small, but she was getting desperate.

'Can I see it?' He stumbled down with a large box in his hand. Holly read on the side that it contained a cloak, cat suit, cat mask and tail. It all looked black and shiny. She couldn't really ask to try it on in the shop. She decided to risk it. 'Oh, she'll love that,' she cooed, handing over the twenty quid (a bargain), and light-footed it home.

The house was empty. She rushed to her room and ripped the box open. This was ridiculous. She could see

151

straight away that the cat suit was too small. It was made out of a thin shiny rubber, cut off at the feet. She undressed and slowly peeled it onto her body. It clung invasively to every pore and crevice of her being. She pulled the sleeves up, squashing her breasts into the straining fabric, and zipped up. It was on. She looked down at herself. It was like a black sheen on her naked body. Even the circles of her nipples were visible, and the fuzz of her bush. She went to the mirror. She was surprised how good it looked, in a pornographic way. The material held in the bits that were bumpy and highlighted her curves. The fact it was too small had a corseting effect. She went to the chest of drawers and pulled a belt from a pair of trousers. It was a thick, black belt with silver studs along it. She buckled it loosely around her waist so that it dropped to her hips. Sexy. Next came the mask. This was important. If they recognised her she suspected they would lynch her. She pulled out the mask, which was black and covered the eyes. It had two dainty cat ears on top of it. She carefully yanked them off, and put it on. It had a flattering shape, with fake-diamonds studded around the eyeholes. Perfect. She got her nail scissors and hacked at the velvet tail, using the pieces to tie around her neck and wrists like weird bondage adornments. She would barely even recognise herself. Shoes? She hadn't got anything sexy enough, she realised, trawling through her collection. She slipped into the Briars' bedroom, feeling naughty. She had caught a glimpse of Mrs Briar's shoes the night before when they were choosing a dress for the party. She opened the wardrobe guiltily. Before her was the perfect pair of shiny, tarty black stilettos, four-inch slender heels, straps at the ankle – ideal. For a moment Holly considered just stealing them and slipping them back in the next day. If she didn't it would mean telling Mrs Briar that she was going out, and Mrs Briar was a nosey soul. Before she could make up her mind what to do, Holly heard the door slam downstairs. Her heart jumped and she hurriedly replaced the shoes and closed the wardrobe. She slipped out of the room, looking like a cat burglar. Ben was on the stairs.

'I – was just looking in your parents' big mirror,' she explained lamely, hoping Ben hadn't twigged that she had a full-length mirror in her own room. Ben wasn't really listening. His eyes were staring in glazed awe at her outfit. 'Oh, this!' Holly indicated the cat suit, aware that her nipples, her pubes, even the outline of her pussy were clearly on show. How could she even have considered going out in this? 'This is for a fancy dress party. My colleague Oberon is taking me. Is it too tarty?' Obviously it was, but nothing is too tarty for a boy of nineteen. Ben's mouth fell open. Holly couldn't help but smile at the image of him practically dribbling before her. He suddenly moved toward her, his hands sliding up the fabric on her hips and gravitating naturally to the large orbs of her bosom.

'What are you – dressed as?' He gulped, the shiny material a perfect aid to the glide of his hands.

'Catwoman. As in Batman. Got it in the joke shop.' His fingers traced the crack of her bottom. Holly felt strangely unmoved. She had expected to feel sexy about her outfit tonight, when she was incognito, but now, on the Briars' landing, she just felt like an idiot. A semi-naked one.

'Where is this party? Can I come?'

'No. Sorry.' He was crestfallen. Holly gently removed his paws from her buttocks.

'Well, can I come into your room now then?' He was a persistent one. Holly mused that it wouldn't do any harm. They had gained a pretty intimate knowledge of each other's bodies already. 'Please. I'll do anything for you.'

'Really?' Holly began to think. Would it be using him to get him to take her to this larch wood? Taxis were few on the ground and she didn't fancy braving the night in this little number. 'You've got a moped, haven't you?'

'Yes.' He looked confused. When he had said he

would do anything, he had fully expected to be given a list of sexual demands. 'Why?'

'If you come in now, would you give me a lift later on tonight? To the larch wood?'

'What do you want there?' She could see from his expression that this place had a bad reputation.

'It's just where I'm meeting my friend.' Ben didn't want to argue with her, not when he could be in her room feeling her up. But he didn't want her to get into trouble either. The dilemma was etched plainly on his face.

'It's not a good place to go. There's a "bad crowd" hang out there.' Even the words 'bad crowd' gave Holly a strange tingle. She reached for Ben's collar and pulled him to her.

'Maybe I want to hang out with the bad crowd,' She whispered. 'Don't worry about me. My friend's a big bloke. I won't get into trouble.' He nuzzled her ear. She couldn't resist that! 'Oh. I think you're the one I should be worried about.' They stumbled backwards into Holly's room. 'I take this is a yes, then? Ben?'

'Yes.' And he was filling her mouth with those ardent kisses again – full on, unsubtle, passionate. Ben slammed the door behind him and pushed Holly down onto the bed. He undressed hurriedly, eventually standing before her naked. He had a lovely body, sinewy and lean, with tan marks accentuating his slim hips. Holly looked at his cock – it was a healthy, smooth specimen, erect in its blond curly nest. A nice size. He obviously didn't have a problem with her looking at him. He walked over to her so she could take a closer look. She sucked the end into her mouth and rolled it around like a lollipop, springy on her tongue. She remembered how much fun it had been last night. She looked up at his face. His eyes beamed down at her, also full of last night's memory. Her kisses trailed down to his balls. She gave a gentle suck on one of them. He breathed in sharply – obviously liked that. She tried it on the other one.

'I want to give you pleasure,' he was saying. Her ears were blocked by her own sucking sounds. She moved her head back. 'It's not my turn,' he continued. She looked at him, leaning back.

'Ben, sweetheart. You don't take turns! Making love isn't like that.' He climbed onto the bed next to her, pressing his nakedness up against her. He slithered around on her, the satiny fabric of her suit turning him on. 'Anyway, you're taking me to this party. And picking me up I hope?' she asked. He nodded. 'So I owe *you* one. And I'll gladly give you one!' He did have the most delicious prick she had ever tasted, she thought, as she sank back down the bed towards it. He stopped her.

'Holly.' This was too good to be true for him. Well, Holly thought, it's about to get better. His cock was at her breasts. Her cleavage was amazing in this outfit, all squashed together and fleshy. She manoeuvred herself forward and pulled her zip down so that his penis nestled snugly in the fold of her cleavage. She pressed it into her and began to move up and down, up and down, so that the foreskin moved over the shaft, which was squashed between her bosoms. Jeff had always wanted her to do this – he had begged for it. 'Let me come all over your tits,' he had urged. And she had let him a couple of times, but she never felt good about it with him. He was already too much in charge, it had made her feel like a slave. But with Ben it felt good. She felt like a goddess.

'My God!' He sighed, grabbing at her to get some traction. 'Oh, Jesus!' His foot fell between her legs, unwittingly rubbing her. The fabric at her crotch was soon hot and prickly at the friction. Holly kept on undulating against him, tickling his balls occasionally to keep him happy. He couldn't keep his eyes off her tits with his livid member drowning between them. This was obviously something he was trying to store in his photographic memory for later use. Holly liked that idea. It was odd how the idea of some men wanking over you was so lovely, while with others it was the most repulsive thing in the world. It wasn't fair really. He took up her rhythm now.

'I wanted . . .' he gasped. 'I wanted to ask you if I could take a picture of you. For when you're not here any more. You look so hot . . .' He swallowed as she added her hand to the melee between her breasts, helping him along a bit. 'So hot in that cat suit!'

'You can take a picture of me.' Holly was slightly breathless too – sexual excitement was contagious. She squeezed her thighs around his foot. He got the message, wriggling his big toe around her slit, which was well defined by the tight crotch of her cat suit. 'I'd enjoy that!' Her own pleasure was a little distracting and she stopped rubbing his cock for a moment. He shuffled down the bed and kissed her full on the lips again. 'I like the idea of you photographing me. But only if you promise to use it when you masturbate.' She pulled him back up to the head of the bed, snuggling into the pillows.

'Oh, I promise.' Ben rolled on top of her, his tongue invading her mouth. She opened her legs instinctively and could feel his cock hitting the spot perfectly. His hips thrust against her. The rubbing was something else. The fact that Holly was still fully clothed in such a slinky outfit was giving her an extra thrill. She wrapped her black shiny legs around him and enjoyed the weight of his erection on her pussy. He couldn't get inside her, but he seemed determined to try. Was he going to tear the material with the head of his cock? He struggled against her for a few minutes until he started to come. Holly could feel his body climbing up the ladder to a climax and she was concerned for her outfit. The last thing she wanted was a white semen stain on her gusset. She wriggled under him, slipping down the bed, and grabbed his cock. It was hovering over her tits again. She unzipped so that her breasts were naked, the nipples looking expectantly up at him, then began to pull on the shaft, slowly at first, but then at a frantic pace. He came in an instant, splashing her with come, leaving white blobs on her tits and in her hair. She had floored him again, she observed, as he rolled onto his back with that recently departed look in his eye.

'We'll leave the photos for another occasion,' she promised, kissing him fondly on the cheek.

'If you ever want taking anywhere on my moped,' he panted, 'do not hesitate to ask.'

When they arrived at the larch wood, the place was already swarming with bizarre-looking people. Ben turned off the moped and the lights at the bottom of a slope and turned to her. His face shone in the darkness.

'Are you sure about this?' he asked.

'Completely,' she lied. For a start Mrs Briar's four-inch heels were already digging into her feet. She had decided to pinch them in the end, as Mrs Briar had been held up at the leisure centre again and hadn't been home to interrogate Holly. She would smuggle them back again in the morning, Holly thought, hopefully not covered in bloodstains from all her blisters.

'You look amazing.' How nice to have an admirer, Holly thought. She was still in the cat suit, nothing underneath, but had pulled a long black coat of Ben's over the top. She would only take it off if she started to feel very brave or very horny. Her hair was pulled back into a severe ponytail, accentuating the sharp contour of her jaw and the fullness of her mouth. Her mask obscured her face. Only the glinting green of her eyes betrayed her identity, and she was sure nobody would get that close to her. She was here to watch. It was research for the play. It was research for life. Max was always going on about sexual abandon. Well, here she was to see what all the fuss was about. Why else would she have come? And yet she kept getting that prick of lust at the memory of Granddaddy sucking on Julie's tits and the lazy fucking she had seen the night before.

Ben rode off with orders to pick her up at one, although she had slipped her mobile in her coat pocket to call him if she couldn't last that long. Looking around, she was quite sure that she wouldn't last. She was glad that somebody knew where she was, just in case a search party was necessary.

She walked slowly and confidently through the dark fields. People were still arriving, forming small groups, laughing, chilled. Beer and gin bottles filled big buckets around the place, and little fires were being started. One group were singing a drunken song, lying on the grass, smoking grass. Dress bizarre, Oberon had said. Some people had ignored that, clad in their trademark leather. Others had weird long velvet capes on, gothic lacy black dresses, ironic pink baby-doll dresses with bovver boots, outlandish make-up, animal costumes. It was going to be a real carnival. Someone set up a ghetto blaster and started pumping out loud rock music into the night. Holly grabbed a beer bottle and forced the top off coolly on the side of the bucket. When she was in performance mode she found she could do things like that, whereas normally she would be fumbling and nervous. But tonight she wasn't herself. She took a long swig and continued walking. A few people had started to notice her now, clocking this serene, beautiful woman. She let the coat fall open and expose her body a little. Eyes were definitely on her now. She moved towards the shadows of the wood. Only a few people were in there, she noticed, and sank down at the edge of the trees where she couldn't be seen. She watched avidly as endless bikes roared up to the spot and more and more characters arrived on the scene. People were in good spirits, laughing and revving engines, taking quick gropes of each other. A couple of women in fairy costumes turned up with their boyfriend, taking it in turns to kiss him. Holly wondered if this was the threesome Oberon had talked about.

After nearly an hour she saw Oberon arrive on the back of Julie's Harley. He had stolen his Derry costume from wardrobe, she saw, a foreign knight with puffy sleeves and a turquoise brocade waistcoat. He looked handsome, and outlandish enough to get away with such an effeminate foppish look at such a macho gathering. Julie's costume was just a medley of leather and silver, all her piercings joined up with chains. Her top was cut away at the bust displaying two pendulous naked bosoms, all chained up like two farm animals who couldn't be trusted. She had large, pale nipples, pinched at the ends by two shiny studs. She thrust them out before her proudly. Holly drank deep as she watched people hotting up. She was pleased to see that this all just seemed to be another hedonistic sex and drugs and alcohol gathering, with a few weird clothes thrown in. And she was ready to get a close up look. She bravely slipped the coat off her shoulders – she was less recognisable without it on, she decided – and left it by the trees. She saw Oberon and Julie disappear hurriedly off to the bushes for some privacy (his request, she guessed, not hers) and took the opportunity to walk amongst the group. She felt stylish and whorish in her clothes all at once, and the shoes gave her a smouldering walk. The more eyes she caught, the more she swung her hips. This was fun. She didn't smile but set her face in a cool, pouting indifference.

She got another beer and used it like a phallic object, sucking the long neck of the bottle in a way that attracted a lot of male attention. She reminded herself that she was here to watch, not to get into any trouble. There was something dangerous about this crowd. She mustn't start something she couldn't finish. She walked around, not meeting any eyes, trying to cultivate the mysterious untouchable stranger image. She soon spotted the two fairies. They were both in tiny pink dresses and wings. Neither wore knickers, Holly noticed, and it looked like they had shaved their pubes for the occasion. The man they had arrived with was lying on the floor, his trousers around his ankles. One fairy jiggled about on his face while the other was humping his crotch. Both the girls were giggling, but he seemed to be struggling to breathe. The girl on his cock started to stimulate herself as she rode him, her pale hand

159

fluttering between her legs. Her wings were jerking up and down. His feet stretched out – was he suffocating? If so, was that the idea? The fucking fairy shrieked out an orgasm, which started to set the other fairy off. Before she got there, the fucking fairy got up and demanded to swap places.

'You're always on the face!' she was complaining. Trouble in paradise. The fairy on the face was trying to ignore her – she was driving against the guy's tongue at a pace that suggested she was near orgasm. His cock was jumping about in the air wanting some relief. 'Get up! Get off, you bitch!' the livid fairy continued. Finally the fairy on the face conceded and wriggled down, slipping the penis deep inside her. She gyrated her hips, leaning forward to get some of the clitoral pleasure she had just been enjoying. The fucking fairy leaped happily on to the guy's face. He had taken a few deep breaths and seemed fine now. She started to wriggle around. Holly was enthralled, watching the whole erotic pantomime with a twitchy pussy. She felt a presence at her shoulder. It was Granddaddy.

'Enjoying the show?' Her heart beat fast. What was she supposed to say to this? Was it good or bad to be a voyeur in this crowd? He didn't seem to recognise her, she noticed. His pale brown eyes skimmed her body, sizing her up.

'Seen it all before,' she said nonchalantly. Her voice came out very husky. Obviously that was the voice she would have to use all night, all part of the new her.

'Know this crowd?' She realised that he was American. He had a slight Southern States drawl to him. Maybe that's what let him get away with being sexually desirable even though he was grey and gnarled.

'Not really. Not many of them.' She was ice cool. She wasn't going to be one of those needy women hanging round the old guy for affirmation. 'I have a crowd of my own. I just came to . . . check you guys out.'

'Let me take you around.' He took her hand. They walked past the fairies (the one on the face was now enjoying her second climax much to the annoyance of the one on the cock) and past a group of blokes puffing on some weed. Around them couples were forming. 'Over there,' Granddaddy pointed to a young couple happily banging away against a tree, 'that's Fiona and Orson. They're new to the group. Newlyweds.' Holly smiled at their fresh passion. 'Not married to each other, I should add.' The guy's white bottom thrust, thrust, thrust and the woman's bare legs flailed hopelessly. 'There's no love in it,' Granddaddy went on. 'Just animal lust.' He eyed Holly, gauging her reaction. She remained expressionless. He pointed to two women lying face to face in the grass, deep kissing each other. One had her legs apart, her skirt up around her hips, and Holly could just see a long black dildo sliding in and out of her. She was groaning into the other girl's mouth. 'Mary and Jo.' He smiled wryly. 'Today they're kissing and making up. Normally we get a cat fight out of them.'

'Which do you like best?'

'What, Mary or Jo?' He thought for a moment. 'Mary is uninhibited, adventurous. But Jo's got real spark.'

'Actually,' Holly had the wry smile now, 'I meant which do you like better – when they fight or when they make up?'

The old guy laughed, chewing on some tobacco. 'I like both. But making up is better, especially when I can get in the middle of it.' He walked her round to the woods. She was glad he wasn't asking who she was or where she came from. She was trying to think of a name for herself. Lola? Vanessa? They came up to a group of men, standing in a ring. They were clapping rhythmically and cheering, spraying beer all over a couple having sex in the centre of the ring. When one man had come, another took his place, fucking her hard. She was naked and seemed vulnerable.

'Is she willing?' Holly whispered, appalled.

'Oh yeah, of course she is. Wouldn't you be?' They

watched as a man heaved his semen into her. She did look delirious.

'Come on, you fuckers!' she cried as he got off her, leaving her legs wide open to the group. Her sex was red and open like a Venus flytrap. It shone with the residue of men who had just come inside her. Another man climbed on, forcing her feet over his shoulders. She liked that. As he started some slow thrusts she moaned, 'Oh yeah, baby. Open me up!' He pushed harder. 'Fill me up, baby!'

'If she doesn't do all ten of them,' Granddaddy explained. 'She has to let them all come on her face. They hold her down and force themselves on her.' Holly tried not to look shocked, but it felt suddenly very dark out here. 'Don't worry.' He had obviously seen her troubled face. 'She loves that bit best.'

'Then why doesn't she just do it straight off?'

'Oh, it's the being forced she loves. You should see her come when they do that to her. It's like a volcano.' Holly felt a gush of abhorrence fill her cunt. Surely that wasn't turning her on? The girl was singing obscenities at her current lover with gusto. Granddaddy moved Holly on, but the screaming stayed in her ears. She suddenly wondered if she was out of her depth. These people were like pack animals, with pack rules. Only this old man made her feel safe, somehow. He seemed to make the rules.

'So, who are you going to pick tonight, Granddaddy?' Holly asked flirtatiously.

'You know my name!' He grinned. 'How come?'

'Just contacts. You have a reputation.' This pleased him.

'I earned it, lady.' He surveyed the heaving mass of bodies around the fields and in the woods, all combinations of people, smoking, drinking, fucking.

'I hear they all want you,' she said teasingly.

'Yeah. Granddaddy's a popular guy.'

A man in a convincing gorilla costume came running up, chasing one of the women dressed in a baby doll outfit. He caught her and pushed her to the ground. She struggled for a bit, her bare legs kicking against his fur, but he was huge and soon overwhelmed her. Holly watched, flushed, as he pulled his cock out from the costume and turned her over onto her stomach. He began to fuck her from behind, grunting like an ape, howling and grabbing at her. He ripped her dress. His big black furry paws travelled around her body, burying under her to stimulate her breasts and her pussy. In the half-light his costume looked so realistic. It was fascinating. Granddaddy was standing behind Holly, watching her reaction.

'You like the kinky stuff, eh?' he said softly, pulling her to lean back against him. Holly couldn't argue – she was transfixed. She felt the old man's hand slip inside her costume and play at her nipple as she watched the humping pair. 'You like to see the maiden being raped by the gorilla. Kind of a romantic?'

Whoever was in that gorilla costume was taking his role very seriously. He was still grunting and grappling roughly at the woman. Granddaddy's hand was quick to stimulate Holly. It was an experienced hand and her breast immediately responded to it. She sighed and leaned back, wondering how far she could go before she made her escape. The gorilla man rolled over so that the woman in the baby doll dress was lying face-up on top of him. He slipped out of her, his oddly pink human cock the only give-away that she hadn't just been fucking an ape. His big hands started to strum at her pussy as she lay there, nestled in his thick black fur. She squirmed, pretending to struggle but loving it. She teased her own nipples.

Granddaddy's free hand unzipped Holly's outfit and sank into the damp tingling nest of her bush. He mirrored the gorilla's hand movements. She focused her eyes and imagined it was the gorilla. Her eyes stared hungrily. If she was going to be a voyeur she should play the part to the hilt. The woman had started to come. But she wanted something inside her, Holly could see; she was struggling and jerking against his crotch. She sat up and lowered herself onto the free pink prick, facing the guy's feet. She bounced up and down on him, his hands still working on her clit. It was hard to see his reaction, his ape mask was unyielding, but Holly was sure she heard him grunting with pleasure under there. Soon the woman came with an animal grunt too.

'He's going to fuck her in the arse now,' Granddaddy whispered. 'She loves that.' He was right. The woman got automatically on all fours and opened herself to the gorilla man. He smeared her own juices and his semen around her bottom to lubricate it, kissing her buttocks and nibbling at her rosebud through his gorilla mask. She was glowing with anticipation.

Granddaddy had slowed down the pace of his hand now. It was just sliding lazily around Holly's pussy as she watched. Holly felt nervous. She wanted to leave. Her juices were flowing and she felt like she was losing control. The women here seemed to be happy to perform any sexual act going, and Holly would soon be shown up if asked to join in. The gorilla man carefully began to enter the woman, using a little force to part her buttocks. She let out a yelp of pain, but her face still beamed, her eyes tight shut. He began some shallow thrusting, then slipped further inside her crack. The further he went the more noise she made, until his big furry pelvis was grinding up right against her bottom, filling her completely. 'She can come like this,' Granddaddy whispered. 'No need to touch her pussy. This is her best way.'

'Have you done this to her?'

'Yes. Oh yes.' His voice was deep against her ear, and she could feel his erection pointedly stabbing at her bottom, his fingers still buried in her. Surely he wasn't going to try to do this to her in the middle of this field. The woman was beginning to scream now, her voice rising with ecstatic fervour. The gorilla's hips thrust maniacally. He was grunting again, his big hand holding her hips still. It had to hurt. Holly wondered what

164

it would be like with a real gorilla – scary and dangerous. She imagined a huge cock thrusting away for
hours, but she was sure the reality would be the
opposite. Still, the idea gave Granddaddy's hand a bath
of her juices.

'You're ripe,' he said and led her away to the centre
of the field, her cat suit now open to the crotch. Her
breasts were nearly spilling out of it and her neat bush
was clearly visible. People were staring as she passed
them, although they had seen all manner of sexual acts
before. But she was with Granddaddy, and that made
her someone to watch.

'What are you doing?' she asked as he laid her down
in the middle of the field. A group gathered around
them – curious males, envious females. 'I don't want
this.' She could get up now and run, she thought.

'Yes, you do.' More spectators gathered.

'What are you going to do to me, Granddaddy?' she
asked, knowing it would be something vulgar and
outlandish. He brushed his moustache against her chin.
Holly adjusted her mask to make sure it was in place.
She didn't want her face to be seen now. She recognised
some of the guys from the night before.

'Granddaddy's going to make you come over and
over,' he said, pulling down the top of her suit. She let
him unpeel it off her body and pull it down her legs.
He brushed her face but she stopped his hand. She
would keep the mask on. Tonight she was somebody
else. And she had been chosen. She secretly wanted to
see what all the fuss was about. He leaned over her
body, taking in the scent. 'Look at these titties.' He
spoke half to the group, half to himself. He sucked her
breasts a little. 'Come and have a taste of these!' Two
men sank to their knees on either side of her.

'What . . .?' Holly started to protest as they each took
a mouthful of her breasts. One was fat with a huge
bushy beard which tickled her nipple. He sucked hard
and liked to nibble. He was groaning like a man who
hadn't had a taste of someone's tits for a long time. The

165

other guy was younger, with slick black hair. He was obviously into technique, flicking his tongue against her at a hundred miles an hour. The air was cool and the mouths were hot. She decided not to struggle. She would never get away, and besides, she was loving it.

'Carry on, boys.' Granddaddy pulled her costume right off her feet. The shoes got caught up in the ankles and came off too. He obviously liked the shoes though, taking the time to put them back on her feet. 'I got to get me a taste of this here pussy. Look at that!' He put both her feet on his shoulders and leaned forward so that she opened up to him. Her stilettos dug into the flesh of his shoulder, but he was busy concentrating on her open sex. He bent down and tickled the area with his moustache, inhaling heavily. 'God, you smell good.' He leered. He took a lick. 'And taste something else.' He began to nurse expertly at her, licking her up a storm in no time. Holly didn't know what was happening to her. She felt more opened up than she ever had been before, desperately welcoming this old guy's agile tongue into her most private part. She couldn't move her legs – she would have liked to wrap them hard around his head, but her feet were glued to his shoulders. She suspected this was on purpose. Like this, the gathered masses had a fantastic view of his tongue moving around her pussy and the gushing quivering response of her swollen cunt lips. The two guys at her breasts were slurping on with relish. There was an electric buzz shooting from her nipples to her clit. She looked down and saw the three strange heads bobbing at her erogenous zones, working to give her pleasure. She couldn't believe this was happening. She had just intended to watch, and now she was the one in view. Holly glanced around the group. All eyes were on her, this strange masked beauty in high-heeled shoes. She gasped and strained to push into Granddaddy's face, but couldn't. His big moustache scratched wonderfully at her clit. His tongue was inventive and serpentine. Within minutes she felt the climax rise through her body, and she shuddered feverishly against his mouth, pressing into him. He continued to lick, tongue-fucking her. The two other guys held her firm as she struggled.

'It's an oil slick down here.' Granddaddy gulped. He started to suck on her, moving up to her bud. A few tugs and flicks and she felt an orgasm suddenly take her over. Just before she came, she looked down her body and grabbed at the heads bowed at her centres of pleasure with clawing hands. She felt her gush of come wash Granddaddy's moustache. 'Lovely. I'll be able to taste you for days.' He leaned back and let her feet fall to the floor, then turned her over into the doggy position and continued to lick her like that, her bottom thrust in his face. His two helpers sat back, leering into her body.

'You liked it when the gorilla did this, didn't you?' he growled, taking a long tongue slowly to the crack of her bottom and licking her there. It was an odd sensation. He was performing the same moves on her there as he had on her pussy. The warm glow moved to her bottom, the quivering starting in her rosebud. He was enthusiastically licking her out. 'You have the loveliest butt,' he said, quickly returning to nibble and kiss it. Holly was overwhelmed with the strange new sensation. He pulled her cheeks apart to get a deeper taste of her. She felt her pussy open up as well. People in the group were starting to get rowdy. A couple of turned-on guys were mirroring Granddaddy's actions with their lovers, or just wanking. A few people broke off to get it on away from the crowd. People were calling things out. Holly got scared. She tried to get up but Granddaddy pulled her down on him and started to lick at her pussy again. His finger snaked thickly into her bottom and began to thrust. She felt weakened by the wonderful sensation. But the fear took over. She had to get out of there. A chant had started up in the group: 'Fuck her! Fuck her!' People were getting restless. Holly's pussy was getting restless. What harm would it do to let the old guy give her one, she thought. She wanted it badly.

'Come on, baby,' he said, responding to the crowd.

'Granddaddy's going to give you the fuck of a lifetime.' He turned her onto her back and crawled on top of her. She saw for the first time the gooey moisture of her cunt sticky in his moustache. His big old face loomed over her, brown eyes filled with cool lust. He unzipped his leather trousers and pulled out his cock. There was applause from the onlookers. She could see why he might be the alpha male in the group, as Oberon had put it. His cock was formidable. It was so large and thick that she wondered if it would fit inside her at all. 'Don't worry,' he read her mind, 'I'll open you up real nice.' He grabbed her ankles and parted her legs roughly, putting a foot over each of his shoulders. When he moved on top of her, her hips rose up and her sex seemed to open like a flower. She was so wet that the head sank in smoothly. They both gasped as he entered her, and the crowd cheered. He bore down on her, pushing his huge shaft further inside her. It burned as it stretched her open. She had never had anything this big to contend with before. She held her breath. Granddaddy paused and bent his head to her chest, nuzzling her cleavage and skillfully titillating her nipples. His hips were moving almost imperceptibly, slowly forging a path inside her. She couldn't escape now, she was literally pinned down, so she gave in to the pleasure of the moment. Her sex was on fire. She was surrounded by eager eyes. She felt like she would explode if she let herself come. 'Say you want it,' Granddaddy urged, his hips moving more.

'I want it.' Her voice was a dry whisper.

'Say you want it,' he repeated louder. 'Tell Granddaddy you want it bad.'

'I want it.' He started to fuck her now. The pain filled her as he thrust himself nearly all the way in. She couldn't take all of it. 'I want it.' She tried to push herself open to welcome the whole of him, but she was full to capacity. His hugeness began to pump inside her. She looked down and could clearly see the thick trunk of his cock sinking into her, his big balls crashing against her bottom. His pubic hairs tickled her slit. She tried to grind up to rub her clit on his pubic bone, but it wouldn't reach. 'I want it!' she cried.

'Tell me,' he growled at her, increasing his pace. Holly wasn't aware of anything now except for the aching need in her pussy. 'Tell Granddaddy.'

'I need it. I want it, Granddaddy.' He leaned harder on her so her legs were pushed onto her own shoulders. He sank in another inch. 'Fuck me,' she whispered into his face.

'Horny bitch!' a woman from the crowd called, coming to watch behind Granddaddy. It was the baby doll woman who had fucked the gorilla. Holly was afraid she was jealous and was going to stop him mid flow. She was near the point of no return now and nothing was going to stop her. The size of him was giving her sensations she had never experienced before. Her clit was feeling a little neglected, but her pussy was full and sated by his big trunk.

'Don't stop,' Holly warned.

'Don't you worry, darling,' he panted, his hips moving a mile a minute. The woman was kneeling down behind him now. She reached around his penis and searched out Holly's clit. 'Sandra's going to help you come.' The woman started to rub firmly against the bud, jigging in rhythm with Granddaddy. The air was filled with the noise of Holly's juices being stirred up. The feeling was overwhelming. Holly was glad she wasn't only watching tonight. She had abandoned herself to the experience and it felt fucking amazing. This enormous cock and this woman's hand were giving her the orgasm of her life. She started to feel the contractions of her climax. 'Come for Granddaddy,' the old man whispered. 'Come all over my big cock.' That was all the encouragement Holly needed. As he fucked her ferociously, her body began to jerk in the throes of ecstasy. She was aware of the flash of a Polaroid camera going off in her face as she came, but she was beyond caring. She cried out and felt the strength drain out of her body

169

as the climax hit her. Granddaddy pulled out of her, still hard as rock. 'You want it in the arse?' he grunted, ready to flip her over. The crowd cheered. Holly baulked at the idea.

'You're too big,' she said, smiling. 'And I have to go.'

'Don't!' He grabbed her, pressing his cock aggressively against her. 'Granddaddy wants to come inside you.' She was tempted to do the whole thing over again, but decided to escape while she could. She had already gone too far and she was sore.

'I don't want to hog you, Granddaddy.' She got up, snatching her clothes from the floor. She stood there naked except for her mask and her shoes. 'All the girls want you inside them.'

'I want you!' He tried to pull her down again, but couldn't. Instead he shuffled on his knees towards her and started eating her out again as she stood in front of him. A few of the girls in the group protested.

'See? All those fresh pussies calling out for you.' Holly jerked her hips away but his big mouth homed in on her like a heat-seeking missile. He looked suddenly very weak and needy on his knees before her, his tongue pointing into her privates. He managed to get it buried up inside her. Her scent was strong now after her climax and he groaned at the taste. There was something soothing about that wet tongue after the friction of his oversized cock. She pushed him off again.

'Don't be greedy, Granddaddy. Next time.' Hopefully the promise of more would cool his ardour. She realised she was never going to get her catsuit on here while trying to fend off Granddaddy. She tied the material round her waist. 'All these babes.' She pulled the first girl she could get her hands on out of the crowd and was astonished to see it was Julie. She glanced around and was pleased to see that Oberon was out of sight. 'Want a piece of the action. Wouldn't you like a go with Granddaddy?'

'Yes, I would.' Julie was stoned. She fell on her knees

before the old man and pouted like a child. 'Can I suck it? Please! You never let me . . .'

Holly retreated through the crowds and ran as fast as she could to the spot where she had left Ben's coat. She was safely in the dark shadows now, and could just see the outline of Julie having a suck of Granddaddy her bulky figure hunched over his crotch. She carefully got dressed and pulled the coat comfortingly around her. She would call Ben and get home as quickly as possible. She had pushed her luck here. She put her hand in her pocket for the phone but couldn't find it. She looked in the other pocket, but all she found was a piece of paper. Her hand froze over it. She was sure it hadn't been there before. The shadows seemed to close around her. It was probably nothing. She took it out slowly and unfolded it. It was too dark to read. She peered closer, angling it towards a distant campfire. The small neat lettering was clearer now. It said: 'I'M BEHIND YOU.'

Her heart stopped. Before she could turn around she felt a hand come out of the blackness and grab at her hair. She struggled, screaming. Whoever it was had been hiding in the wood. She flailed her arms, trying to turn around. Another hand swung roughly at her face – a woman's hand, pale and ghostly. Nails tore at Holly's lip. The clawing hand now pushed her to the ground. Holly staggered to her feet, the adrenalin rushing to her muscles. She turned on the woman, but the figure had retreated swiftly back into the woods. Her silhouette was just visible darting silently amongst the trees. Holly was bleeding and shaken. She stumbled hurriedly back towards the group for help, but they were no safer. They were clapping and howling like animals. She couldn't see Oberon there. She had to get out. The phone wasn't in her pocket. Her attacker must have taken it. She looked back towards the shadows of the woods. It was possible that the phone had just fallen out of her pocket, she thought, trying to be rational. She had to phone Ben and ask him to collect her. Especially now, when a walk home on her own seemed like the most terrifying proposition in the world. She walked nervously back towards the woods. Her eyes tried to pick out moving shapes among the trees but she couldn't see any. Just blackness and silence. She kept alert as she neared the spot where she had left her coat. If someone was going to attack her now, she would be ready for it. Barely breathing, she got down on all fours and patted the grass, keeping her eyes wide and watching all around her. Her hand soon landed on the hard familiar shape of her phone. She rose like a coiled spring and ran like the wind away from the woods. She felt as if a trail of ghosts were chasing her, unhappy spirits oozing from the wood and snatching at her heels. She found a safe spot on the side of the road where Ben had dropped her off and dialled the number with trembling fingers. Ben's voice on the other end of the line was a welcome, familiar sound.

'Promise not to ask any questions when you get here,' she said, tasting the blood on her lip.

'No questions. But you're scaring me.' His voice was concerned. 'I'm coming straight away.'

Chapter Eighteen

Monday morning had never come as such a relief, and the idea of work had never been so sweet. Holly had spent Sunday in bed, cursing her stupidity for getting involved with a set of people she couldn't trust and nursing her broken lip. She had laid out her two notes on the dresser and went occasionally to study them. 'I'M WATCHING YOU' and 'I'M BEHIND YOU.' Both designed to terrify her. Mrs Briar didn't ask what had happened, why Holly looked like she had been attacked by a wildcat or why her black stiletto shoes were caked in mud. She just came in with a steady stream of hot tea and comfort food, closely followed by Ben with a succession of cuddles and soft kisses. Holly had felt like a sickly child in the bosom of her family.

Oberon was the first face she saw when she arrived at the theatre. He looked up at her and instantly clocked the injury, which had puffed up and blackened, making it look more dramatic than it was. Holly wondered if he had spotted her that night. She had basically given a sex show to a group of strangers with some dirty old man – she wouldn't blame him if he didn't want anything to do with her. But if he did know about it, he wasn't letting on. He rushed to her side.

'What happened to you?' How much could she tell

him? If she told him where she had been on Saturday night, he'd know everything. But she wanted someone to know that there appeared to be a deranged person in her midst.

'I don't really know.' She wanted to sit down. Oberon led her to a seat and took her hand.

'Is it that fucker Jeff?' He looked angry.

'No! It's weird, Oberon. Someone wants to scare me. And they're succeeding.' She told him about the notes and about the woman who had come out of nowhere and attacked her, although she didn't mention where she had been. She said she had just been on a late-night stroll to get some air.

'Well, obviously you have to go to the police.' He was right. She hadn't thought of that. But in her heart, she felt it was someone she knew, someone playing a game with her. So many people had gone to great lengths to toy with her feelings of late – especially Jeff – that she wouldn't be surprised if this was one big hoax. 'Look, Holly. Acid little notes are one thing. But getting your face ripped open – that's no joke.'

'You don't think it's Nikki, do you?' Holly couldn't believe it herself, but she had to consider everyone.

'No!' He thought for a moment. 'Why, did she look like Nikki?'

'I didn't see her face or her hair. She was behind me and then it was so dark in the wood. She had long nails though. Does Nikki have long nails?' Oberon shrugged.

'Can you think of anyone with long nails?'

Holly could – Mrs Briar. She had those heavy manicured talons that all beauticians seemed to favour. They made her plump hands look even rounder. But it couldn't be her, could it? The figure had looked slimmer than her, although she had worn a long coat. Holly remembered it flapping behind her as she ran into the forest. Holly didn't mention Mrs Briar to Oberon. She would have to say how naughty she had been with Ben and Caleb Briar to explain motive, and she didn't relish that.

'Oh, never mind.' The others were arriving now. Max and Nikki had seemingly had a wild and wet weekend; they were glued to each other. She seemed to have become more voluptuous, her breasts stood out as if to announce they had never had it so good, and she wiggled more when she walked. Jeff seemed OK with it, coming in with them and even patting her on the bottom. What kind of a timeshare was going on there? Max saw Holly's lip and sneered.

'Finally drove someone too far?' Then he muttered to Jeff, 'Doesn't surprise me.' Holly pretended not to hear. Was Max in one of those moods? 'Where's Nathaniel?' he called out to Adrian, the harassed stage manager, who quickly went to call Nathaniel's digs to check he hadn't overslept. 'Honestly, these older actors can't even get out of bed on their own; what's he going to be like on stage?' Max sat up on the stage with Nikki in her usual pose, curled on his lap like a kitten. She was smiling and chatting with Jeff sitting on the bed opposite them.

'Maybe tonight . . .' Holly could hear her saying. Jeff flashed a look at Max who gave a dirty laugh.

'How's your sex life?' Holly asked Oberon, who was also watching the scene on stage with some curiosity. 'Any new piercings I should know about?' He laughed and rolled his eyes.

'No. No. I went to that party I told you about.'

'Oh yeah?' She tried to look disinterested. 'Any good?'

'It was mad. There were even more people than usual, all in a crazy mood. It was odd. I remembered you telling me to be careful, and I could suddenly see your point. I mean, some of those guys are out of control.' He shook his head. 'Julie wanted to have some kind of gang bang with a group of her mates, but I'm not into all that. I said we could go off on our own or forget it.'

'And?' Holly wished she knew her mind like Oberon did. Maybe that way she would have stayed out of trouble.

'Well, naturally she wanted some of my special loving, so she came with me into some bushes and we did it a few times.' He puffed his chest out. 'I was pretty sensational.'

'Yeah?'

'Of course. Once she'd got it out of her system, she wanted to go back and join the group. She wanted to see if Granddaddy would let her in on the action.' He sighed. 'It's all just too weird for me, Hol. I said to her, 'Look, it's either me or him and a gang of blokes. But you can't have a combination of all three.' She didn't like that much. She gave me a lift home and we said our goodbyes – up against the front of my digs – so she wasn't too pissed off at me.' He smiled. 'Parting is such sweet sorrow.'

'And then she went back to the party did she?'

'I think so. God knows. Back to her precious Granddaddy. Thinks he's God's gift.' Holly almost commented that he was pretty gifted in certain departments, but stopped herself. Poor Oberon. If he had a crest, it would have been fallen.

'I think you made a good decision,' she comforted him. 'That lot are bad news. Although it's all very seductive, at the end of the day you can't trust one of them.' He raised an eyebrow. She suddenly seemed very expert on the subject. 'I can tell from what you've said. All that Granddaddy stuff. It's sick.' A good healthy dose of hypocrisy, she thought to herself; nice one, Holly. Nathaniel arrived a little out of breath, his clothes obviously assembled in a hurry.

'I'm so sorry, everyone. Unforgivable. Completely overslept.'

'Don't tell me even he's getting some!' Oberon whispered to Holly. Max looked up from nibbling Nikki's neck.

'At last!' He got up, handing Nikki to Jeff like a toy. 'Well, we were going to do the Lord Hunter scene today, but something tells me a certain actor's mental preparation is somewhat amiss...' he said bullishly, stabbing a finger at Nathaniel.

'I do apologise!' The poor actor was distraught.

'So we shall continue to fine-tune the work we have done already.' Max glared at Nathaniel. 'But be advised, you are the one who will look a fool up here on stage if we never get to rehearse your scene.'

'For God's sake, leave him alone!' Holly couldn't help herself. She hated to see someone bullied, and Max's power had lost its strength for her now she knew his little secret. He turned his fire on her.

'You, Miss Parker, are a waste of my time! How dare you talk back to me.'

'Shall we get on with the work, Max?' Her calmness irritated him beyond belief. He gave her a look that told her she was in for some bad treatment today.

'Now you've done it,' Oberon whispered. Jeff was looking at her curiously. He had just noticed the bruise on her lip, and was also wondering what gave her this sudden feistiness.

'I just think a little less shouting and a little more rehearsing would be good for the production.' She looked levelly at Max. 'Don't you?'

'You'd better watch it, you little cow.' His voice lowered to a gravelly warning.

'You see, that's just the sort of comment I don't find helpful.' Holly was enjoying this.

'What are you doing?' Oberon hissed in her ear.

'Now, shall we get up and start running scenes, or do you want a little time alone with your new squeeze. Again.'

'I don't know what's up with you, but you better watch it.' This was Jeff putting his oar in.

'Thanks for your concern.' Holly got up and walked to the stage. 'I know you can be relied on in a spot of bother. Can't he, Max?' The two men glanced at each other. Did she know about the prostitute? She had planted just enough of a seed in Max's mind to take the wind out of his sails for a moment. He rallied the cast onto the stage and commenced rehearsals. Holly flowed effortlessly through the sexual scenes that had so scared her at the beginning of rehearsals. Everyone in the room had seen it all before, had seen her naked no less, had seen her on the brink of a climax straddling another woman's face. What was there left to be shy about? In her scene with Oberon she found a new sense of adventure, enjoying the bodily contact. He responded, trying new things. Probably things Julie had taught him, Holly pondered. She was going to enjoy playing this character.

When it came to her scene with Nikki she was aware of Max's eyes penetrating her with more than a directorial interest. Nikki was his new plaything and he was getting possessive over her, although Jeff was allowed a go. Obviously Jeff was using his famous debt of gratitude. Holly decided to rub salt into the wound, publicly relishing her scene with Nikki, taking liberties with her body. They had kept to the idea of Holly wriggling up Nikki's body during the scene, and Holly made the most of it, happily wriggling around on her co-star's face. Max didn't know whether to be turned on or jealous. After the scene he broke the actors for lunch.

'That's enough for one morning!' he called, running up onto the stage. Nikki was lying back on the bed. He sat next to her, placing a possessive hand on her breast. 'We will take an hour. No,' he kneaded at her, 'make it two hours. I need to . . . make some notes. Go on then!' Nathaniel, Oberon and Holly were ushered out of the building, closely followed by a nervous Adrian who had only the faintest clue what was about to happen on the bed on stage. He had tried to tell Max that props and scenery were only to be used for rehearsal purposes and had been threatened with the sack.

'Pub?' Nathaniel asked, hopefully. Oberon was obviously reluctant to see Julie so declined. Adrian gladly tagged along though, off to get a stiff drink. Holly decided to join them. It would be interesting to get another look at Julie, although she was worried the girl might recognise her from Saturday night. She suddenly remembered that her purse was in her coat in the auditorium. She rushed back to get it.

'Don't worry, won't be long,' she called behind her. She slipped back into the darkened auditorium, seeing that someone had put the sharp stage lights on. She was too late. Something had already started on stage. She got her coat and turned to go but was curious to see what these three got up to. Nikki was lying on her back between them on the bed, still wearing her short summer dress, which had been unbuttoned to the waist. Max on one side had a hand on her nipple and was kissing her deeply, his tongue playing with hers in a snake dance, sometimes sweeping across her face, sometimes duelling with hers. He ground himself against her hip. On the other side, Jeff had his hand down her knickers and his mouth clamped tightly to her other nipple. Holly could hear the familiar heavy breathing he always started up when he was getting excited. She had heard it a million times: his alarm call of passion. Sometimes he had started it when they were just kissing. It warned her that more was to come. Once upon a time that heavy breathing had been enough to flood her panties, wherever she was. But now it just seemed vaguely comical. He was rasping for England into Nikki's pert bust, gyrating against her. Her face was a picture of pleasure. A delicious smile spread on her face, like a little girl with a double helping of ice cream. She opened her legs to invite Jeff's fingers in. Holly wished he would pull her panties off so that she could get a good look. What was he doing? How many fingers were up her? As if reading her mind, he yanked the flimsy material down Nikki's legs and threw them off the bed. She giggled a bit at this and looked his way, transferring her deep, wide open-mouthed kisses to him and bringing her knees up so that Holly now had a fantastic view of her. She seemed to have shaved her pubes off, just leaving a tight, compact little smooth pudenda for Jeff's hands to explore.

Jeff did have clever fingers, Holly remembered. He

had easily made her come in the most inappropriate places. They had once gone on holiday with his family to Menorca and they had all gone into the sea to play with a beach ball. He had swum up behind her and given her a bear hug. Little did his whole family know that under the water his fingers were buried inside her, trembling in all the right places. She had caught the ball and chucked it back to Jeff's dad while his son was diddling about inside her bikini bottoms, setting her off like a firecracker. She had gone under when she came. A mouthful of sea, a pussyful of sea – it had been amazing. Now Nikki was responding with the same speed. Max, not to be left out, was suckling her breast, his hand resting on her knee. He slipped it up towards her crotch, and finding Jeff's already busy there, moved towards her buttocks. Jeff had four fingers jiggling about inside her and Max started poking inside her other hole. Soon they had both holes covered, a fingerful in each orifice. Nikki was that crimson colour again, her tongue going mad against Jeff's mouth. She was making little helpless noises. Max moved his mouth to her ear and started to whisper things – Holly strained to hear. Whatever they were they filled Nikki with naughty pleasure – she turned and kissed him again. Jeff was now freer to really concentrate on frigging her pussy. His hands vibrated feverishly inside her shaved cleft. Nikki came like that, her mouth glued to Max's, her body in spasm against Jeff. She let out a long, deep sigh. The men smiled to each other, sickeningly self-satisfied. Their fingers slipped free from their respective holes. Nikki lay, legs open, in the weakness of afterglow, catching her breath. Max slipped off the bed now. The rise of his cock was clear in his trousers. He was looking through his briefcase, getting out a small jar. Nikki looked surprised.

'What is it, Max?'

'You know, little one.'

'Don't worry.' Jeff laughed, and hugged her. He whispered into her hair, pulling her dress up over her hips.

He unzipped himself and pushed his trousers off, leaving his bottom half bare. His prick was familiar – not huge but nicely formed. Nikki automatically started to caress it. She certainly was obedient, Jeff would like that in her.

'We're going to have a Nikki sandwich.' She glanced back at Max who was spreading oil from the jar over his genitals, lubricating his cock. 'Nikki's going to love it.' Holly wasn't so sure. Max was better endowed than Jeff. If anyone was going to perform anal sex on Nikki, it would have been fairer for Jeff to be the one. Jeff had begged Holly for it enough times, and she had tried it, but never liked it much. It had hurt and felt odd. Her cunt had always felt left out and they had never done it for long. He had made her feel like a failure for not loving it. 'My exes all went mad for it,' he would sulk. Max was on the bed now. They turned Nikki on her side so that she faced Jeff and curled her top leg over Jeff's thigh to open her up a bit. Max's dick rammed up against her backside, impatient.

'Open yourself up for Max,' he said into her neck. 'Push down to let me in.' Jeff stroked her hair as Max held her open and slipped the head of his cock into her bottom. She gasped. 'Just a bit more, sweetheart. Relax.' He pushed a little, an inch further. Nikki's mouth opened in pain. She didn't look sure about it at all. The men took a moment to caress her body, Jeff sucking on her tits, Max flicking her clit. They were trying to warm her up like an engine, Holly thought, teasing her so she could take no more, revving her up. Max stabbed at her again, sinking further in. She let out a groan. Was it pleasure? 'Yes, baby. Be a good girl and take Max all the way in. Push down, baby.' He pushed again. 'Oh, you're so tight!' He was taking some pleasure for himself now, beginning to gently thrust. 'Love it, baby. Good girl.' She had her mouth and eyes wide open. Jeff kissed her.

'OK, Nikki.' That was Jeff. 'Ready for more fun?' He slid his hand between her legs to open her lips up.

'You're so wet! Look, Max.' He brought a gooey pair of fingers up to Max's face. This set Max off to thrust a bit harder. Jeff held the base of his penis and guided it into Nikki's pussy, having trouble because Max's movements were jerking her around. 'Wait a minute, mate.' Max paused, frustrated. Obviously they had yet to hone this technique down to a fine art. Jeff slipped inside her again, pushing his way up. Nikki cried out. She suddenly looked so small between these two hulking men. Holly was worried for her. She looked crushed and helpless. But she was there willingly. She was wrapping her leg around Jeff's hip and inviting him all the way in. The three of them were pushed up right against each other, Max and Jeff's feet constantly touching and their knees clashing. Did they not notice or just not care? Both men started to thrust carefully, slowly. Nikki was moaning. Holly was jealous of her – all that attention, all that cock inside her. Her two holes must be filled to the hilt, she thought, leaning against the back wall and rubbing herself. Nikki was panting and whimpering.

'Good girl,' Max was saying. 'Take us both in. Let us fuck you. You love it.'

'Yes,' she answered. 'Harder, please.' The men glanced at each other, smiling. They could let go a bit now. They both increased their pace, Jeff pumping harder than Max. Nikki was being jerked around between them like a rag doll but she seemed to love it. The pain must have given way to pleasure, Holly thought, remembering last night and the size of Granddaddy. She rubbed herself harder. They were like a six-legged beast on that bed, writhing, pumping, moaning, crying, jerking.

'Oh God.' Max was going to come soon.

'Wait! Don't stop!' Nikki cried, stepping up her breathing. They all went up a gear, Nikki starting to let out one long whine that shook with every thrust. 'Ooooh! Ooooh!' Jeff's hips went wild. He pushed his tummy into her, trying to push against her clit. Thoughtful of him, Holly thought. He was breathing in

182

his pre-climax mode now, deep grunting breaths, 'captain caveman' she used to call him. 'I want to come!' Nikki was whining. 'Ooooh!' The men could barely take it any more. Max pushed a hand round between Jeff and Nikki, finding her little button of pleasure. He obviously found it because she began to cry out even louder.

'Good girl, baby. Come for Max. Let it go for Max.' The whole street must be able to hear this, Holly thought, two men grunting and a woman screaming blue murder. They'd certainly be getting an audience if this was what everyone expected to see on stage. Jeff's belly slapped rhythmically against Max's hand, but they were both beyond caring. Jeff came first, suddenly losing it and making that final 'hrrrghhh' noise he did when he hit a particularly good orgasm. Holly could almost feel the hot shot of his come inside her. She began to strum harder on herself. Max was still going like a trouper, his hand dancing against Nikki's clit. Jeff didn't withdraw, but watched with renewed excitement as Nikki started to come.

'Fuck me! Fuck me harder!' she was shouting.

'Come on. Come on,' Max urged. 'Come on, you little tease. You little whore.' His cock was going wild inside her butt, his fingers never leaving her clit. She soon dissolved into a juddering, wailing orgasm. Max shot off into her bottom, thrusting hard with each jerking spasm, pushing her harder onto Jeff's wilting cock, filling her to the hilt. The threesome lay out of breath for some time. The men were still inside her, Nikki still moaning softly.

'That's the hardest I've ever come.' She beamed. Jeff ran his fingers through her hair. Holly saw from his expression that he must be hardening again. He always did have a short recovery period. He began a gentle pumping again with his hips. Nikki looked surprised, smiling up at him. 'Hello!' she gasped. 'You're so big again.' Holly wondered if Max could keep up with the younger man. Jeff had once come inside Holly five times in one night at the beginning of their relationship. He had been insatiable then. Sometimes, like now, he didn't even have to pull out before he started up again. He was very proud of that fact, she remembered; he had even bragged to her about it before they had ever made love. He was back in full thrust with Nikki now, and she welcomed the second coming. Max was looking very turned on, his cock still lodged up Nikki's behind.

'You want another go?' Max grinned at her. 'You know, I'll take a lot longer to come this time.'

'Me too,' Jeff said, thrusting hard. 'I can go on for hours like this now.' Nikki was flushed with anticipation. She had the glow of a woman with power over a man – or in this case, two men. They wanted her so much that they had stiffened again before their come had even dried.

'We've got some natural lubrication now,' Max said. 'It's hotter and wetter up there. I can fuck you harder.'

'Yes!' she gasped. 'Fill me up again!' Jeff kissed her hard on the mouth as his hips started off. Once again the three of them were jerking away like a six-legged monster. All three of them were insatiable.

'We've got another hour and a half.' Jeff grinned. 'Another hour and a half to fuck you, sweetheart. You'll be full of my come.' Nikki sighed, her face glowing.

'We'll make your little pussy and your little bottom quiver,' Max whispered. 'Would you like that?'

'Yes, please.' She wrapped her leg harder around Jeff's hips. Holly wondered at her stamina. She obviously felt safe with these two, safe enough to let go. Or maybe she was just so turned on by the situation, she didn't know when to stop. 'Fuck me,' she was saying, over and over again. 'Fuck me fuck me fuck me.' The pumping and grinding started up again in earnest now. It was more confident this time. There was no hurry.

Holly's fingers trembled as they made her come, and for a flash her imagination put her down there on that bed, being urged on to come by two men. She made a small noise as she climaxed. They didn't seem to hear her, too wrapped up in their own compulsive fucking. Holly thought she'd better make good her escape.

She picked up her coat and silently slipped out into the street, the cries of lust still audible from within. She walked across the shore to the pub, occasionally peering behind her. The woman from the larch wood played heavily on her mind. Whoever she was, she hated Holly enough to hide out in a forest and run back through its dark grotto to escape afterwards. Whoever it was must have somehow found out where Holly was going that night. Only Ben knew that, and she was sure he would do nothing to hurt her. It was, however, possible that he had told his mother where she was going out of concern. Did Delilah have that much venom in her?

The pub seemed like the best option now, a bit of normal conversation with Nathaniel and Adrian. Two steady guys and a pint of lager. Safety. She soon found them in a corner, Nathaniel dragging happily on a cigarette, Adrian doing the crossword.

'Drink anyone?' She smiled.

'How lovely.' Nathaniel seemed very pleased she had come. Obviously conversation with Adrian was limited. 'Mine's a brandy.'

'Just a Coke for me.' Adrian obviously felt he needed to keep his wits about him. Little did he know what was really going on back at the theatre.

Holly went to the bar and held a tenner up, trying to get some attention. It was full of local men on their lunch breaks, all pushing in before her. Finally Julie came over. She studied Holly's face intently.

'A brandy, a Coke and a G&T please.' Julie kept eyeing her as she poured the shots. Surely she couldn't recognise her from the party? Holly looked down.

'Ice and lemon? In the Coke.'

'Yes, I think so.'

'You're that friend of Oberon's, aren't you?' Julie said, taking her money.

'That's right.'

'You were in here the other night. Having a row with

185

that guy?' She must have meant when she stormed in after Jeff. Julie handed her the change and looked deeply into her face. 'Did he do that to you?'

'What? Oh!' Holly had almost forgotten about the bruise on her lip. 'No, no. That was just an accident.' She fingered it. The cut had risen up, the scab harder.

'Really?' She looked fiery. Holly thought she was about to go and offer to beat him up for her, which was quite a tempting idea if she thought about it.

'Really. It was some woman. Some mad stranger.' Holly took the drinks and sat down. She spoke with Nathaniel about familiar things: London, theatre, the weather – all safe and comforting. Back at work, she knew, Nikki was in the throes of mounting passion, all of them in a heap of hedonistic abandon. And somewhere on that hill was Joshua Delaney, getting on with his life, not thinking about her. But here, it was just a nice drink and pleasant conversation. She felt eyes on her and looked up. It was Julie, standing at the bar, watching her. Julie smiled. Holly felt that she was somehow on her side. She would remember that, if ever she needed a friend.

Chapter Nineteen

*T*he sound of Holly's mobile ringing startled her awake. It was a high-pitched, jolly song designed to penetrate any peace and at this time in the morning, it worked better than any alarm. She stumbled in the half-light to her bag. The clock on her bedside table said 07.30 in neon letters. She fell over her shoes, swearing, and eventually found the phone. She finally put the annoying noise to death with the flick of her finger.

'Yes?'

'Holly.' It was Josh's voice. She was stunned. A minute ago she had been asleep, dreaming about the man. What was he doing calling her at this ungodly hour. She sat on the bed. She had been trying to put him out of her head in the five days that had passed since their last meeting. She had tried everything, but it hadn't worked. Work, drink, sex with strange bikers, none of it had stopped the warm image of him from flooding her imagination every time she closed her eyes.

'Hi,' she said hoarsely. He wasn't very forthcoming about the reason for this ridiculously early call.

'Did I wake you?'

'It's OK.' She cleared her throat and rubbed the sleep from her eyes, wishing she could rub it from her voice.

She wanted her wits about her for a conversation with Josh.

'Listen. What time do you have to be at work?' Perhaps he was going to declare his love for her? 'It's important.'

'Eleven.'

'Can you come over?'

'I'll be round in half an hour.' She hung up. She staggered though the shower, trying not to disturb the Briars, and dressed in what she hoped were attractive clothes: tight jeans, cropped green T-shirt, boots. She brushed blusher on her cheeks and moistened her lips with gloss. No need to look as tired as she felt. She stood before the mirror – yes, she looked perfectly acceptable. It was amazing how quickly you could wake up, she thought, if the right person calls on you.

The beauty of morning really was wasted on the world, Holly mused, marching through the pinkish, optimistic glow of dawn. The air was so sharp, the sky so bright. She never normally saw this time of day. Her natural time to rise was about ten o'clock, later if she was performing in the evenings.

Joshua seemed to be waiting for her at the door. He hadn't made the same effort as Holly, still in his dressing gown, his hair a mess, his face pale and disquieted. Freud ran down the path to greet her, jumping up and wagging his tail demonstrably.

'Morning!' she called. 'This better be worth it, Joshua.' He didn't smile. He looked so drawn and pale – maybe the decision to declare himself to her had given him a sleepless night. She got to the door and smiled up at him, her heart full of fresh air and curiosity. 'Well?'

'Come in.' He looked at the trace of a bruise on her lip. She followed him through to the kitchen. He indicated for her to sit at the table and sat opposite her, his hands sweeping through his hair. He really should get that cut, Holly thought. Freud sat happily in his basket chewing on a rubber ball.

'Spit it out.' She was beginning to feel nervous. He didn't have the look of a man about to shout his love from the rooftops, more of a doctor about to tell you that you have a month to live.

'OK. This isn't an easy one.' He passed her a large brown envelope. It was opened. 'Have a look, I got it this morning.' Holly slowly looked inside, pulling out a ten by eight inch black and white photograph. At first she couldn't make it out, it was such a mass of activity. Then she saw it. It was of her, naked, black stilettos in the air, with Granddaddy bent over her. You could clearly see his cock sliding into her. People around were shiny black shapes, clapping, hollering, grinning. Her face was a picture of ecstasy, whorish lust. Her mask was on, her hair back, her mouth wide open. She looked different.

'How did you know it's me?' she asked, shamed. She could feel the tops of her cheeks burning.

'I didn't for sure. Until you just said it. But I had an idea.' Her eyes searched the photo. How must he have felt when he first received it? She tried to look at it with his eyes. She looked like a slut. She looked deranged. Eventually he took it away from her. He tore it up.

'My God,' she whispered. She put her face in her hands. 'That's me but it's not me.' He didn't say anything. She felt the need to explain herself to him – not as a therapist but as someone she cared about. 'I went there just out of curiosity really. I wanted to see what went on. I'd seen the gang on Friday night and they'd kind of taken the piss out of me. I just wanted to see if they would accept me as one of them. I didn't intend to . . .'

'What happened?'

'It was like an orgy. It was powerful. I got involved.' Her voice cracked. 'I went too far. I know. I'm sorry.'

'You don't need to apologise to me,' he replied hurriedly.

'Yes I do.' Her eyes met his. They were spoked with

189

gold in the morning light. He shifted, as if he felt she was trying to bewitch him.

'You said you would seek out pleasure if you couldn't get what you wanted from me, and you did.' He was so matter of fact, but she was sure there was pain in his eyes. He looked at a fragment of the photo. It was her foot flung over the old man's shoulder. 'This looks dangerous. This situation. You could have got hurt.'

'I know.'

'Did this man hit you?' he asked, indicating her swollen lip. 'Did they beat you up?' Now his voice trembled slightly.

'No. I was attacked by someone.'

'Who?'

'I have no idea.' She realised her life wasn't sounding particularly sorted. 'I keep getting hate mail from someone. I think it was her.'

'A woman?' He leaned forward. 'What does she look like?' Holly shrugged. What did that matter? It was only now she saw his worried face that she realised that she could be in real danger.

'I'm sure it's nothing to really be scared of,' she said. 'I just need to find out who it is. Whoever it is has had access to my address in London and my filofax. And she was there on Saturday night.' She suddenly had a thought. 'Hey! Who sent you this? Have you got spies on me?'

'No, I haven't.'

Holly considered the implications. 'Well? Who was it? Do you have friends in this little gang?'

'No,' he said, his voice loaded. 'That's what worries me the most. I'm somehow involved here.'

'I'm so stupid,' she whispered to herself. What had she been thinking? Running round some dark woodland in a catsuit with a weird group of sex-crazed bikers. She was mad. 'I just get curious sometimes. Especially when someone seems to think I'm a prude. That's like a challenge to me, Joshua. I'm not a prude.'

'I know you're not.' He smiled now, looking at a

square of the photo with her face on it – contorted with pleasure. 'It's evident.' She smiled too. 'Why would someone send me this, Holly?'

'To make you hate me?' She wondered after some thought. 'Do you hate me now?'

'No, I don't. But I am worried about you.' Holly was relieved. 'I don't know what worries me more – that you have someone trying to scare you on your tail, or that you let yourself get into this kind of situation.' He pointed to the photo. Holly looked at the writing on the envelope. It was the same neat, childish hand that had penned her hate mail.

'Well, whoever sent you this is the same person who keeps writing me little notes. The same person who attacked me, I'm sure.' He studied the writing.

'I don't know it. But looking at it, it could have been written with the left hand. It's so careful.' Holly leaned on the table. His hand was just inches from hers. She had the overwhelming desire to take it, fold it in hers, hold it to her cheek, kiss it. What was wrong with her?

'Who would want me to dislike you, Holly?' he asked.

She wished he would drop it now and look at her properly.

'I don't know. Maybe Jeff. Maybe Max. But the person who struck me was definitely female.' She loved the crumpled scruffiness of his dressing gown. His old dog-chewed slippers. 'Maybe they'll stop, now. Maybe this is what they wanted all along. I haven't had any trouble since Saturday.' He sighed, reluctant to let the matter rest. 'When you saw that photo,' she asked him tentatively, 'how *did* it make you feel?' He looked down. She braced herself.

'Honestly?'

'Honestly.'

'Rather ... envious.' She smiled in surprise. 'But, Holly, please don't make me regret saying that. I'm a red-blooded male. Obviously the sight of a beautiful woman having an orgasm is going to do things to me.' Beautiful? What things? Her mind raced with wanton images. She wondered what Josh's cock was like. When he masturbated, was he in bed or in the bath? Was he picturing her?

'Perhaps you shouldn't have torn it up?' she teased.

'Tearing up was the only thing to be done with it. That's not how our relationship is.'

'Look.' She felt like Nato negotiating with Russia whenever she embarked on a conversation about their relationship. 'What if you weren't my therapist? What if I fired you? Then would it be OK to think about me in that way? Would it be OK for me to want to kiss you all the frigging time?'

'No. I can't go running off with patients or ex-patients. Otherwise, all therapists would be getting in there with their prettiest clients and just saying they'd been fired.'

'I don't see the problem.'

'Holly,' he warned. Freud looked up and whimpered. This was obviously the same tone of voice he got when Josh was reprimanding him. 'The reason we got so intimate so quickly was because we talk about sex in our sessions. It's natural for you to associate me with sex, because you've been open with me in my professional capacity. Now, I'm not going to take advantage of that intimacy. That's abuse, and it's serious.' Holly wished he would seriously abuse her. Why did he have to be so bloody proper? 'I told you. I've made a mistake before and the consequences were huge. I've just got over it. I had to move away from London, I had to give up my practice. I made a big mistake. I learned my lesson, and however attractive the temptations to make the same mistake again, I am not going to change my mind.' He could be quite eloquent when he wanted to be, Holly noticed, but she was too hung up on the stuff about him finding her attractive and a temptation to really take in what he was saying. He pushed his chair back. That was obviously the end of the matter.

'OK,' she conceded. 'But I'm pretty pissed off with

192

this other woman, whoever she is, who got to have you when I don't.'

He smiled. 'You're not exactly short of offers.' He was right there. She would have to keep venting her passions on Ben and Caleb. But she hankered after the day she would wake up in Josh's house, in Josh's bed, in Josh's arms. She would make love to him very gently. She would suck him and kiss him and nuzzle him all over. They would bury themselves in the covers and laugh and eat and kiss all day. She sat in silence while these images twirled in her mind. From the pensive expression on Josh's face, maybe he was having the same wistful thoughts. He had practically admitted that he fancied her, at least. Unless he was just trying to let her down gently.

'Do you want some breakfast?' he asked, getting up to put the kettle on.

'As long as it's in the rule-book,' she retorted. 'I'll have toast and honey, if that's not breaking the Hippocratic oath.' He laughed.

'Quite the little comedian.' At least he was being affectionate now. Holly sat with Freud pretending to steal his rubber ball, hiding it behind her back, making him fight for it. It was funny, she noticed, that if she hid it from him and made it look like she really wanted it herself, he got crazy and was desperate to get it off her. But when she showed no interest in the toy, he lost interest too. Things were only as valuable as other people made them, she thought. Perhaps she had made Joshua too valuable, openly seeking out his approval. And maybe she should remind him how valuable some people made her.

'Can we have an impromptu session?' she asked suddenly. 'I've still got half an hour.'

'What, here?'

'Why not. Over brekkie. Relaxed.'

He looked reluctant. 'We should really go into my study,' he began, but then stopped himself. 'OK, no

more rules and regulations. What did you want to talk
about?'

As they ate their toast, Holly filled Josh in on Ben. She
explained how he had fixated on her, how his stepfather
had set her up as a learning tool for the boy's sexual
prowess. She described him caressing her to sleep, how
she had gone down on him in the fields. Josh listened
intently.

'I think he's in love with me,' she said. 'I feel a bit
responsible.'

'Well, you are responsible,' Josh said plainly. 'You
should obviously stop it now. Let him have a healthy
reciprocal relationship with someone who finds him
genuinely attractive.'

'Oh, but I do!' she cried. 'He's gorgeous. He's young,
but he's going to be a great lover. I like teaching him.'
She was pleased to see Josh looking mildly uncomfortable with that. 'He's very adoring. I've never had that
before. Jeff always made me think I should be grateful
to him.' Josh snorted. He had little time for Jeff from
what he had seen of him. 'But Ben's dad is also always
coming on to me. I've given in a couple of times, but
more out of frustration than lust for him. Although he
has a rough charm.'

'All very D. H. Lawrence.' There was an acidity in
Josh's voice.

'I suppose so. He does have some tenderness, but
with him it's mostly animal sex.' Was she making
herself more valuable, she wondered, or was she just
sounding like an arrogant slut? 'I mean, he was the one
who relieved me after you and I ... well, you remember.' He nodded quickly, looking down. 'I needed some
satisfaction and he gave it to me. It might not have been
the exact relief I wanted, but it made me feel loved.' He
looked at her sceptically. Yes, maybe that was going a
bit far. 'Or at least, made me feel like a woman.' That
was more realistic. 'He's very natural. No games. With

him what you see is what you get.' This was an obvious jibe at Joshua and he looked up sharply.

'I've been more than honest with you, Holly.' He almost looked hurt.

'I know,' she said softly. Why did she have the constant desire to make things better for him? She was supposed to be making him suffer.

'So where do the biker set all fit in to this scheme of things?' he asked, snapping back into an impersonal mode. She gave that some thought.

'Sometimes,' she replied, 'you just want to see how the other half live. The half that don't analyse and question everything, or live by the rules, who just follow their instincts like pack animals.' Again, he looked like he might be taking this personally. Good – she wasn't going to pander to it this time. 'I found that I liked it. I loved it, actually, as you saw on the photo. But it was a one-off. I couldn't live like that.'

'So, it was more of a fantasy?'

'Yes. One I lived out.' She looked into his eyes. If she just leaned across the table, she could brush that lock of hair away. She could slip her hand inside those warm pyjamas and stroke the curly hairs on his chest. 'Other ones will just have to remain as fantasies.' His eyes skimmed the curve of her breasts beneath her cropped T-shirt. The word 'angel' was spread across her chest. They flickered quickly back up to her face. The silver letters strained against the full swell and puckered slightly at the nipple.

'Yes,' he agreed.

Freud moaned when she got up to leave and followed them to the door with his tail between his legs.

'Yet another admirer,' Josh joked, indulgently.

'It's mutual.' Holly kissed the dog's snout and ruffled his golden head. When she bent over she made sure she did it in the most attractive way possible, long at the hip, round at the bottom.

'I don't know if you'd be available, but I've got to go

up to London next Monday night. I know it's not part of the therapist/client relationship . . .' He grinned. At least he could take the piss out of himself, Holly thought. 'But would you be interested in coming up here overnight to keep an eye on him. I don't like to leave him.' A chance to sleep in Joshua's bed, to wake up in his house, albeit without him there. The idea filled Holly with naughty delight. 'I mean, it's OK if you can't. It's just you are the only person in the village who doesn't set him off barking. He never keeps quiet with a stranger, otherwise I'd pay someone to keep and eye on him.' Freud looked at her perkily, knowing that he was somehow the subject up for discussion.

'Of course, I'd love to.' She tried not to sound too keen, in case he thought she was intending to take the opportunity to rifle through his drawers and masturbate on his bed. Which of course she was. Josh smiled in relief.

'Great. Sorted.' He opened the door for her. 'I'll call you to drop off some keys and explain what he eats and stuff.'

Holly didn't linger over goodbyes this time. That had always got her into trouble and looking foolish. She flicked her hair and strolled breezily down the hill. This time when she looked back, there he was, dog at heel, watching her go. Just as it should be.

Holly got to the theatre early. She changed into her long practice skirt and sat in the back watching Nikki go through her scene with Oberon. She played her part flirtatiously, with a girlish coyness that Max obviously adored. It was the kind of acting any woman in the audience would baulk at though – it was for men only. Oberon wasn't immune to it, Holly noticed.

At eleven it was time for her and Nathaniel to have the first stab at their scene. They went with some trepidation up onto the stage, aware that Max was about to subject them to some of his sexually explorative improvisation work.

'Finally, we come to this scene!' Max rubbed his hands together. 'Can you tell me why this is a great scene? An important scene?'

'Because it gets you off?' Holly heard Oberon mutter to himself in the auditorium. She sniggered.

'What is it, Dolores, that makes this a big scene for you?' He glared at Holly as if she was an imbecile. 'Come on!' he barked. He was back to his old tricks again. Max glanced at Jeff who was sitting in a box in the auditorium. 'For Christ's sake, have you no brains at all?' The heat was obviously back on her. Maybe the honeymoon period with Nikki was wearing off, leaving him grumpy again. Holly looked up at Jeff too. His face seemed to be urging Max on. 'How you ever work in this profession is beyond me, Miss Parker.' So, Jeff was back to making her life hell via Max, was he? Knowing the game, Holly felt that it had lost its threat. Just a sad old man being manipulated by a younger one to get at his ex-girlfriend. How pathetic.

'Why don't you tell us why it's such an important scene, Max? You're the font of all wisdom it seems,' she snapped, airily. 'And please don't talk to me like that. Even if it does score you brownie points with Jeff.' There was a stunned silence in the room. Holly didn't care. If she pushed it too far and Max lost his temper completely, she would simply expose the truth. What a powerful weapon the truth was! Just knowing that you had it loaded in your holster made you feel like you were top cowboy, ready to shoot. Max measured her up, just like a bandit at the OK Corral, eyes squinting. Obviously he wasn't ready for a duel just yet.

'It's important,' he began calmly, 'because it's the only scene in the play where she is not in charge. She's not "on top" as you say. She's following orders. Something you seem rather reluctant to do.'

He busied himself with setting up the scene, ordering people about and trying to look important. Nathaniel, as Lord Hunter, was to sit in the large, throne-like chair and teach Holly, as Dolores, the facts of life – except in

197

this scene the facts of life were how to hook in a man, how to tease him, how to turn him on. The scene was to end, Max said, with Holly curled in Nathaniel's lap being stroked to orgasm as a reward for being such a good pupil.

'You may use the dialogue for this one,' Max conceded, perhaps not wanting to inflame his leading actress again. 'It's not such a physical scene.'

'*My dear niece,*' Nathaniel began, entering the space with a foppish flourish, '*if you are to go fishing for suitors for your Mistress Rachel, you will have to find better bait than your more obvious charms.*' He came up to Holly sitting on the side of the bed and indicated her breasts. He cupped his hands over them. '*If you are to keep them interested, these womanly wiles of yours will soon become mere trifles to be won and discarded.*' He had the steady, authoritative presence of an experienced player, Holly thought. Totally in control.

'*My dear uncle,*' Holly replied, '*if my bait is not fine enough to keep the fish nibbling, you must tell me where I can purchase something more tempting. Although, I have not found the little fishes' mouths reluctant to gobble at these mere trifles, as you call them!*' Nathaniel sat back in the chair and indicated for Holly to get up. She stood before him obediently.

'*To begin, you must not let the man know that you are pursuing him. All men are hunters, my child, and need to know that they are the one firing Cupid's arrow, not being fired at. Make them believe they are chasing you! You must laugh when he entertains you, but look away before he does, as if in thought about some other lost love.*' He patted his knee and she sat down on the ground before him. He tapped her bottom with his walking cane. '*You must let him wonder about this wondrous posterior, but never see it.*'

'*Never?*' Nathaniel was caressing it with the hard shaft of his stick. '*But I have such a delightful posterior, Uncle. I have caught many a fish for my mistress with that fulsome bait.*' He gave her a resounding thwack on the buttock for this remark.

198

'It must be seen only when the fish is struggling helplessly in the net. It is your greatest asset. Do not use it prematurely. Bend over!' Holly got onto all fours, her bottom facing Nathaniel. 'Yes, most becoming, my dear. Like this my imagination is running wild with possibilities.' He lifted the edge of her practice skirt with the cane, exposing her bottom. He eyed it. 'Marvellous, my dear. This is the jewel in your crown. Only the most intrepid explorer must find it.' He flicked the skirt up so it fell over her back, leaving her bottom uncovered. He slowly guided the rod between her legs and played it over her panties, stroking her back and forth with its smooth cane. 'Ah yes, this other jewel. Ah, my dear niece, what a treasure you have hidden there. The small twinkling diamond of pleasure . . .' He pressed against her clitoris. Good aim, Holly thought happily. 'And the deep tight passage of liquid gold.' The end of the rod started to play around the entrance to her hollow, pressing against the white fabric of her panties. He pushed and it sank slightly into her. Nathaniel's experience clearly wasn't limited to on-stage antics. He sure knew his way around a woman's body.

'When a man is allowed a peek at these, my dear, be coy. Close your legs around his gaze and make it a forbidden vision. Then when the gates are finally opened to him, he will never want to leave his new palace of delight.' The rod eased up another inch. Yes, Holly thought, Dolores would like this, push it more. She widened her legs and bowed her head to the ground so that her bottom stuck up in the air. The rod was removed at this. 'Come sit on your uncle's knee, my dear.' She complied quickly, curling on his lap as she had seen Nikki do with Max. She glimpsed them in the auditorium, in that self-same position. Max had his hands slipped under Nikki's shirt, stimulating her breasts. Nikki's head was resting back on his shoulder, her half-open eyes watching the action on stage. Holly tried to mirror the pose – it looked sexy. Nathaniel buried his hand in her skirts. 'You learn well, my dear, but I fear you will always have the lusts of a whore. You must come to your uncle regularly, and he will relieve *you of your need for gratification.*' His hand found her knickers and pushed them to one side. He had obviously taken Max's rule about no faking to heart. Holly squirmed a little as his cold fingers melted into her warmth. *'Then you will not be pressing your jewels into the hands of any old stranger.'* The frigging started. Her skirts shook as his hand worked on her. *'Or let any suitor carry off your diamond on his tongue, for that is your weakness, niece, I know that well. It is easy to succumb to the delight of a tongue on your treasures.'*

Holly could feel the stiffness of his prick under her and moved so that it could spring up. She ground around in his lap to encourage it. Nikki wasn't the only one who could be a horny little bitch. Nathaniel's hand was persistent against her. She opened up to him but he didn't slip a finger inside her. Obviously he drew the line at that. Could they hear her squelching in the third row? *'But hold back, my dear, be the hunted. Be like a deer in the forest, running from the bow and arrow. Let him have you in his sights, desire you, win you. Even though you may want to impale yourself against his arrow or run onto the spear that will send you to a thousand little deaths.'*

God, his hand was going at her like crazy – how could he remember his lines at a time like this? Faster, Nathaniel, she thought, let's show them how it's done. Oh God, can I get this every night on stage? Can I lose it like this, let go in front of everyone, gush on his hand like I'm doing now?

Nikki was rising up and down on Max's lap in the third row, bouncing on his prick with the buoyancy of a blow-up doll. His hands were still fixed on her little tits, but his eyes were fixed on Holly.

'Come to your uncle whenever you need the fire to be quenched, my dear.' He was still saying the lines! Holly just wanted to scream. She felt the climax coming. Don't stop, she thought, keep going. *'I will impale you on my spear and shoot you with my arrow.'* Just as she was jerking out an orgasm on the word 'impale', he stuffed his fingers inside her. Her pussy clenched around them like

a hungry mouth sucking them in, foaming at the mouth, swallowing a climax. She gasped, jolting forward. No one would have heard his last line over her panting orgasm. She lounged in his lap and he stroked her softly. *'And when the deer is ripe to be hunted, I will release her into the forest. And she will do her best not to be caught.'* Was he still going? Holly felt his firm fingers on her tender clit. She couldn't listen to any more stuff about deer. *'But when the time is right, she will take the arrow and die with pleasure.'* It was her line, she knew, somewhere in her brain. His fingers were still on her, though, re-igniting her. She was more aware this time, a true exhibitionist, wanting to show what a fine climax she could have.

'What if my uncle is not here to dampen me . . .' No that wasn't right, *'To dampen the flame!'* Nice finger work, she thought. She would have to know her lines better than this if it was going to be like that on the night. She could see Nikki's blonde mop of curls shaking wildly – she was coming. Max growled an orgasm out, still watching the stage. *'I am a deer that will often be hunted, and I can take many arrows and many deaths, dear Uncle.'*

Jeff was watching steely-mouthed from his box. She let go a bit just to spite him, inviting Nathaniel's hand to press harder against her. There was another figure, she noticed, right at the back. Nathaniel was still con-tinuing with his lines and his handwork, but she wasn't listening. The figure was a man, sitting guiltily, slouch-ing down in the shadows. The messy shape of his hair was familiar. It was Joshua! She stared at him open-mouthed. Nathaniel was saying something about spears, his hand moving fast against her. She was coming again. She was going to show Josh how well she came. She opened her legs wide and pulled up her skirts, showing the humped shape of Nathaniel's hand vibrating against her. She kept her green eyes steadily fixed on Joshua. He couldn't leave now – she was watching him closely. Don't move, she thought. She was like a lioness circling her prey. If they ran she would be able to see them better. They knew to freeze, to be invisible. Josh was stuck there.

'*You're a delightful little fawn, of course the men will be aiming their arrows at you.*' Nathaniel was saying. His prick was hard against her thigh. '*Let your uncle take a shot at you sometimes, my dear.*' He went on, his voice rising with urgency. Holly stopped listening, her pussy awake with the knowledge Josh was there. This was the closest they had come to having sex, she thought, the most intimate. He had seen a still photo of her in action, well, here was the real thing. And he had sought her out, come to find her. He had crept in to catch a secret glimpse and got more than he bargained for. All the men in the room were hard at the sight of her – why shouldn't he be? Her green eyes dilated with shuddering joy. Watch me, Josh, watch how I come, she urged silently. This could be you up here, your lap, your hand. Oh God, she thought, go faster, go faster. When she came it was silent, but fierce, her eyes flashing like a cat's, her full red lips opening with pleasure. There was a silence. Josh stood up and left immediately, unnoticed. Holly wanted to go after him.

'*It's your line my dear.*' Nathaniel whispered. Holly came back to reality.

'Oh! Er . . .' Max gave her a pointed stare. '*My lord, my Mistress Rachel is coming – I hear her carriage on the gravel. Perhaps you will come again tomorrow to dampen the flame of my whorish lust, for there will be suitors arriving from foreign parts.*' If she ran she could reach him, find out why he came. Catch him while he still had the image of her coming emblazoned on his memory.

'*Suitors?*'

Holly sighed. She couldn't leave. She was at work, even though it didn't feel like work. And Max was glaring at her again.

'*A foreign Knight. And I am already anxious for the arrow to strike.*'

'*Then I shall visit in the morning.*'

'*Good day.*'

The scene finished. Max bounded up on stage, his trousers obviously stained and smeared. He paced the stage.

'If we are to do this right, Miss Parker, you will have to be able to think and come at the same time. Is this too much for your little head?'

'No.'

Jeff was leaning forward, grinning.

'Good. Because tomorrow we have a visitor and we will run the play for her. You all know you can do it with the safe eyes of your colleagues watching, but I wonder who will go to pieces with a foreign eye on the proceedings?' He looked at Holly in a way that let her know his wonderings didn't stretch much beyond her. 'It's about time we got some fresh input. Please be word perfect. I will not be happy with the kind of line-dropping Miss Parker has displayed today.' This was a strange sport, this Holly-baiting.

'Who's our audience?' Nathaniel tried to deflect the attention off her. His fingers were all gooey, she noticed. He hadn't made any attempt to clean them. Holly's mind slipped back to Joshua. She had an overwhelming urge to go after him.

'Our audience is my wife,' Max was saying. He looked momentarily proud. 'Lady Eleanor.' Nikki was pouting and sulking away in the stalls. Obviously she would have to be on her best behaviour tomorrow.

'Well, she's got to be a kind and tolerant soul,' Holly commented. 'I look forward to meeting her.'

Chapter Twenty

L ady Eleanor was poised, rather like royalty, in a box on stage left. She had somehow been furnished with a cup of tea in a bone china teacup and wore a blue floral dress. Holly suspected she was wearing white lace gloves, although she couldn't see. She had the slim, sexless frame of many an elegant lady, along with remarkable posture. Holly couldn't imagine what she was doing with Max. He seemed like a frantic Russian bear beside a cool, graceful English swan. Like royalty, the cast was not encouraged to talk with her before the run. The air was tense with the status of this new visitor. Holly and Oberon dropped their bags at the back of the theatre and sneaked off to the dressing rooms to have a bitch about her.

'Who does she think she is?' he hissed, giggling.

'I'm scared!' Holly felt a naughty hysteria come over her. 'What if she chops off my head?' They collapsed into laughter. 'Does she know what she's come to see?' Holly went on.

'Crikey. It'll be like doing it in front of the queen.' Oberon didn't relish the sexual scenes. 'I won't be able to get turned on with her staring at me.'

'Ah, remember. No faking,' Holly corrected him sternly. They suddenly heard Max's voice in the corridor and closed the door. They shushed each other like naughty school kids. He was talking to Jeff.

'You're letting her off too lightly,' Jeff was saying. His voice was quietly angry. 'It isn't much to ask that you go at her a bit harder. She's got to realise her weakness. That's the fucking point of all this.' Holly glanced at Oberon. Were they talking about her?

'Look, I've got a lot to think about, Jeff. Eleanor's here.' Max's voice was uncharacteristically timid.

'So?' There was a silence. 'Look, Max, Holly's got to realise how much she needs me. She's weak. It won't take much to break her.'

'Really?' Max spat. 'That's what you said at the beginning. But the therapy, the trust game, the shouting, it's all running like water off a duck's back.' Oberon was stunned. He looked at Holly for an explanation. He hadn't had an inkling what was going on but to Holly, this was just a final confirmation. 'She's tougher than you think,' Max was explaining.

'Bullshit. Get another therapist. One who'll play the game.'

'He's the only one here, you idiot.'

'Watch it.' They calmed down. Did Max say 'sorry'? Jeff whispered something inaudibly.

'He wouldn't be manipulated, I told you,' Max replied. 'He said he'd treat her, but only for her own good, not ours. I don't think it's helped your cause at all, Jeff. I think that's backfired. I couldn't find a bent therapist down here. It's not London, you know. Not everyone has a price.' So they had hired Joshua to try to weaken her. Of course he wouldn't be used as a tool against her! Holly wondered how much Josh knew of Max and Jeff's overall plan to bring her down.

'*You* have, though, Max, and I own you,' Jeff threatened. 'Do what you have to do.' They moved on, still talking, leaving Oberon and Holly to mull over what they'd heard.

'Bastards,' Oberon said eventually. 'So all those mind

205

games were just a way to drive you back into Jeff's arms after all?'

'Don't you worry, Oberon.' Holly smiled. 'It isn't going to work. Let's get the show on the road. I'll sort those two out later.'

They ran the play under Lady Eleanor's cool gaze, barely stumbling over lines, valiantly trying to stir up the sexual tensions. Holly had a fire in her belly after what she had overheard, and played her part with a raw passion that Max had to admire. Everyone else responded to her sparky energy, and by the end the performance was pretty rousing. When it had finished they all bowed to the slow, dull clap of the few people gathered in the auditorium – Max, Adrian and Eleanor. They were exhausted. All the actors congratulated each other and turned to Max for his approval. They weren't going to get it.

'That,' Max said, coming up onto the stage, 'was pure, unadulterated shit. You!' He stabbed a finger at Holly. She braced herself. 'What were you doing out there? You inadequate, prim, talentless . . .' The word he wanted escaped him. His head went red trying to find it. 'If it wasn't too late to fire you I would.' Holly looked up to Lady Eleanor, whose face registered no emotion. Not a drop of sympathy. She even seemed to be enjoying this spectacle. 'How you ever got into this profession amazes me. You have no passion, no fire, no heart!' He advanced on her. Was he going to hit her? Everyone was stunned, except for Jeff who looked like the cat who got the cream. Holly was cool too. She was waiting for her moment. If that moment happened in front of his wife, all the better. 'Only Nikki gave us anything to go on!' he bellowed. 'Nikki and Jeff,' he corrected. Holly saw his wife take this on board, raising a perfectly plucked eyebrow. He had inadvertently revealed his two favourites. Did Lady Eleanor know how intimate he got with his favourites?

'What exactly was wrong with my performance,

Max?' Holly wanted to bait him now, give him a spade so he could dig himself the biggest hole to stand in, give him enough rope to hang himself for good. 'I mean, most directors give you specifics, not just a load of old rant.'

'How dare you!' He lost it. 'Specifics, you want specifics.' Saliva shot from his mouth. He looked like a rabid dog, Holly thought. 'You stink! You give nothing! You're frigid from the start, weak, sad, pathetic. You fawn with Oberon, you are scared of Nikki, you are uptight with Jeff, you are laughable with Nathaniel, you will be the laughing stock of everyone who comes down here!' He picked up a chair and threw it across the room. 'You make everyone on stage look like amateurs.' Lady Eleanor was smiling slightly, her fingers at her lips – that was probably the raunchiest she ever got. Nathaniel and Oberon looked as if they were about to attack Max, Holly noticed. But she wanted this moment all to herself.

'You know, Max,' she gave her sweetest smile, 'I love the way you do this for Jeff. I really do. What a loyal friend you are.'

'I don't know what you're talking about.' He staggered a bit, unbalanced by her lack of emotion. She glanced up to Lady Eleanor.

'To put yourself out to be so awful to me, just so he can get his jollies from it. To make yourself look so foolish. All for friendship.' She went up to him. 'Anyone would think you had some kind of, I don't know, debt of gratitude to him.' Max sank back onto the bed on stage, mouth open. She could see the slow computer of his brain whirring behind his eyes, working out how much she knew, if anything.

'I don't know what you're talking about,' he repeated quietly. He looked at Jeff, panicking, then at his wife.

'I only know a few things. I know that Jeff thinks you're pathetic.' She smiled at her ex. 'Weren't those the words you used, sweetie. In that letter? You remember?'

He shifted on his feet. 'I've got it at my digs, Max, if you want to see it.'

'What's going on?' Nathaniel didn't like a scene and this was getting dangerously close to one.

'I'll tell you, shall I?' she said helpfully.

'No!' That was Jeff.

'Yes, I think I will,' she contradicted and turned to Nathaniel as if explaining it to him. 'Our director got into a spot of bother. In Northampton of all places. Tried to do a prostitute who was legally underage. Isn't that right, Jeff?'

'Shut up, you bitch.' Jeff made for her but Oberon restrained him.

'Not just yet, sweetie,' she said. He looked like a rabbit in the headlights. Max looked like one that had already met a nasty end under the wheels of a lorry – squirming on the bed, grimacing. 'He likes them young-looking. Doesn't he, Nikki?'

'Please.' Max was barely audible.

'Anyway,' she continued, 'Max got into some bother. This girl's big brothers did him over. Jeff saved him, like the hero he isn't. But it's really been a sad little tale of blackmail ever since, hasn't it, Jeff?'

'I would like to speak to my husband.' Lady Eleanor's cut-glass voice was icy as a glacier, calm as a lake. She was standing in the box. It was a summons.

'Of course,' Holly said. 'I think these things are better out in the open, don't you? Now Jeff can't control you like a puppet, Max, and I don't have to put up with this mindless abuse all the time. We can get on with the play and make it halfway decent. And your wife can keep an eye on you and your . . . strange desires.' She smiled up at the lady. 'I know a great sex therapist if you need one.'

'You poisonous cow,' Jeff spat, helplessly. He was livid, although he knew better than to struggle with Oberon. He turned to Max. 'She's lying, mate. I never told her that stuff.'

'How could you?' Max looked at Jeff like he was

208

going to cry, curling up on the bed. Holly almost felt sorry for him. He reminded her of the lion in *The Wizard of Oz*, who started out all fierce and blistering but was soon reduced to a quivering wreck. If he only had 'the nerve', she smiled to herself.

'I didn't tell her.'

'He only told me some of it, Max, to be fair.' Holly was all magnanimous. 'I'll show you the letter, if you want.' She couldn't wait to turn the knife. This was going to be the best bit. 'Mandy told me the rest. Remember Mandy, Jeff? She's great, actually. Only too willing to help me out. No time for you, apparently.' Jeff lurched forward, but Oberon quickly landed a sharp blow to his left cheek. He spiralled to the floor like a leaf in autumn.

'I've been wanting to do that for ages.' Oberon grinned.

'Me too,' Holly agreed. 'Greasy spoon, anyone?'

The cast, minus Jeff, arrived at the usual café buzzing with adrenalin from the morning's events. Max had dismissed them for the day, grim-faced at the idea of explaining himself to the frosty Lady Eleanor. Holly was grilled over her burger about how she knew all about Max, and she took great relish in describing her adventure in minute detail. At the end of the meal, she generously offered to foot the bill. The actors didn't put up much of a protest. She fished in her bag for her purse and opened it up. There was a strange black card in there.

'What's this?' They watched as she pulled it out. She didn't recognise it. In her heart she knew what it was.

'What does it say?' Nikki asked, peering at the silver lettering.

'It says: "You're dead." ' She swallowed the jolt of bile that rose in her throat. The card was passed around the group, who read it in grim silence.

'Is it some kind of joke?' Nikki gave a nervous laugh.

'No. No joke.' Holly kept swallowing.

'Well, it's Max obviously,' Nathaniel said. 'I'd take it to the police.'

'No. It isn't Max.' Holly stutteringly told them of the other hate mail she had received, and of the woman in the woods. They had clearly been wondering about her cut lip, most of them confessing they had feared that Jeff had beaten her up. She felt better for telling everyone, as if the group were a safety net to break an inevitable fall.

'Well, think, Holly,' Oberon said. 'Someone has your home address, access to your filofax, to your purse . . . it's got to narrow it down.'

'Where did you leave your bag today?' Nikki asked. Holly thought – it had been lying by the door. Anyone could have slipped into the auditorium if they wanted to enough and put it in her purse. Her filofax was always in her bag too.

'I wasn't careful enough, basically,' Holly conceded.

'Could the woman have been Lady Eleanor?' Nikki asked, wide-eyed and excited, as if playing *Cluedo*. 'Was she the right height?'

'Maybe.' If Eleanor had been wildly angry, Holly imagined, she would probably be capable of all kinds of cruelty. 'Why, though?'

'Why would anyone want to scare you, Holly?' Oberon asked. 'Or hurt you, even?' It was a very good question.

Chapter Twenty-One

*S*he didn't know why she was walking to Josh's house. It was like a compulsion. The thrill of her confrontation with Max was subsiding like a tide going out, leaving all the worms and debris and seaweed to deal with. She felt like her mind was a long beach troubled with everything that had been washed up on the shore. Josh was always reminding her that he was her therapist – well, she was going to use him as one. The black card cut into her hand as she held it tightly in her fist. The pain made her feel alive. She concentrated on that as she climbed up the hill to his house. If she kept her mind on the corners cutting into her hand, maybe she wouldn't dwell on all the other things.

He opened the door wearing nothing but a towel and a look of surprise. His face was half foamed up with shaving cream and his shoulders glistened with water. For a moment her heart dropped like a brick. He must have a woman in there – why else would he be getting washed in the middle of the afternoon. His body was firmer and more toned than Holly had imagined – and she had spent some time imagining it. He was tanned, broad. It had the glow of someone who had just had a lot of sex. She tried to look at his face.

'I didn't expect you.' He looked confused.

'Sorry.' He waved her into the house. 'Is this a bad time?' Say no, say no, she thought. She listened for sounds of a woman in the bedroom, sniffed for a sweet smell in the air.

'No, I had a late night.' His eyes were dark. 'Well, a sleepless one actually.'

'Oh, no.' Holly was dismayed. Either he meant that he'd been making love all night, or that he'd had insomnia. She could see it was the latter. 'Shall I knock you up some breakfast?' she offered. He thought for a moment. He looked vulnerable.

'I'd like that, actually. You know where everything is.' He turned to go up the stairs. 'I'll just cover my modesty.'

She felt a little bit like she was auditioning to be his wife, trying not to burn the eggs, trying to scoop the coffee grounds out of his cup. She had never been much good in the kitchen. Well, not much good at cooking anyway. Freud watched her clumsily scrabbling around the kitchen with amusement in his big black eyes. She slipped him the odd corner of toast to keep him happy.

'Tell your daddy to give me a chance,' she said to him, popping a bite of peanut butter on toast in his mouth. Joshua chose that moment to come in. She couldn't tell if he had heard her – he was the model of discretion if he did. He came and sat down looking younger and fresh-faced after his shave, pulling the plate of food towards him.

'Thanks, Holly. It's nice to have someone to look after you.' He took a sip of the coffee and choked on it slightly. 'Did you do this in the cafetière?' She nodded.

'Was I ... not supposed to?' He laughed and shook his head.

'It's fine. Just – next time do it in the filter!' He valiantly drank another slug. Next time, he had said 'next time'! Holly tried not to read anything into it – it was a slip of the tongue, a manner of speech.

'So, why didn't you sleep? Funny noises again?' She poured herself a generous glass of orange juice and leaned against the kitchen counter in what she hoped was a casually seductive pose. He chewed on an egg (obviously a bit overdone, she realised) without answering. He avoided her eye.

'There were a few noises, actually. No more than usual.' He dismissed the subject quickly. 'How are you, anyway? How's the play? Not long now, is it?' She gave him a potted version of the morning's events, which he listened to with intent admiration, laughing at her description of Max's downfall.

'I always thought he was a bit of a tosser,' he said, shaking his head. 'A very strange man to deal with.'

'I think he'll be subdued from now on.' Holly smiled back. She was rather proud of herself now that she recounted the story to Joshua. It made her sound rather heroic and feisty. 'Too late to sack me. Too late to cancel the show. He'll just have to put up with me.' He nodded and smiled, tearing his bacon with his knife.

'What have you done with this bacon? Boiled it?' He obviously found this wildly funny and fed the whole thing to Freud with a big grin on his face.

'Well, at least you look a bit less serious than when I got here,' she said shirtily. She hadn't had to make him his sodding breakfast, she thought.

'Yeah, I am.' He carried on laughing in the way only a man who's had no sleep can. Freud wagged his tail at his master's uncharacteristic hysterics. 'Go easy on that bacon, Freud. Don't want indigestion, eh!' Holly took a long drink of her juice. She knew how to shut him up.

'I had another one of those poisoned letters,' she said abruptly. 'A poisoned card this time.' He stopped laughing and looked up at her. The colour drained from his face. She got it out of her pocket and put it on the table in front of him. He looked more worried than even she had been.

'Christ, Holly,' he said quietly. The silence sat around them until she couldn't bear it.

'Oh, come on, this is making me even more bloody nervous!' she cried eventually. She wanted to make light of it, to laugh about it until it went away, but his face told her it wasn't going to go away. Why did he have to take all the serious things so seriously?

'Will you go the police?' This seemed to be the standard advice; maybe she should take it. Holly was just a bit embarrassed to go to some country plod with a load of childish hate letters. *I hate you, I'm watching you, I'm behind you, You're dead.* It was a pretty chilling commentary.

'Should I? I should have kept the first letter. I screwed it up in the taxi.' She trawled through her mind for the lingo of all those cop serials she'd sat through. 'That was vital evidence.' She took the card and carefully slipped it back into her purse. It had the colouring and gilt of a greetings card. 'At least they made an effort this time,' she joked. 'Last time it was really scruffy. You've got to have standards.'

He wasn't laughing. She walked over to him and stood behind him. His shirt was thick blue cotton. His hair (it so needed cutting) was brushing the back of his collar, thick and chestnut. He was compellingly touchable. She gently massaged his shoulders, just as a friend would do, she hoped. He was tense. It was just lovely to touch him, to feel him release under her expert hands and sigh when the first wave of relaxation hit him. She expected him to make her stop at any minute, but he didn't. He bowed his head and leaned back instead – an invitation to go on. She teased out the muscles in his neck – a fine, sturdy neck she noticed – and pushed out the knots in between his shoulder blades. Then she squeezed with open hands. She couldn't resist it. She brought her fingers to his temples and slowly combed them through his thick hair. His head fell back against her chest, a lovely pillow. His upside-down face was irresistible. She caressed his forehead and played with the curls at his cheek. He wasn't struggling! Holly steered the massage away from the medical and into the erotic. Being allowed to touch him at all had made her tingle, and the back of his head buried in her cleavage

214

was divine. She pushed her breasts forward so he couldn't ignore them, cupping his face and running her thumb tenderly along the thick line of his lip. His eyes were closed. She supported his head with her hand as she slipped beside him and knelt on the floor. His face, like the sleeping face of a child, needed to be kissed. She leaned forward slowly and took a soft, tender taste of his mouth. It was like sucking a strawberry. She kissed again. His response was subtle, dreamy. She took his hand and placed it over her jersey top on her full breast. Her nipple puckered tightly with gratitude.

'I saw you,' she murmured. 'In the theatre, watching me.' Little kisses on his lips, little kisses on his eyelids. His hand came to life and started to caress her breast. She sighed. 'I loved it when you were watching me, Josh.' He kissed her then, scooping her towards him and eating her mouth like hungry man with a ripe peach. He sighed full of relief, the way men do when they know it's finally going to happen. Stars seemed to fall off her tongue when he kissed her. His eyes were closed all the time. Maybe if he didn't open them, then it wouldn't be like it was happening.

Holly broke away first. Her body was melting into her panties like an ice-cream suddenly blasted by the sun. She had to be licked up soon before she was pure liquid. She leaned into his knees, her breasts resting on them like offerings on a plate. He opened his eyes for the first time, dousing her in blue.

'I couldn't sleep because I was thinking about you, Holly,' he said. She looked up at him, her hand on his thigh. Oh, keep talking, she thought, slipping her fingers between his legs, keep talking. 'I couldn't get the image out of my head.' With a heavy sigh she came into contact with the promising shape of his erection. She wanted to straddle him now and take it inside her, but he was like a nervous horse being coaxed into a warm barn. He wanted to go, but wasn't to be forced.

'You like watching me?' She parted his legs and crawled between them, kneeling up between his thighs.

She pressed forward, and started to suck and kiss at his neck. He tasted delicious, clean, salty, heady. He moaned and bent his head, finding her mouth, kissing her deep and long again. They ground their bodies together, his hands finding her breasts. He let out a strange gasp of excitement at their wonderful size and shape, the magic points of her nipples. She pushed into his palms. She wanted him so badly, her body was going to implode with need. Her pussy dry-humped the air, jealous of her breasts getting all the attention. Touch me, touch me, she wanted to scream, push yourself into me. They were as tight into each other as they could go in this position, but Holly was frantic for more. If she didn't take this chance, maybe the fear would come for him again and he would hold back. If he made love to her now, then she knew she would have him. She rose to her feet and positioned herself over him, sinking onto his lap with a leg on either side, her skirt rising. This way she had the feel of his hard shaft exactly where she wanted it, pressing through the fabric of his trousers into the centre of her panties. They stared at each other intensely as she began to rock against him. Her mouth was open, her pussy was open, her eyes were open, all of her ready to take him inside.

'I was thinking about you all night,' he breathed. 'This just feels like part of the dream.' His hands scanned her bottom possessively, holding it, controlling its pulse. She moaned into his ear, nibbling a little as she liked to be nibbled. He would find that out about her soon, she thought as her hips drove harder, all the little things she loved. He would gently tongue her ear, lovingly suck her toes, tease an orgasm out of her pussy with his mouth, let her suck his cock with his hands in her hair, flick his tongue against her nipple, tell her all the dirty things he wanted to do to her, watch her as she masturbated, come in her face – oh, they were going to have a great time. She shivered against him, constantly on the brink of coming. She reached down to open his fly and release his cock. His eyes came into sharp focus.

'No!' he said suddenly. He pushed his chair back and shoved her hard off his lap. She fell back against the table and clutched her shoulder where she felt a bruise spreading. She was sprawled on the floor, stunned. He was backing off. She had lost him. 'God, this can't happen, it can't.' He got up and adjusted his clothes. 'Holly, I'm sorry.' Her heart sank, she wanted to scream, she wanted to come, she wanted to hit him. 'I've told you, it's impossible.'

'Why?' she was wailing. Everything hurt so much, her shoulder, her pride, her heart.

'I made a promise to myself . . . after last time . . .' He clutched at his hair, leaning against the far wall for support. She sat up on her ankles.

'What was so awful last time?' The emotion shook her voice. 'What was so fucking bad that you have to keep doing this to me?'

'God. Where do I start? The only good thing that came out of that episode, Holly, was Freud. This woman, this patient, she was the one who gave me Freud.' He indicated the dog, who was sitting alert in his basket, baffled and blinking at the high emotion in the room, ears pricking up at his name. 'Her name was Maria Kelly. She used to come to me for sexual problems. She was frigid with her husband. She was a disturbed individual.' He sighed. 'We were attracted to each other. She thought I was the answer to her prayers, she knew she wouldn't be frigid with me. I was flattered into thinking that it was love, that I was some kind of saviour. I was an arrogant, vain shit.'

'I don't think you're my "saviour", Josh!' Holly was indignant. How could he compare her with some mad, frigid woman. She was his equal.

'I know, I know!' He sank onto a chair. 'We had an affair. It was amazing. She found she could come with me. For a while it was great. Then she got fixated. She got mad. She started talking about bumping off her husband.' Was he really comparing her to this lunatic? 'One day, I read in the local rag that he had died. The brakes had failed in his car.' He trailed off. He buried his head in his hands. Was she allowed to go over and comfort him? She got up and went to him. She poured her arms around him and felt him shaking. 'She insisted it was an accident, but I don't think it was.' He continued quietly, 'When I refused to see her again, she reported me, shamed me, had me struck off. She stalked me for a while, but it stopped when I moved down here. She couldn't trace me then. That's the whole reason I hide away in this tiny place.' Holly squeezed him.

'I'm not her,' she said. 'I don't see you as a therapist, a saviour, or even the answer to my prayers. You're just Joshua. Joshua Delaney.' She held him for a while. 'I'd like to know you better, that's all.' He fell back onto the chair and pulled her onto his lap and they began to kiss again. It was comforting. He held her as tight as a drowning man holding on to a raft. His hands moved over her body as if trying to find some flaw, some dark force, some indication that she was going to hurt him as he had been hurt before. All he found was pleasure. She pulled her top over her head, her naked breasts bouncing free. She brought his mouth down to her nipple and he suckled her. It was soothing to both of them. Holly sighed as he nursed, stroking his hair, feeling safe. She had wanted his mouth on her for so long, and it was as warm and gentle as she had imagined. His handsome face was intent at her breast, sending shimmering darts of pleasure to all the nerve endings in her body. He began to lick and nibble at her. His vulnerability again gave way to lust. She sighed, desperate for him to let go. He couldn't keep blowing hot and cold, at some point he would have to stay on hot. His hands grasped her bottom again, slipped over her thighs, finally – ah, finally – sinking between her legs, urgently pushing her skirt aside and edging under the fabric of her panties. 'Yes,' she urged as his fingers dissolved into her. He moaned, sucking passionately at her breast. This time she was going to climax quickly. It was as if her body didn't trust him not to change his mind again. The pleasure mounted within her.

'I've been so jealous. Jealous of the men who are allowed to do this to you.' He sighed darkly into her neck. 'The men who have tasted you, made love to you. Even the man who had sex with you at the station all those years ago; even he tormented me for days.' She smiled, his words sending creamy delight down her thighs. 'That boy, that Ben, God, I would have loved for you to be my first. For you to take me in your mouth. Oh!' His fingers greedily explored her pussy, whipping her wet pleasure into stiff peaks. His words were like a tongue in her ear. 'Holly, don't ever think I haven't wanted to, because I have.' She sighed and sighed and came all over his hand. She turned to face him in his lap, dying to kiss him, suck him, fuck him, whatever. 'But, I don't think I can do this,' he said sadly. 'I don't think this can go any further.'

The slope was easy to run down, especially with anger in her feet. She pulled her clothes straight as she went, her bag dragging along the ground. She had slapped him, she remembered that, she had seen red. She had felt like a tornado, and now here she was, twisting her way to find Ben, or Caleb, or Granddaddy. Any man. Josh was jealous, was he? Good. She'd make him so jealous he couldn't contain it any more. He was running after her. But he was tired and frustrated and even sadder than she was. He couldn't keep up.

She reached the shore under the cliffs of Joshua's house and saw Ben drinking beers with some of his mates. She recognised George, the Italian-looking one from the dance, and there were two others; she hadn't seen them before. They were laughing, boards under their arms, sea in their hair. They'd do. She looked up and saw Josh's figure on the edge of the cliffs watching her. He had a bird's-eye view.

She ran up to Ben and grabbed his arm. He smiled broadly and started to introduce her to the group.

219

'Hi, guys,' she said before he had finished. 'Ben, ready for lesson four?' She pulled him away, down to the sea front, over a ridge of rock, away from the tourists and the school kids skiving. He was hard by the time they got there, he was pretty much hard every time he was in her presence. She pulled her top up to expose her breasts, still swollen and blushing from their recent excitement. He fell on his knees before her and sucked on them gratefully. The other boys had followed gingerly and were peering over the rock. Ben started to show off – he kissed down her body, yanked her skirt off her hips. Her panties came down with it. She kicked the clothes impatiently off her feet, her sandals flying into the sea. She didn't care. She opened her legs to him and stood naked and shivering as he hungrily lapped at her, holding her round arse and sucking out her juice like a watermelon. He was very excited, he could feel she was sopping wet. He didn't know another man had got her like that; he thought it was all his own doing. Just that thought made him ready to come. She grabbed his head to steady herself.

She could still see Josh up on the cliffs, watching her. She hoped he would suffer. He'd made her suffer. He'd told her enough to make her let herself go in his lap. She'd let him put his fingers inside her, thinking that was just the beginning. But he'd known all along that it was the end. Ben's tongue was slithering up inside her now, her gush was pouring down his cheeks, his neck. The other boys were leaping over the rock-face, getting in on the action. She pulled one in to her bosom and let him have a suck on it. Why not? She was so horny she'd fuck every one of them. They all thought all their Christmases had come at once. Another boy was attached to her other breast now. The fourth boy, George, stood before her, watching intently. Ben's tongue was magnificent. Her knees buckled, she collapsed onto the sand, coming, coming. Ben pulled off his trunks and climbed on top of her.

'Can I?' he asked.

'Yes yes yes,' she moaned into his hair. His prick was long, rubbery, eager. When it sank into her he groaned as if he was going to come. He wasn't going to last long. The other boys knelt at her side, watching Ben's cock dive in and out, in and out. Holly's body closed happily around it, finally something inside her, something passionate. She wrapped her legs around his hips and clasped him to her. He nearly came at this. He was ready to go off like a rocket. His thrusting was erratic, desperate, his pubic bone was pounding against her clit. She opened her legs into a wide V, her feet in the air. 'Yes yes yes yes yes.' George and another boy, a dark one with longish black hair, grabbed at her ankles and pulled them back, opening her even wider. The fourth boy ran round to see her open rosebud and her hungry sex.

'God, look at this!' he cried, wanking over his shorts. 'Her pussy's fantastic!' Ben's balls were bashing against her bottom. She stared to cry out in climax. 'She's fucking gushing down there!' the boy shouted. 'He's in all the way. He's going to fucking rip her open!' Ben couldn't take it any more. He heaved his semen into her in five massive violent thrusts. She was on the brink of coming each time.

'Don't slip out!' she begged, grabbing his buttocks, pushing his body against her, urging his weight over her clit, squirming, wriggling as his cock diminished inside her. She couldn't get it. She was exasperated. 'Someone, please.' The guy with long dark hair pushed Ben off and climbed on top of her. Ben didn't like this but was weak after his orgasm and just lay there watching. The boy took his place and sank easily inside her. He resumed thrusting at exactly the frantic pace Ben had finished off. Ben lay beside her, stroking her hair as if nursing her through an ordeal. The tide had started to roll in – Holly felt the occasional cool bath of a salty wave pull at her hair. Her ears trickled with sand and sea. This boy's penis was small but as fast as a bullet. She let her legs fall open and enjoyed the hammering pressure on her clit, although her pussy ached for more. She glanced at the other two boys' crotches. George wasn't well-endowed, but the other boy, the talker, seemed to have a healthy package.

'You're next,' she mouthed to him. He grinned in delight. Josh was still watching, a statue on the hill, but this wasn't for him any more. This was for her. The long-haired boy was grimacing and sweating over her, pounding away, trying feverishly to make his cock fill her, failing. Her pussy was contracting against him, needing an orgasm badly. He felt the grip of her muscles and suddenly came, overwhelmed. That was the problem with young men and virgins, she was realising, it was all too much for them. He grunted and yelled at her throat, pouring so much come inside her that she thought his balls would implode. Her pussy happily drank it all up, hot and sticky.

'My turn,' the well-endowed boy was saying. He had whipped his shorts off, and the cock in question hung heavy and engorged in front of him, like a heat-seeking missile, like a stud horse's dick sniffing out his mare. It was too big for his body, she saw, opening her legs delightedly. 'No, I want you doggy,' he said.

'Frank!' Ben was ready to valiantly defend her, but she was already eagerly scrabbling onto all fours. Her pussy opened up in the guy's face, pouting, sulking, wanting satisfaction. He took a sneaky lick at it, probably tasting the other guys' come, but not caring. His tongue snuffled around, finding the nub of her clit. He lapped at it. She groaned long and deep. He giggled.

'It bloody works!' he shouted to the others. He positioned himself over her, pushing her head down to rest on the sand, her arse in the air. He had trouble finding the hole. The bulbous head of his young prick stabbed at her lips, her arse, the space between her legs. Eventually, sighing in exasperation, she reached round and guided it in.

'Oh. Yes!' he moaned as it sank in slowly. Her pussy was tighter in this position, and he was wide. Holly felt like she was being slowly entered by a donkey. He pushed a little more, sliding up a few inches. 'Oh sweet Jesus. Oh God. Oh, she's a wet bitch.' The sand moulded itself to her cheek as her face was pushed down. This guy was a real talker. 'I'm fucking her, the dirty bitch. She's so tight. Christ!' He was obviously a fan of porn films, or telephone sex lines. He shoved his way up to the top of her pussy, until she was impaled on his hugeness. 'My balls are right up against her crack.' He began to fuck her then, slowly, earnestly. George, who hadn't had a turn, came to sit next to the humping pair, his envious eyes fixed on her body. He had opened his fly and was massaging his cock, the black hairs of his bush a perfect backdrop for his weeping head. He looked a little forlorn. What a waste of a spare cock.

'Come here,' Holly panted. 'Lie in front of me.' She positioned him so that his crotch was at her head. She lifted herself up on her arms, and lowered her face to his shaft. All eyes were on her as she lovingly popped its excited head into her mouth and began to give the boy the blowjob of his life. Now both ends were occupied, she sighed contentedly. The long-haired boy was fiddling with her nipple as it hung beneath her, trying to get in on the action again, his little penis desperate to be sucked like a lolly. Ben was just watching, jealous and proud. Holly felt the big cock inside her pumping harder as she sucked and licked feverishly at George's prick. She wanted a splash of his excitement on her face. Her pussy wanted to come with this large cock inside it. She wanted to satisfy all of them.

'Oh, she's a horny bitch,' the talker was saying as he fucked her harder. 'Oh, she's a whore. She's a dirty whore.' Her pussy twitched and spat in response. She bore down on his cock, inviting him to go harder. He became more aggressive. 'She's sucking and fucking like a fucking whore!' She was, she loved it. The harder thrusts forced her head down further onto George's erection. His penis hit the back of her throat. Both her orifices were filled to the hilt with juicy cocks! She wriggled and moaned in delight, a human kebab sizzling and sweating. The hands at her breasts were getting rougher; obviously the long-haired boy thought she deserved harsher treatment. He grabbed and kneaded at her.

'Suck them!' she ordered, letting go of George's prick for a moment. 'Suck my tits.' He eagerly shuffled underneath her and stuffed a boob in his mouth, inexpertly sucking away, practically suffocating every time she was thrust into and bore down on him. He had a great view of his mates being sucked and fucked by Holly; his eyes darted up and down taking it all in. She was worried that the talker was going to come and leave her stranded again – he had gone awfully quiet and his cock was like a piston inside her. She pulled her mouth off George and begged Ben to touch her.

'Where? Where, Holly?' He jumped up.

'Find my clit and rub it, please. I really want to come! Please hurry!' He sat beside her and buried his hand under her pussy, rummaging around in the mushy heat.

'Watch it!' The talker grunted as Ben accidentally touched the base of his prick.

'Higher,' Holly said.

'Please suck me again,' George whined, having to rub at his own dick for a moment. She felt a bit like a kindergarten mistress. The mouth at her nipple was getting more experienced, though, lapping and nibbling like a real pro, sucking a little too hard, but he'd learn. Ben hit the spot.

'I feel it!' he breathed, wondrously.

'Ah! Gently rub it.' He was too gentle, too slow. The thrusting inside her was getting frantic. 'No, faster, side to side.' He was like Aladdin rubbing for the genie of the lamp then, vigorous but respectful. It was a huge responsibility. He was the one who was going to make her orgasm. She returned to George's needy prick, suckling with gusto. He groaned at her hot wet mouth. All five of them were intent and concentrating, now, emitting only the occasional groan or whimper or sigh. It was a carnal carnival and her body was the main attraction. The talker was fucking her hard, holding onto her hips and forcing her back onto him. Ben's hand was working its unselfish magic on her clit. The long-haired boy was flicking his tongue against one breast and his fingers lightly against another, sending sparks of joy between nipple and clit, clit and pussy, pussy and mouth – which was happily sucking young George dry. Holly felt the climax start to rumble through her loins. She moaned and cried with her mouth full of cock, ramming her hips back against the talker.

'Oh, fuck. I'm going to fucking come,' he cried. 'That bitch is going to make me come.' He thrust manically inside her, Ben mirroring the speed of his hips, his hand tired and cramping up. 'I'm going to fucking come up her cunt. Her sopping cunt!' And he started to jolt and jerk uncontrollably. Holly pushed back and let Ben's fingers whip her into a shuddering orgasm, her pussy, her clit, her nipples, her mouth alive and on fire. She gave a muffled wail and grunted, gagged by George's penis. It was all too much for the boy. He filled her mouth with his hot, bitter semen. Her pussy and her throat drank come at the same time, swallowing, contracting, sighing, trembling. She was flailing about like a fish on a line. She was exploding. She contracted onto all the foreign bodies inside her. She yelled and grunted like an animal. When her orgasm subsided, Ben slowed down his hand, eventually pulling it away and sniffing at its musky glue. All five of them lay groaning and sweating in the sand. Holly lay back, legs wide, her pussy dripping with semen. The sea washed at the crown of her head.

'Look at that cunt.' The talker was amazed at her. 'It's like an oyster shell.' He fingered her sex softly, circling the small, engorged bump of her clit. 'With a lovely pearl inside.' He was waxing all lyrical now, Holly smiled to herself, now that he'd come. Ben lay next to her, hugging her to him. George, feeling left out again, lay on the other side, thankfully kissing her ears. Long-haired boy and the talker knelt before her, taking in her body, better than any porn mag. She opened up her oyster up to give them a better view. Come poured out of her like sea water from a shell.

'Beautiful cunt,' the talker said, leaning forward and giving her a lick. He lapped at her pussy like a cat at cream. She sighed. Her body was on a loop of climaxes now; she seemed to come and come, like the waves of the sea, not crashing and dramatic any more, just rolling in. His tongue was soft and tireless. 'Delicious cunt,' he murmured, swallowing yet another of her orgasms. 'Nice tits too.'

On the hill, Josh was still frozen to the spot. He was probably disgusted and aroused at the same time, Holly imagined. He never seemed to know his own mind. He was hard, she was sure, as she lay there letting the talker's tongue tease her over and over again. Josh must regret that he had turned her on then sent her into the arms of four young men who all willingly had their way with her. He would go back and masturbate about it, think about it, dream about it. He would lose sleep over it. But he would never do it. Holly drew her knees together and kissed Ben sweetly on the lips.

'Thanks, my darling,' she said.

'Can we go again?' the talker asked, still hovering at her hips. Four young pricks sprang up in agreement. 'I want to fuck you up the arse.' His hand searched out her pearl again. She opened her trembling legs and let him play with it for a while. He fell silent. The sea whooshed in and filled her ears.

'Another time.' She sat up. 'Ben, will you walk me home?' she asked and they kissed again. He was eminently kissable. They got up and dressed themselves. Holly had water streaming down her neck, clinging to her breasts. The other boys eyed Ben enviously. Her shoes were bobbing about in the ocean, she noticed, laughing. Ben was all for diving in and getting them for her, but she refused.

'I like going barefoot,' she said. The ground was still

warm from the heat of the day, lovely sand trickling between her toes. Ben and Holly started to walk along the shore, leaving the boys to brag about their adventure.

'If Mum and Caleb are out, can we go into your room?' he asked politely when they got to the strand. Why not, she thought, although she was exhausted. They could make love all evening, he could fuck the memory of Josh out of her body. 'I want to make you come with my mouth. I never make you come that way.' Holly looked up at the cliffs. Josh had gone. She felt her heart sink a little. 'George seemed so good at it,' he sulked on.

'Well, we can keep trying.' She smiled up at him weakly. Her pussy was still hot and liquid from all those boys. A nice, soothing tongue on her would be just lovely. 'We can do sixty-nine,' she promised. 'That's one of my favourites.' She looked back at Josh's house. It looked lonely and empty on the crest of that hill, exposed to wind and rain. Even on a mild evening like this it looked somehow windswept. There was a light in his upstairs window now that dusk was falling. Holly wondered if he was in there, what he was doing. She was annoyed at herself for even caring. She slipped her hand round Ben's waist and squeezed their bodies together.

Caleb and Delilah were snogging in the kitchen when they got home. He had her rammed up against the kitchen units, her fat thighs engulfing him. They were fully clothed but Holly still felt embarrassed. Ben didn't seem to be – he was obviously used to it. His face only fell when he realised his evening of indulgence in Holly's bedroom would have to be postponed.

'There'll be other times,' she whispered to him. 'Or even other girls.' Joshua was right – she should stop using him, although he was dying to be used. She hated it when Joshua was right.

Chapter Twenty-Two

'It's me. Josh.' Wow. It had been two days since they had seen each other. Two days of Holly fantasising about an 'It's me, Josh' phone call. 'It's me, Josh, I've made a terrible mistake' or 'It's me, Josh, my God I need you!' had played on an endless, subconscious loop all through rehearsals and all through the night. Holly looked at the clock – it was 9 a.m. What kind of a person calls to declare their love at 9 a.m. on a Saturday morning? Maybe he'd had another sleepless night and couldn't wait any longer.

'I thought you might be rehearsing later. Sorry if I woke you.'

'Yes, I'm rehearsing and yes, you woke me.' Oooh, her voice was coming out as prickly as the bramble path; that was a surprise. She was expecting to be gushy. She sounded all efficient and pithy like a businesswoman on an American soap. He fell silent. Come on, Josh, spit it out, put me out of my misery. Two days of mooning over him, what a waste of time. Ben had been knocking constantly at her door, but she was abstaining. In her water she knew that Josh would be calling to beg her forgiveness. No one could leave her feeling that rejected, surely. She had tried to reason herself out of hope and waiting, but she had known all along. 'Josh? What do you want?' she asked eventually. Good, not too expectant.

'I just wondered – I know this is a bit cheeky . . .' Yes? Yes? '. . . If you were still on for dog-sitting on Monday? It's just that, if you don't want to I'll have to get someone else and I need a bit of notice.' She was stunned. This wasn't the fucking fantasy. 'Sorry. I completely understand if you don't want to.' She tried to get a hold of her breathing. She wanted that pithy businesswoman back. She had dissolved into a choked-up London girl.

'Oh.' Was that all she could say? 'Of course. No probs.'

'Sure?' He sounded quite rightly awkward.

'I love Freud. You know that.' See, I'm loyal to the hilt, she thought. I'm consistent. I'm honest.

'Thanks. I'll leave the keys at the stage door of the theatre for you.' So you don't even have to see me, she thought contemptuously. He couldn't even bear to hand his keys over in person. She wanted to think of some breezy goodbye, but she just cleared her throat instead. 'Take care.' He said it darkly, as if he meant it, not in the trendy, flippant way it was bandied about as a goodbye. He was talking about her enemy, her poison penfriend. Thanks for reminding me, she thought. With friends like these . . .

'You take care,' she said, in the flippant, trendy way. They hung up. What a fucking awful start to the day.

The change in Max was nothing short of miraculous. He was like Samson with his hair cut off, like a middle-aged Lothario who'd run out of Viagra. If he'd had a tail, it would have been between his legs. Whatever Lady Eleanor had said or done, it had well and truly taken the wind out of his bullying little sails, and now rehearsals were like a dream. The play was shaping up under this new humble regime. Jeff and Max were frosty with each other. In fact, Jeff seemed to be the only actor not delighted with the change. He blamed Holly completely, which Holly took as a compliment. Even Nikki didn't seem to be missing her sugar daddy too much.

Lunchtime at the pub had a celebratory feel, with everyone speculating on how the play would go down. Nathaniel got in a bottle of champagne. Julie brought it to their table, eyeing Oberon enigmatically.

'You OK?' he muttered. Why are men so awkward after they've shagged you, even a lovely one like Oberon, Holly wondered.

'I'm great.' She handed out glasses and popped the cork with an unceremonious shove. 'Enjoy.'

'Julie!' Holly called her back. This wasn't right, the girl just serving him and sloping off. 'Can't you join us for a moment? More than enough for all of us.' Oberon looked at her askance as if sizing up what trick she was about to play. Julie's expression opened up though, and she smiled, flashing her silver tongue stud.

'Don't mind if I do.' Holly chatted with her as the bubbles started to go to her head, asking her about the biker set, getting the gossip. Apparently Granddaddy had had his birthday party in a deserted warehouse a few nights before, which sounded like the same debauched fun as all their other parties. As his present he had been sucked off by three girls at the same time, and when he came they had all been sprayed with champagne.

'Were you one of the girls?' Holly asked. Julie's slow naughty smile said that she was.

'For God's sake don't tell anyone in here. My family all know him. They'd go ballistic.' She drained her glass, her eyes resting on Holly. She had nice eyes – navy blue with sticky black eyelashes, almond-shaped. 'Your lip's healed up nice. Ever get the bitch who did it?' Holly suddenly remembered their conversation.

'No.' Her face clouded over. It was so easy to forget about that woman, the weird notes; they seemed completely unconnected to real life.

'Tell me,' Julie urged, seeing the change in Holly. So

Holly poured it all out, even admitting quietly that she had been at the orgy at the larch wood. She spoke of Josh, how he'd reacted. Julie reacted with the same gravity as Joshua, instantly feeling protective. 'We need to find her. Before she does something really stupid.' Holly knew the advice off by heart.

'Go to the police?' she asked. Julie sniggered.

'Christ, no!' She poured herself another glass of champagne, thinking. 'No, they're useless round here. No. We'll think of something.'

'Maybe.' Holly went off her drink, despondent. She felt safe in the presence of Julie – there was something strong about her – but Julie couldn't always be there. 'It makes you scared to be alone, that's all.'

'You don't have to be alone.' Julie was implying something – was this a come-on?

'I do!' Holly laughed. 'I have to dog-sit for Josh for a start – Monday night. That's going to be a bit spooky. I've got to be there till Tuesday afternoon.' She shivered. That house, venue of many a humiliation, without Josh in it.

'Say no – don't do it!'

'Actually, I'll be OK. Freud the dog will protect me. He barks at strangers.' Julie looked dubious, but Holly felt better for that thought, she really did.

She went there straight after Monday's rehearsal, her little overnight bag packed with all the essentials. Josh had left the keys and a nice note at the stage door, advising which room she would be sleeping in and what keys to use in what doors. Not mentioning anything else, not saying sorry, but suitably grateful.

It was still light when she got there; she was glad not to come up that hill in darkness. Freud was doing a dance of joy at seeing her, wagging and panting and jumping up. There was a note in the kitchen saying he needed feeding in the evening, but not to let him pig out too much. She did that first, aware of her responsibility, spooning an unappetising glob of dog food into his bowl. He looked at her as if to question whether she *really* expected him to eat that, like a child with a babysitter, knowing he could push it.

'This is what daddy gives you, Freud,' she admonished, mashing it up as if that would make it look better. He half-heartedly began to nibble at it. 'Good boy.' The first odd thing she noticed was that the back door wasn't shut properly. It seemed strange that Josh wouldn't just leave it open, but slightly on its hinges, like he'd left in a hurry out the back way. She pushed it to and turned the key. Freud wasn't eating. He had tried and failed to go for the rabbit-and-heart-flavoured jelly.

'Poor thing.' She could be indulgent; she was like a granny or an auntie. She fished a packet of biscuits out of the larder and offered him one. He sniffed it and turned his head. 'Not hungry, little one? Missing daddy?' She crouched down to kiss his head and he snuggled into her. Then she saw that there was another bowl on the kitchen floor, under the table. It was a china bowl, willow-patterned. It had the remains of what looked like a steak in there. She picked it up and put it in the sink. The remains seemed to be slightly tepid. 'That's odd.' She rinsed it out. No wonder he wasn't hungry, he was digesting. She shrugged off a nervy feeling and decided to treat herself to an explore upstairs.

She tried to make harsh judgements on Joshua, she really did. She tried to pick fault as you do when someone has rejected you. But she liked his style. He obviously didn't like clutter – it was clean lines, white walls, wooden floors. But it had a cosiness too. His bed was a king-size antique oak affair with a big white duvet that looked like it could send you to sleep for a year. His walls were occasionally adorned with family photos, a painting of Freud, a Monet print. He had an en-suite bathroom – clean but a bit messy, not many products, just aftershave (smelling it she nearly swooned, it was so like being pressed up against his neck). She looked in his mirror, her face framed by old oak. She went well with the decor, she thought, thumbing his electric toothbrush. She smelled its head – all minty and warm – putting it on the tip of her tongue. When she pressed the button it buzzed and whirred in her hand. She turned it off again. She took it into his room and lay back on the endless bed, smelling him on the pillow. His pyjamas were tucked under there – she pulled them out and snuggled her face into them. Then she lifted her knees and put the electric toothbrush against her panties. That brush had been in his mouth. She sighed as she turned it on, feeling its bristly head vibrate directly against her clit. She looked around as the sensation built up inside her, taking in what he saw every time he went to bed. She hooked her panties to one side and applied the brush to her skin. It was harsh at first against her tender bud, but she pushed it against her and somehow that dulled the points of the bristles. It buzzed and turned until she came. She knew it had taken two minutes, because the toothbrush's timer stopped it just as her last spasm jerked her head off the pillow. Timing.

He had a living room upstairs too – a long, warm room with ochre walls and a big blue sofa. The TV was large, but the hi-fi larger. Music was obviously his thing. Holly thought she heard Freud scratching at the kitchen door. Funny, she had meant to leave it open for him. She didn't like the idea that he wasn't allowed out of his 'leisure quarters'. She hopped down the stairs and opened the door for him. He did his doggy version of a grin.

'Keep me company?' She smiled, leading him into the study. There was her red leather chair, there was his famous video camera. She considered taping herself for a laugh – stripping or faking an orgasm – but after what had passed between them it didn't seem fun any more. Instead she scoured the bookshelves for videos to put into the machine. The monitor was where she had seen it that night, the night she had spied on Josh spying on her. The videos were amateurishly labelled with names:

'Mrs Murray, Miss Holmes, Miss Parker' – that was her! She decided to have a look at her handiwork, quickly working out the video recorder and slipping her tape in. She looked pretty. She fast-forwarded to the spot where she had flashed herself to the camera. Brazen. She craned forward and paused the video, really examining her own genitals for the first time. They were really attractive – a delicate pink flower with two petals lightly dusted with soft brown hair. And shiny – she must have been quite wet. No wonder men liked it. Freud started to snore in the corner as Holly searched the shelves for other videos. She tried out various ones.

'He wants to tie me up, but I'm scared,' one middle-aged woman was saying. 'If he loved me surely he wouldn't want to do something like that . . .'

'I don't see what's wrong with incest.' This was a sharp-featured young blonde. 'I mean, we're consenting adults. Why should society dictate who I can and cannot fuck?' Holly took that one out quickly.

'My virginity is like an albatross round my neck.' A chubby lady in her forties, pretty, shy. 'I just want to be rid of it, really. But I think it's too late.' Sad individuals, Holly thought, feeling uncomfortably voyeuristic. Still, she'd look at one more.

'I love you.' The woman was in her late thirties, skinny, long black hair. She looked familiar. Her pale green eyes were intense. 'When you touch me, I know I am not made of ice.' She was attractive in a wild way, beautiful even. 'Your hands are like the sun on me, Joshua.' She was leaning forward, her small breasts clearly visible under her gaping low-cut shirt. Holly looked at the case. It said 'Miss Kelly'. This was the woman – the woman who had ruined him! 'You're special. And I know I could be special for you too.' Her lips were so red, but it didn't look like make-up. She began to unbutton her top. Holly could hear Josh saying 'please' in the background – was it 'yes please' or 'please stop'? The woman had amazing tits – small but round, upright, livid tiny nipples. They seemed to point right at you and ask for attention. 'Come and nurse at me,' she pleaded. She fondled herself. 'I love your mouth on me. It's like waking up after a hundred years' sleep. I'm like Sleeping Beauty, Josh, and you're the prince.' She laughed. 'I know you say it's wrong, that it shouldn't have happened, but it has happened, darling. We can never undo it. It was magical, beautiful . . .' Holly was really jealous of this woman now. Josh was muttering something. The woman's voice hardened. 'Don't lie to me. You love me as much as I love you. You wanted me – more than I wanted you. You fucked me like a tiger, you brought out all the sex that had been locked away in me and now you want me to shove it all back in? Well, it won't go!' Her tits wobbled as she spoke. Then she plunged a hand between her legs. 'When *he* touches me I feel nothing. I'm dry. But when you touched me, oh, sweetheart.'

It was then that Freud began to bark. She had never heard him bark in earnest before and it was quite alarming. He growled, his teeth showing, standing up, alert. Holly snatched the video out of the machine and shoved them all back on the shelves. She looked out of the window but all she saw was blackness

'What is it, Freud?' she whispered. The dog meant business. 'Has she come to get me?' Holly felt sick. She grabbed a poker that was resting in the fireplace and went to the front door. Through the glass she could see the figure of a woman. There was long black hair, pale skin. A hand suddenly pressed against the glass, one white palm. She screamed.

'Holly. It's me.' It took Holly a moment to place the voice.

'Julie?' She trembled as she tried to unlock the door. 'Sorry.' Eventually she opened it. Freud carried on barking. 'It's OK, baby, Julie's a friend.' Julie held out a greasy hand and the dog was appeased.

'Needn't have worried about you. He's a better guard dog than I thought.' She kicked off her biker boots and walked in. 'Nice place. Mr Rich.'

'Why are you . . .?'

'I didn't like the thought of you being on your tod.' She strode in as if she owned the place. 'Not with mad women with long nails about.'

'I see.' Holly was glad Julie was there, but also felt invaded. She had wanted to spend this night in Josh's house alone, nosing through his stuff, absorbing him. Julie read her mind.

'Look, you need me here. I'll lie low, you don't have to see me if you don't want to. I'll hide out, just in case the woman comes back.' She threw her leather jacket to the ground. 'Cup of tea would be nice though.'

They sat in the upstairs living room making conversation. Holly was desperate to go back downstairs and see more of the video of Maria Kelly. She wanted to suss out her rival, her predecessor. Julie put the TV and started watching some dreadful Monday night series. She rolled a joint, which must have made it more palatable. Holly refused one, saying she had some stuff to do downstairs.

'Holler if you need me,' Julie said.

'I love your tongue. His tongue is like an icicle, yours is like a lick of sun. I think we could be magical together . . .' The video went on, with her often exposing herself, kneeling before him. At one point he came over and kissed her, caressing her breasts, fondly succumbing to her. He did look younger there, more vain, as he had said. His face was chubbier and his blue eyes brighter. Holly could see the wet pink stub of his tongue gliding into the woman's mouth, the big square of his palm pressing against her crotch. Their legs got tangled up. He was visibly erect, the woman's hand resting on it proprietarily. Then she bent to it and worshipped it with her red mouth. Holly's pussy was dripping with envy, her appetite whet. He had a beautiful cock, and the woman ate at it as if it was a delicious fruit. A forbidden fruit. The look of heaven on his face melted Holly, she almost couldn't watch. She turned the video off and replaced it quietly. She switched off the monitor and then decided to straighten up the room. She went to draw the curtains. A face, white, sharp, loomed at her through the window. A woman's face pressed against the glass. Holly gasped. It was a grimacing, pained face, pale green eyes shooting deathly stares. It was Maria Kelly's face. Holly's voice caught in her throat like bile, she choked.

'Freud,' she called weakly. 'Julie.' The woman was holding up a brick, grinning. Holly recognised her now – she had met her walking home once from Josh's house. She had been picking wild flowers. The brick smashed against the window, shattering the glass. A cold gust of air whirled in, followed by a thin white arm. The woman clawed at Holly's throat through the broken glass, grabbing her round the neck.

'Take your eyes off me!' the woman hissed. Holly pulled away, kicking, gurgling. The woman's eyes were as cool as a cat's and she had a thin red smile as she dug her talons into Holly's skin.

'You evil little bitch, you little whore, you witch, you dead little shit,' she muttered and spat as she strangled Holly. Her wrists were grinding against the jagged glass of the window frame, welling up with blood. But she didn't seem to feel it. Freud walked into the room to see what the noise was about. He recognised Maria and let out a strange, confused bark. Were they playing? Seeing him gave Holly her voice back.

'Get off me!' she screamed, yanking down on the woman's arms. Julie came thundering down the stairs. The woman had large shards of glass embedded in her skin. She didn't even wince. Julie ran in and unpeeled the stiff claws from Holly's throat, shouting obscenities. Freud decided to join in now, barking and yelping. He didn't know whose side he was on. Blood was streaming down the walls. Finally the woman unclenched her fists and flew backwards out into the night. Julie made sure Holly was all right and jumped through the window, chasing the dark figure. Holly stood trembling and blinking in the wind. She sank to her knees and Freud came to comfort her.

'Some good you were,' she whispered. 'Trust you to have the best memory of any dog. Trust you to remember *her*.'

Julie came back an hour later, flushed and frustrated. She had lost the woman at the cliff edge. The woman had seemed to disappear over the side, maybe climbing down the rock-face.

'She won't get far. She was bleeding like a river. She's got glass in her arms.' They started to clear the room, scrubbing down the bloody walls and sweeping up the glass. Holly couldn't speak. 'Shall we call the police?' Julie asked.

Holly considered it. If this was the patient who had got Josh in trouble, would it be somehow bad for him to call the police? She couldn't think straight. But in the end, they did.

'A strange woman you say?' The policeman was young, but spoke like someone out of a fifties crime novel. He surveyed the window. They gave him a description and the name Maria Kelly. He still looked dubious. 'We'll do a hunt tonight, but I have to say it'll probably be morning by the time we catch her. Daylight. Perhaps you can come down the station tomorrow to do an incident report?' He called out a man he knew to fix the window and asked if the girls wanted a guard for the night.

'We're fine,' Julie said. 'We're together.'

That night they slept curled around each other in Josh's big bed. Every gust of wind or creaky tree sounded like Maria Kelly coming back to get Holly. She slept fitfully, constantly waking up with a shudder.

'Shhhh,' Julie said. It was 4 a.m. and Holly had just jolted upright with fright. Julie pulled her back down and pulled her in tight. Both girls were wearing Josh's

T-shirts, big, baggy, warm things. Julie's bare legs tangled around Holly's. 'It's OK. She's gone.' Holly was shivering. Julie covered her with her fleshy body, running her hands over her arms and thighs, encircling her small waist. 'Relax.' Her hand slipped under Holly's T-shirt and played sweetly at her nipples. Holly sighed as she began to release her tension. Julie put her mouth to Holly's ear and started to lick tenderly inside it. The shortcut to Holly's pussy was through her ear – how could Julie know that? Holly began to squirm a little. Julie's hand moved lower, ribs, belly-button, hip, pussy. She idly pulled Holly's knickers off, followed by her own, and stroked at her softly. Holly tensed up slightly. She wasn't a lesbian, and if she were Julie wouldn't be her type. But the girl was so sure, so confident, so strong. She was making Holly feel better and that was all that mattered. The tongue stud was surprising in Holly's ear. She could imagine it in other places. She moaned. Julie took this as invitation and rolled on top of her. She was a fulsome, hefty girl with wonderful tits. Holly cupped them and they spilled over her hands. Holly pulled Julie's T-shirt over her head to get a better look. In the moonlight she marvelled at their generous size and the lovely big nipples, one pierced with a stud.

'Did that hurt?' she asked, her finger gently playing with it.

'Not really. It was worth it.' She lowered her tit into Holly's mouth and let herself be sucked. It was a nice, milky taste, sweet and warm. Julie liked it hard, Holly noticed, and increased her suction. There was something wonderful about the fact all this was happening in Josh's bed. If only he was here to share the joy. They would squash him between their four wonderful breasts and he could feast till morning. Julie was getting horny. She ground her naked pussy against Holly's. It was stubbly and prickly. Holly reached down and felt it – it was like a little hedgehog. The pubes she had shaved off were growing back. The bristles felt good against

Holly's clit. Holly took a handful of Julie's full bottom and pulled it towards her.

'I like you.' Julie said. It was a bit of an understatement if the slipperiness of that little hedgehog was anything to go by. 'When I watched you with Granddaddy I was ready to cream myself. You were foxy.' She slithered down Holly's body and wholeheartedly lapped at her cunt. She was like a fat kid at Burger King, gobbling, slurping. Holly enjoyed the ride, clutching Josh's pillows with delight. Holly gasped with surprise when Julie lifted her knees up and pushed them back to reveal Holly's tight rosebud. Julie licked from hole to hole, taking it all in. She knew what buttons to press and her tongue stud gave it all an edge. Holly's first climax took them both by surprise.

'I guess that silver thing speeds things up,' she panted. Julie moved back up her body, her breath heady with Holly's come. She writhed around on top of Holly, trying urgently to get friction between their pussies. She gave her a deep tonguey kiss and massaged her breasts, sighing.

'Can I tie you up?' She grinned. Holly didn't know what to say. The light was turned on and Julie was soon fixing her naked body in a star shape to the bed post, two wrists and two ankles firmly secured. She used four of Josh's ties – they were expensive silk ones. Holly hoped they wouldn't get damaged. The bed was a perfect size for that – Holly wondered enviously if Josh had ever tied any of his women up there. Or if he had been tied up himself. That image gave her a gush of lust. 'Ooooh, you like that, don't you?' Julie grinned, stud glinting. 'Let's see what our host has that we can play with.' She scouted round the room, turning drawers out and looking on shelves. Finally she emerged from the bathroom with a bottle of baby oil.

'What are you going to . . .?' Holly began, before she was squirted all over with copious amounts of the stuff. It was cold and it trickled down her sides onto the covers. Will it stain? she wanted to ask, but was distracted by Julie spreading herself with the shiny oil, her tits and tummy, her little hedgehog, her face, her legs. She climbed on top of Holly and lay on her, holding on to the side of the bed to stop her slipping off. Then she began to gyrate and slide all over Holly's body. Up and down, left to right, like a kid on some weird ride at Disneyland, sliding in circles, sitting up and sliding her pussy the length of Holly's torso, so Holly could feel Julie's hot, open sex all over her. It was a weird feeling. She gave Holly's tits an extra squirt and landed on them, circling her open cleft hard on each nipple, masturbating herself on them. Holly looked down and could see the lips opening and enveloping her breasts. Finally she slipped down to crouch on Holly's triangle and gyrated on that, rubbing their two pussies together like a caveman trying to make fire. Holly watched her arse pump and shudder away. Her own arousal was slow and astonished, just getting used to this bizarre routine. The juices in her awakened and joined the oily bath of the bed. Julie had her eyes closed, her head thrown back. Her wobbly belly was tightening. Holly watched as she came raspingly, butting Holly's private parts with each spasm. She didn't scream or whine. Afterwards she lay back next to Holly and kissed her.

'That was fun!' She grinned. Holly smiled back, still vaguely turned on, but tired. She was concerned about the bedclothes, the state of the house. She didn't want Josh to come back and find a trashed place like a parent returning from holidays to find their naughty teenager has had a house party.

'You're still not relaxed,' Julie said. She went to turn off the light and slipped back onto the bed. She let her hand play between Holly's legs. Holly was still tied up and couldn't close her knees together. 'Come on, let me,' Julie said. 'It'll help you sleep.' Her hand was so slippery from the baby oil, it slid around Holly's lips like a tongue. She pressed her palm to Holly and gently rotated it on her. It was soothing. 'You've got such a pretty pussy,' Julie whispered, fondling it. Holly felt hotter, she began to melt. 'No wonder Granddaddy liked it so much. You should come back to the clan one day and let him lick you out again. He's the best.' Holly steamed up at the memory. 'You should ask him to fuck you on his bike. With the engine on. That gives a great vibration.' Her fingers slipped inside. 'You should get two of the biker boys to see to you at the same time. You'd like that, wouldn't you? They can be as rough or as gentle as you like.' She was rubbing Holly's clit, pouring naughty words into Holly's ear. She had one hand inside Holly and the other going mad against her nub of pleasure, describing wonderful things to her. Holly bucked and strained against her bondage. 'I've fucked them all, Holly, except Granddaddy. Once I had twenty fuck me in one night.' Holly shivered feverishly, pouring hot lust. 'They tied me up like I tied you up tonight, then lined up and had me. Everyone was cheering. It was fantastic. You'd like that, wouldn't you. You'd love that.'

Chapter Twenty-Three

'*H*ello?' Through her thick dream Holly barely registered Josh's voice and the slam of the front door. She turned in the bed and sighed herself asleep again. He went straight into the kitchen and was surprised to see Julie sitting there in her leathers with a cup of tea and a piece of toast. 'Who are you?' He was ready to be very indignant.

'Julie.' She smiled, munching away.

'Where's Holly?' Josh couldn't believe this. 'Where's Freud?'

'Upstairs.' Julie got up to go, inserting her head in her helmet. 'It was a pretty big night.'

The bedroom was a state. Four of his best ties were lying at the foot of the bed. His favourite two T-shirts were in a crumpled heap on the bedside table. There were weird oil stains all over the sheets. And his big bed was occupied by a naked unconscious woman and a snoring dog.

'It's nearly midday, you know.' It was all he could think of to say, although he knew it made him sound like his dad. 'What the hell's going on?' Freud woke up first and beat his tail against the bed like a prize bass drummer. Holly stirred then, tentatively opening her eyes against the light. 'What's going on?' he repeated now everyone was listening. He dumped his small suitcase in the corner and took his jacket off. Reality trickled into Holly's consciousness, memories of all last night's events. Josh looked like he was about to explode, like he didn't know her at all and he was just realising it.

'I can explain,' she croaked. This wasn't how she imagined waking up in Josh's bed – her all puffed up from sleep, him all edgy and mean. Only Freud was playing happy families. Josh let out a sardonic laugh. 'Where's Julie?'

'Oh, our unexpected guest? She helped herself to breakfast and is now riding off on her Harley into the sunset.' His voice had a sarcastic quality that Holly didn't like much. He fussed about the room, tidying up and tutting.

'Hang on,' Holly warned him. 'You don't know what happened last night.'

He snorted again. 'I can guess.'

'No you can't.'

'Look at you – naked, oil all over the sheets, strange dykey woman in the kitchen. I wash my hands of you, Holly, I really do,' he blustered, then a look of total disgust swept his face. 'Oh my God. You didn't . . . with Freud . . .?' Now she was angry.

She got out of bed, oblivious to her nakedness and searched for her clothes.

'How dare you?' she spat. She was putting her panties on the wrong way round. 'Shit.' What had she seen in him? He watched her get dressed, unable to take his eyes off her despite himself. She didn't want him to watch her. 'Can you look away please?'

'Oh, suddenly shy, are we.' But he turned his head anyway, sinking onto the bed. In the silence he had time to calm down a little. 'Look, if you'd wanted someone to stay with you, fine. But you should have asked me. It's common courtesy.' Holly marched up to him now, pretty much dressed, fiery with the knowledge that she had the upper hand here.

'There wasn't time to ask you,' she said coolly. 'Your lovely ex Maria Kelly was here. She tried to kill me. Julie saved my life.' His mouth fell open. He looked suitably shocked. 'Now, we have to go to the police station. They need statements. OK?'

They were put in a neon-lit incident room, sparse and functional, with one potted plant. Josh couldn't stop apologizing. Holly couldn't bear to look at him. The policeman from the previous night came in and smiled at her.

'Hello again.' He nodded and shook Josh's hand. 'Police Inspector Howard.'

'Joshua Delaney.' They sat there like guilty children as Josh told the Inspector all about Maria Kelly. He said he had been in court the day before, trying to get a restraining order against her, in case she ever came near him again.

'I was afraid she would find me, you see,' he told the man. 'I think I may have shot myself in the foot by bringing it to court. I made myself traceable through my solicitor. I'm so sorry.' He turned to Holly again, who stared stony-faced before her.

'Well, I hope we will find her soon. I know she's injured. We've informed the hospitals and are searching the area. I'm sure we'll get her soon, sir.' He looked quizzical. 'But why would she be out to harm Miss Parker?' he asked, genuinely baffled. 'You say Miss Parker is a client of yours. Seeking treatment. Why would this Miss Kelly seek to harm her?' Josh and Holly sat toying uncomfortably with this question for a while. Eventually Holly tried to explain it.

'I think she must have observed how Mr Delaney and I were – appearing to grow intimate through our sessions. I think she – misconstrued our relationship as more than therapist and client. The notes she sent me were obviously to warn me off him.'

'One of these notes was sent to your house, is that correct?' he asked. 'How would she have your private address?'

'I don't know.' Holly thought about this. 'She seemed to have access to Josh's – Mr Delaney's – house. I mean, the back door was open when I got there yesterday. I assume now that she'd opened it. I think she'd fed the dog a steak too.' It all came into focus. 'Maybe she went through my records?'

'But she somehow thought you two were an item?' he asked again. He wasn't buying it. Josh cleared his throat.

'We are, you see, Inspector,' he said finally. 'We are an item.'

They were silent in the car. Holly didn't dare ask him if he had meant what he said, or if he was just trying to make the interview easier. She looked at him driving, confident, determined, looking in his rear-view mirror more than he needed to. Looking for *her*. Holly wondered where he was going to drop her off. She hadn't asked him to take her anywhere. But they drove past her digs and back to the house on the hill. They went in and greeted Freud. She followed Josh through to the kitchen, not knowing what to say. His face was fixed, impenetrable. Was he angry with her? He went straight for the back door and rattled it to make sure it was locked.

'Change the lock first thing tomorrow,' he said to himself. Suddenly Holly realised – he was scared. She wanted to go over to him and hold him, but just couldn't face another rejection, so she put the kettle on instead. She handed him a tea.

'Are we?' she said eventually. He knew what she meant.

'Yes, I think we are. I think we are an item.' He took her hand. 'But until Maria gets put away, I don't want you round here. It's dangerous.' He caressed the bruises on Holly's neck, his fingers slipping into her hair. 'I've been an idiot,' he said. 'Not just recently, but for ever.'

246

She wasn't going to argue with that. He pulled her in to hug him – his thick jumper smelt of sandalwood.

'So I can't see you?' she murmured into his chest. Even in this shaken, muted moment, just his presence made her body yearn.

'No, not till she's out of the picture.' He kissed her head. 'I can't risk that. I can't risk you.' She felt so safe with him now that it seemed ridiculous, but part of her knew he was right. The image of Maria Kelly's white, feline face and her ghostly claws still flashed in her mind whenever she closed her eyes.

'But it's my first night on Saturday,' she said. 'Surely you'll come to that.'

'Oh, I wouldn't miss that for the world.'

Chapter Twenty-Four

'*T*his is your quarter-hour call everybody.' Even Adrian's voice sounded terrified over the intercom. 'You have fifteen minutes.' The actors all applied make-up and laced corsets furiously in their dressing rooms, anxious to forget the ordeal they were about to go through. 'Just enjoy it!' Max had said, and they had all laughed. What a ridiculous notion. Nikki knocked on Holly's door and peeked in. She looked great in her costume – a white frilly affair with a big high wig.

'Break a leg,' she said, smiling tensely.

'It'll be great,' Holly replied, unconvinced, and Nikki disappeared off down the corridor singing scales to warm up. Oberon was out there too, going over a line he always stumbled on. Holly saw him dressed up in the same costume he had worn to that mad biker orgy. The memory of that night gave her a tingle. She welcomed that – Max was always going on about how she had to be constantly aroused to play this part and at the moment, nerves had obliterated any chance of that. She went to the mirror and adjusted her full creamy breasts so they sat buxomly under her green satin costume. The full skirt had a big hooped petticoat that made it swing when she moved. She glossed her lips and admired herself. Josh was going to be out there and she wanted him to fancy her like this. Ben and Caleb would be there too, and Delilah, and Julie for that matter. She wanted to look great for all of them! There was a mousy knock at the door.

'Come in.' Nathaniel crept in, looking drawn.

'Oh, I'm too old for this,' he groaned. 'I know it's not the done thing, but what I wouldn't give for a dram of whisky right now!' Holly embraced him warmly, and he leaned his head on her fleshy cleavage for comfort. 'I knew you'd make me feel better. Take my mind off the blasted thing,' he said. His breath was hot on her bosom, pleasant. 'You know, I really enjoy our bit in the play. It's my favourite part. I'd like to be your uncle for life, my dear, and continue to teach you.' Was he coming on to her? 'I think you like it too.' He was right. He made her come every time, even when they rehearsed it three times in a row. It was a strange intimacy, though, not quite real life. 'I think it would calm me down to do something like that now.' He looked at her with pleading eyes. 'Let your Uncle Hunter take succour from his pretty niece,' he said, suddenly in character. She smiled. It would be nice – a bit of relaxation, a bit of titillation. Nathaniel dropped to his knees and lifted up her skirt. He pulled up the hooped part and crawled under it, deliriously happy in his little cage.

'Oh my dear, you smell delicious,' he said, pushing aside her panties and taking a sniff. Holly leaned back against the wall as she felt Nathaniel's tongue edge tentatively inside her crevices. What an unexpected pleasure! She pulled her skirts down so he was invisible, hidden in the fullness of her costume. Now he was like a secret lover, a burrowing animal, rooting about with his wet tongue, sniffing and lapping at her. She could feel him groaning into her pussy, the sound vibrating up her and into her belly. He had a fast tongue, a strong one. She began to pant, widening her legs to admit him more. Suddenly there was another knock on the door.

'Nathaniel!' she whispered, but he just carried on. Was he deaf or just enjoying himself too much? 'Stop –

someone's here!' The tongue tickled her clit in reply. She gave up and tried to regain some composure.

'Can I come in?' It was Jeff.

'Yes!' she said, a note of eagerness in her voice. He closed the door behind him.

'You look amazing,' he said. She nodded a thank-you, pulling at her skirts so they covered Nathaniel's feet. 'Really incredible.' The tongue was slowly lapping at her now, tantalising long licks along her slit. She flooded his face with appreciation. 'I wanted to say, I'm sorry. I know I was hard on you. I know we had some tension back there. But, babe, I know there's still a lot between us.' He came towards her, pleased to see a blush rise in her cheek. 'I know we could still have a lot of good times, babe. I think about it a lot.' He touched her throat and slipped his fingers down to the tempting swell of her bosom. 'God, this thing makes you look pneumatic.'

He pulled one of her breasts free so that the nipple popped out over the top of the costume. Holly let him. She was rendered powerless by Nathaniel's wonderful, tireless tonguing. 'Babe,' Jeff whispered and took the nipple on his tongue like a drop of acid. His mouth fell around it greedily, and he flicked and swirled his tongue just as he knew she liked it. Meanwhile Nathaniel's tongue was doing pirouettes on her pussy. She was ready to explode. She sighed and began to let out quiet little cries of excitement. 'Oh babe.' Jeff hardened instantly at the thought his touch could do this to her. He licked frantically at her tits.

'Oh, yes.' She was louder now, grinding her cunt into Nathaniel's grateful mouth. 'Oh yes!!!' Jeff couldn't believe his powers.

'Baby, that's right, come for me,' he urged, returning to her breasts with renewed vigour.

'Oh, I'm coming!' she cried out, and her pussy slathered and quivered and jerked into Nathaniel's face. She thought she was going to wet herself. She climaxed loudly, performing to her audience.

250

'Oh baby!' Jeff started to kiss her and she pushed him away, laughing. She pulled up her skirts to reveal Nathaniel, grinning broadly with a dripping chin. Jeff got it immediately and stormed out, leaving Holly and Nathaniel giggling like naughty kids.

'It's going to be a great night.' Holly announced, sure of it now.

And she was right. The audience – a mixture of curious locals and London glitterati – were seduced by the raw sexuality and full-blooded realism of the production. They even laughed at the jokes, which surprised the actors who hadn't realised there were any. Max was glowing up in a box, with Lady Eleanor perched beside him. Holly had spotted the Briars too, Ben with a pretty girl from the village whom he had started seeing. Julie was there with some biker friends. Even Police Inspector Howard was there with his wife. She couldn't see Josh though. Perhaps he had sat at the back to not put her off her lines.

When the curtain came down there was rapturous applause and a few people (encouraged by Ben – what a sweetheart!) gave a standing ovation. They had pulled it off. Holly scoured the room for Josh in the curtain call. He wasn't there. Her heart dived with disappointment. She was sure he would come. He had said he wouldn't miss it for the world.

She changed quickly and made her way out into the foyer flanked by her co-stars for the first-night drinks party. Champagne and oysters was the theme, and everyone was invited. People were kissing her from all sides, congratulations bandying about her head, but she was distracted by Josh's absence.

'Well done.' This was the police inspector. 'Bit risqué, but most enjoyable.' Seeing his face, the truth slid into focus.

'Please. We have to go!' she urged him, much to the consternation of his wife. 'It's Josh. He isn't here.' It took him a moment to twig, then he turned and ran with Holly through the crowds and out of the theatre. His car was parked outside and they got in swiftly. He called the station for backup as they screeched up the road.

Josh was tied to a chair in his study. The video was playing – a tape of Maria Kelly and him, the tape Holly had watched. He had scratch marks down his face. Holly and the inspector spied through the window. Maria Kelly didn't seem to be there. Freud was barking somewhere which made Josh look up. He saw Holly at the window, relief etched on his face. He nodded towards the door. She was obviously still in the house.

'Come on!' Holly said, leading the inspector to the back door. He kicked it open, sending Freud into a frenzy. They ran in and went to the study. Holly sat by Joshua untying his binds, while the inspector searched out the woman.

'I'm sorry,' Josh said, inexplicably. 'How did it go?'

'God, don't worry about that now!' His hands were free, now she was at his feet. The knots were tight and complicated. He bent down to help her. She was momentarily aware of a shadow over her back. She swung round to see Maria Kelly bearing down on her with a knife, crazed turquoise eyes clear with hatred. Josh caught Maria's wrists and Holly screamed for help. The woman was skinny but strong, flailing against the couple, kicking and screaming.

'You stole him, you fucking bitch!' She jerked away from Joshua's grip and the knife lurched downwards. Holly rolled out of the way and Maria stabbed herself in the leg. Her blood was redder than anything Holly had seen before. Her arms were covered in gashes. 'I'll fucking kill you,' she hissed, raising the knife above her head again. But the inspector was behind her, grabbing the weapon and wrestling her to the ground. Four other policemen rushed in and pulled her to her feet. She was spitting and grimacing like a panther as they cautioned her, but they dragged her away.

'Got her.' The inspector smiled. 'It's been a very successful night all round, hasn't it?'

After making lengthy statements to the police, Holly and Josh returned home and shared a large, welcome brandy. They sat upstairs in the sitting room, curled together on a blue puffy sofa with Freud dreaming noisily in front of the fire.

'I have so much to apologise for, I don't know where to start,' he said softly into her hair.

'Then don't,' she replied simply. 'It's over now. I feel like that woman was a demon of your past, the demon that haunted you. And now she's gone.' She turned and kissed him. 'So it's a new start. Yes?'

'Yes.' He kissed her, his mouth burning with brandy. 'I'm glad you came here. To exorcise my ghosts for me.' He showered her brows and eyelashes with kisses. 'My angel. My little devil.' He put the glass down and pulled her into the bedroom, trying not to wake Freud. He closed the door softly and they both undressed in the warm light. Holly felt oddly nervous. She was hardly inexperienced, but this meant something. And she didn't want to be a disappointment. She stood naked before Joshua, trembling slightly. Her skin was tingling with anticipation. He walked up to her and ran his eyes over her body. He looked taller naked, and more muscular. He had a beautiful penis, thick and long with a smooth, promising head. It was hard at the sight of her and the thought of what was about to happen. He pulled her down onto the bed and their bodies tangled up as they kissed, his hands finding hers and pushing them above her head so she was stretched out helplessly underneath him. He was heavy, that lovely solid weight of a man, his thick thigh pressing insistently between hers. His mouth explored hers gently, his tongue seeking her soft tongue, as his body pressed against her. She was ready, ready for whatever he wanted to do to her. Weeks of desire and longing ached in her pussy. She kept opening her legs – a big V-shaped hint, but he didn't enter her. He wanted to enjoy all of her first.

'Please,' she pleaded quietly, pushing her hips up in the air, her petulant wet cunt-lips pouting at his cock. He smiled and moved his pelvis away, caressing her ear with his mouth.

'Oh no, not that,' she groaned helplessly as his tongue shot in, flushing her body with hot pleasure. He chuckled a little as he had to steady her with his hands, enjoying his control. She was panting out little sobs of excitement. He moved his mouth down to her breasts.

'Oh, these,' he whispered. 'I think about these all the time.' And he licked at them in a dream-come-true kind of way, losing some of his composure, moaning into her skin. She thought she was going to come, the electricity in her breasts was so strong. She wrapped her legs around him, her pussy sucking wetly at his belly. 'Not yet,' he said.

'You are always making me wait,' she complained. He laughed and sank between her legs, going for gold, hitting the jackpot with a big growling groan, drinking the elixir of life, sending Holly into a giddy spin of delight. His tongue on her was a dream, but better than that was the vision of his handsome head buried between her thighs, worshipping at her.

'Joshua,' she murmured happily. 'Joshua Joshua Joshua.' His tongue enquired at every hollow and tasted every crevice, every slippery fold, every lip, licking her thoroughly. His cock was pressing against her leg as he devoured her. She wanted to squeeze his head between her thighs and keep him lapping at her for ever, but he had her legs pinned down. Instead she grabbed his head and pushed it into her greedily. It still wasn't enough. She rolled them over and scrabbled down the bed so that she was straddling his face in the sixty-nine position, taking his lovely cock into her mouth with a large sigh.

'Oh, my God.' His voice was muffled. His penis sprang up in her mouth and begged to be licked and sucked. She tasted it like a lollipop – it was sweet and salty, filling her mouth with its wide girth. She played softly with his balls as she suckled on him, feeling him respond with lusty, strong licks at her clit. Her mouth was wet, hot and velvety against him. He was groaning now, desperate for her, licking madly at her juicy pussy, swallowing her up, flicking against her until she came and came and came on his tongue, his hard cock pulsing in her mouth all the time. He sat up, holding her pussy to his lips so that her arse rose in the air and she was supporting herself on her elbows. His cock slipped further into her mouth and she almost gagged. Her thighs were hooked on his shoulders as his tongue started up on her again but she wanted his hard cock inside her now. She struggled to release herself but she was stuck. She couldn't even speak for her mouth was impaled on his penis. She wriggled and flailed until he let her go and she fell sideways onto the bed. She lay back and pulled him on top of her impatiently.

'You have to make love to me now, Josh,' she panted. 'I can't wait any more.' His blue eyes were dark with desire as he held the thick head of his cock at her pussy lips and gently pushed his way inside her. They both let out a gasp as he stretched her open. His face hovered over hers, smelling of her, dripping with her juices. They locked eyes as he moved inside her. She could lose herself in those eyes. Occasionally he blinked with the overwhelming sensation of being with her and inside her.

'God. I can't believe I waited so long for this,' he breathed, beginning to thrust. 'You feel amazing.' She wrapped her legs around him at the words, holding him to her.

'We'll just have to make up for lost time.' She smiled, and grabbed his firm buttocks as they pumped hard against her. She wanted to say more but all she could do was whine and whimper. The whole night was going to be like this, she thought. No more words.

* * *

She was sitting back on the train, empty this time, the last service from Plymouth to London. She leaned back and opened her legs a little, erotic dreams lapping at her knickers. The play was over for now – just until it was to transfer to a London theatre – but it had been quite an adventure. So here she was with her suitcase and a head full of slippery memories to torment her at night. Over the past few weeks she and Josh hadn't been able to keep their hands off each other. She had taken him to the stage and they had made love on that big bed. They had done it on the beach, they had done it in the sea. She had borrowed *Delilah*, the Briars' boat, and done it in there. Her whole body rang like a bell with sense memories of him. How could she let that go? She opened her legs a little and imagined a man there, licking at her. His breath tickled at her thighs. He was pushing the white cotton away. He was fucking her with his tongue. Some fantasies never change, she thought, but looking down and seeing Joshua there kneeling between her legs, she knew the reality would always be better. He looked up at her with the adult equivalent of a milk-moustache.

'You OK?' He smiled. It was sweet of him to come to London with her, to see her flat. They were going to be spending more time there, although it wouldn't be fair on Freud not to spend at least half the year down in Cornwall, with all those open fields and beaches to run along.

'I'm amazing.' She smiled back, as the rolling hills gave way to little towns and industrial estates. She was going to have a taste of it all from now on, the green glow of Cornwall and the silver sheen of London. She and Josh both needed the two extremes, the two worlds. His face was a picture of contentedness. The cat that got the cream. That image reminded her of what he did best. 'Now come on, that's enough mooning,' she said and pushed his face back down to her sex. The train rocked her around on his tongue. 'As a special treat I'm going to get you a new electric toothbrush,' she added, mostly to herself.

'Huh?' he murmured into her.

'I used your old one.' She sighed. He lifted his head up and crawled up her body, kissing her.

'I know.' He grinned. 'Do you think I didn't notice? It had hair in it, for God's sake!' She blushed, slapping him with a rolled-up newspaper. It was one of a pile sitting there with the reviews of her show. Most were glowing, although the tabloids were a bit shocked at what the world was coming to. If they could see her now.

'Why didn't you say something?'

'I rather liked it.' He smiled, his head disappearing again. She laughed and sighed, looking absently at the review in the *Guardian*. *'This is going to be Holly Parker's year,'* it began. And she wasn't about to argue.

BLACK LACE NEW BOOKS

Published in June

SUMMER FEVER
Anna Ricci
£6.99

Lara Mcintyre has lusted after artist Jake Fitzgerald for almost two decades. As a warm, dazzling summer unfolds, she makes the journey back to her student summer-house where they first met, determined to satisfy her physical craving somehow. And then, ensconced in Old Beach House once more, she discovers her true sexual self – but not without complications.

Beautifully written story of extreme passion.

ISBN 0 352 33625 0

STRICTLY CONFIDENTIAL
Alison Tyler
£6.99

Carolyn Winters is a smooth-talking disc jockey at a hip LA radio station. Although known for her sexy banter over the airwaves, she leads a reclusive life, despite the urging of her flirtatious roommate, Dahlia. Carolyn grows dependent on living vicariously through Dahlia, eavesdropping and then covertly watching as her roommate's sexual behaviour becomes more and more bizarre. But then Dahlia is murdered, and Carolyn must overcome her fears in order to bring the killer to justice.

A tense dark thriller for those who like their erotica on the forbidden side.

ISBN 0 352 33624 2

CONTINUUM
Portia Da Costa
£6.99

Joanna Darrell is something in the city. When she takes a break from her high-powered job she is drawn into a continuum of strange experiences and bizarre coincidences. Like Alice in a decadent Wonderland, she enters a parallel world of perversity and unusual pleasure. She's attracted to fetishism and discipline and her new friends make sure she gets more than a taste of erotic punishment.

This is a reprint of one of our best-selling and kinkiest titles ever!

ISBN 0 352 33120 8

Published in July

SYMPHONY X
Jasmine Stone
£6.99

Katie is a viola player running away from her cheating husband. The tour of Symphony Xevertes not only takes her to Europe but also to the realm of deep sexual satisfaction. She is joined by a dominatrix diva and a bass singer whose voice is so low he's known as the Human Vibrator. After distractions like these, how will Katie be able to maintain her serious music career *and* allow herself to fall in love again?

Immensely funny journal of a sassy woman's sexual adventures.

ISBN 0 352 33629 3

OPENING ACTS
Suki Cunningham
£6.99

When London actress Holly Parker arrives in a remote Cornish village to begin rehearsing a new play, everyone there – from her landlord to her theatre director – seems to have an earthier attitude towards sex. Brought to a state of constant sexual arousal and confusion, Holly seeks guidance in the form of local therapist, Joshua Delaney. He is the one man who can't touch her – but he is the only one she truly desires. Will she be able to use her new-found sense of adventure to seduce him?

Wonderfully horny action in the Cornish countryside. Oooh arrgh!

ISBN 0 352 33630 7

THE SEVEN-YEAR LIST
Zoe le Verdier
£6.99

Julia is an ambitious young photographer who's about to marry her trustworthy but dull fiancé. Then an invitation to a college reunion arrives. Old rivalries, jealousies and flirtations are picked up where they were left off and sexual tensions run high. Soon Julia finds herself caught between two men but neither of them are her fiancé.

How will she explain herself to her friends? And what decisions will she make?

This is a Black Lace special reprint of a very popular title.

ISBN 0 352 33254 9

Published in August

MINX
Megan Blythe
£6.99

Spoilt Amy Pringle arrives at Lancaster Hall to pursue her engagement to Lord Fitzroy, eldest son of the Earl and heir to a fortune. The Earl is not impressed, and sets out to break her spirit. But the trouble for him is that she enjoys every one of his 'punishments' and creates havoc, provoking the stuffy Earl at every opportunity. The young Lord remains aloof, however, and, in order to win his affections, Amy sets about seducing his well-endowed but dim brother, Bubb. When she is discovered in bed with Bubb and a servant girl, how will father and son react?

Immensely funny and well-written tale of lust among decadent aristocrats.

ISBN 0 352 33638 2

FULL STEAM AHEAD
Tabitha Flyte
£6.99

Sophie wants money, big money. After twelve years working as a croupier on the Caribbean cruise ships, she has devised a scheme that is her ticket to Freedomsville. But she can't do it alone; she has to encourage her colleagues to help her. Persuasion turns to seduction, which turns to blackmail. Then there are prying passengers, tropical storms and an angry, jealous girlfriend to contend with. And what happens when the lascivious Captain decides to stick his oar in, too?

Full of gold-digging women, well-built men in uniform and Machiavellian antics.

ISBN 0 352 33637 4

A SECRET PLACE
Ella Broussard
£6.99

Maddie is a busy girl with a dream job: location scout for a film company. When she's double-booked to work on two features at once, she needs to manage her time very carefully. Luckily, there's no shortage of fit young men, in both film crews, who are willing to help. She also makes friends with the locals, including a horny young farmer and a particularly handy mechanic. The only person she's not getting on with is Hugh, the director of one of the movies. Is that because sexual tension between them has reached breaking point?

This story of lust during a long hot English summer is another Black Lace special reprint.

ISBN 0 352 33307 3

If you would like a complete list of plot summaries of Black Lace titles, or would like to receive information on other publications available, please send a stamped addressed envelope to:

Black Lace, Thames Wharf Studios,
Rainville Road, London W6 9HA

BLACK LACE BOOKLIST

Information is correct at time of printing. To avoid disappointment check availability before ordering. Go to www.blacklace-books.co.uk

All books are priced £5.99 unless another price is given.

Black Lace books with a contemporary setting

THE TOP OF HER GAME	Emma Holly ISBN 0 352 33337 5	☐
IN THE FLESH	Emma Holly ISBN 0 352 33498 3	☐
SHAMELESS	Stella Black ISBN 0 352 33485 1	☐
TONGUE IN CHEEK	Tabitha Flyte ISBN 0 352 33484 3	☐
FIRE AND ICE	Laura Hamilton ISBN 0 352 33486 X	☐
SAUCE FOR THE GOOSE	Mary Rose Maxwell ISBN 0 352 33492 4	☐
INTENSE BLUE	Lyn Wood ISBN 0 352 33496 7	☐
THE NAKED TRUTH	Natasha Rostova ISBN 0 352 33497 5	☐
A SPORTING CHANCE	Susie Raymond ISBN 0 352 33501 7	☐
TAKING LIBERTIES	Susie Raymond ISBN 0 352 33357 X	☐
A SCANDALOUS AFFAIR	Holly Graham ISBN 0 352 33523 8	☐
THE NAKED FLAME	Crystalle Valentino ISBN 0 352 33528 9	☐
CRASH COURSE	Juliet Hastings ISBN 0 352 33018 X	☐
ON THE EDGE	Laura Hamilton ISBN 0 352 33534 3	☐
LURED BY LUST	Tania Picarda ISBN 0 352 33533 5	☐

Black Lace books with an historical setting

INVITATION TO SIN £6.99	Charlotte Royal ISBN 0 352 33217 4	☐
PRIMAL SKIN	Leona Benkt Rhys ISBN 0 352 33500 9	☐
DEVIL'S FIRE	Melissa MacNeal ISBN 0 352 33527 0	☐
WILD KINGDOM	Deanna Ashford ISBN 0 352 33549 1	☐
DARKER THAN LOVE	Kristina Lloyd ISBN 0 352 33279 4	☐
STAND AND DELIVER	Helena Ravenscroft ISBN 0 352 33340 5	☐
THE CAPTIVATION £6.99	Natasha Rostova ISBN 0 352 33234 4	☐
CIRCO EROTICA £6.99	Mercedes Kelley ISBN 0 352 33257 3	☐
MINX £6.99	Megan Blythe ISBN 0 352 33638 2	☐

Black Lace anthologies

CRUEL ENCHANTMENT Erotic Fairy Stories	Janine Ashbless ISBN 0 352 33483 5	☐
MORE WICKED WORDS	Various ISBN 0 352 33487 8	☐
WICKED WORDS 4	Various ISBN 0 352 33603 X	☐

Black Lace non-fiction

THE BLACK LACE BOOK OF WOMEN'S SEXUAL FANTASIES	Ed. Kerri Sharp ISBN 0 352 33346 4	☐

-------✂------------------------

Please send me the books I have ticked above.

Name   ....

Address   ....

          ....

          ....

          .... Post Code ....

Send to: **Cash Sales, Black Lace Books, Thames Wharf Studios, Rainville Road, London W6 9HA.**

US customers: for prices and details of how to order books for delivery by mail, call 1-800-805-1083.

Please enclose a cheque or postal order, made payable to **Virgin Publishing Ltd**, to the value of the books you have ordered plus postage and packing costs as follows:

UK and BFPO – £1.00 for the first book, 50p for each subsequent book.

Overseas (including Republic of Ireland) – £2.00 for the first book, £1.00 for each subsequent book.

If you would prefer to pay by VISA, ACCESS/MASTER-CARD, DINERS CLUB, AMEX or SWITCH, please write your card number and expiry date here:

....

Please allow up to 28 days for delivery.

Signature ....

-------✂------------------------